PLAY

WILD CARD
BOOK 4

NIKKI HALL

Thanks for picking up this copy of Play Maker! If you'd like to go back to where the series begins, grab your FREE copy of Game Changer, the prequel novella for the Wild Card series.

For a FREE copy of Game Changer, go to www.nikkihallbooks.com/signup.

For everyone whose life feels just a little too tight.
Give yourself the space to grow.

1

Mac

Something was wrong with me. Not physically—these abs didn't quit—but something in my brain. I stood in the sun-splashed backyard of a sorority house, surrounded by beautiful women frolicking in bikinis, and I didn't give a shit.

The summer before my senior year should have been spent honing my skills to a razor-sharp point and enjoying the notoriety that came with a national football championship. Instead, I'd fucked up and gotten involved with my best friend, Eva. Former best friend?

I sighed and grabbed a beer from the cooler on the patio, trying to blend in as I meandered my way across the yard. A snippet of song floated through my head, but it was too faint for me to catch more than the down beat. I let it go in favor of brooding.

She was avoiding me by spending the summer at her family's beach house, and I was trying to give her the space she clearly needed from all the feelings I'd tossed at her. Stupid, I know. The worst part was that I couldn't stop wondering what if I'd left things the way they were. What if I hadn't given in to the itch to change something and jumped at her hookup offer.

Our relationship was one big question mark at the moment, kind of like my plans for the next few months. I usually spent the summer training with the cheerleaders when I wasn't busy with football stuff or classes, but I didn't need to be told that Eva's squad was off-limits now. The gaping hole in my schedule was nothing compared to the Eva-sized chunk missing from the rest of me. She had her ways of coping, and so did I. Except my usual strategy wasn't working.

I frowned down at my junk—immobile under my lucky pink cargo shorts—and pointed out the abundance of opportunity, but no amount of pep talking got Big Mac to pay attention. Honestly, I didn't even think he was listening.

Fuck, this summer was going to suck.

"This game makes no sense." The familiar husky voice stopped me in my tracks.

Eva's friend, Blue, was somewhere at this low-key back-yard party, and I desperately hoped she was alone. Not for any sexy reasons—my dick was officially on hiatus—but because I needed a break from Eva.

From all of them, really.

I'd picked a Chi Omega party specifically because this sorority didn't pander to athletes. They went for the high-powered business type, which should have guaranteed me obscurity among the crowd.

None of my crew knew I was back at TU, and I wanted to keep it that way for a few more hours. I couldn't explain the sudden feeling like my life didn't fit any more, and I didn't need the sad looks and the pity. Bad enough my mom had gone on and on about how unfortunate it was Eva couldn't make it home with me.

My family had always been careful not to put pressure on our relationship, but everyone knew Mom had been planning our wedding from the day Eva had gotten suspended in first grade for punching the asshole kid who stole my lunch.

No one knew, but that day was the beginning of my love affair with Wonder Woman. Eva had worn her star-spangled dress and lasso of truth when she defended me. As much as I loved Gal Gadot, my first Wonder Woman was tiny and blonde.

And now, she's gone.

I took a long pull of my beer, raising the bottle to my mouth as I scanned the people milling around on the grass, enjoying the sunshine. It took me two passes, but I finally spotted Blue in her tortoiseshell glasses, standing with her fists propped on her hips next to a cornhole setup.

My hand stilled with the cool glass pressed against my lips. The sun brought out a pink flush on her bare shoulders, and her black tank top clung to her curves. Curves I hadn't noticed before, but I was sure as hell noticing now.

Rainbow streaks peeked between strands of her dark hair as she tilted her head to glare at the little beanbags littering the area around the boards. Shorts rode high on her thighs, and my gaze traveled down the long length of her legs to her pink-tipped toes.

Blue was a smokeshow...when had that happened? Every time I saw her, she looked like a different person. Overalls, a slinky dress, yoga pants—she'd worn it all. Usually lurking on the fringes when she showed up. I knew Chloe invited her out a few times after Eva left, but I hadn't considered Blue having a social life outside our crew.

Today's outfit fit right in with the sorority, relaxed and uncomplicated. For some reason, the kaleidoscope of Blue drew me. I wanted to peel back her chameleon layers until I found the real person beneath.

Belatedly, I checked the faces around her and relaxed when I didn't see a tiny blonde cheerleader holding court. If Eva were here, she'd be with Blue and surrounded by her adoring fans. Her absence meant I could have the afternoon to myself if I wanted it.

Suddenly, the idea of being alone in a crowd wasn't nearly as interesting as finding out what Blue was doing at a sorority party. Preferably somewhere away from the half-drunk co-eds. I chuckled as I finished off my beer. The guys would definitely give me shit if they knew I came to a party and planned to hide from the ladies.

Almost as much as if they realized I still had my shirt on when there was a bright yellow slip and slide stretched across the large backyard. I trained hard, and I liked the effect my efforts had on the female population. No shame in my game.

Two girls wearing almost nothing shrieked as they launched themselves over the slick surface, but my gaze landed back on Blue. Unlike most of the women I knew, Blue had never shown any appreciation for my body. As a matter of fact, I wasn't sure she'd said more than two words to me in the months since she'd started coming around with Eva.

Another mystery I wanted to solve. Some part of me insisted I was focusing on Blue as a distraction from my splintered insides, but my interest in her was real. It was nice to feel something other than misery and exhaustion.

I bided my time, watching like a creeper until Blue

shook her head in disgust and abandoned the game to head for the big house. She slipped through the sliding glass doors, and I took the opportunity offered to me.

The entrance from the patio led to a large white kitchen, empty except for the girl I was suddenly obsessed with digging through the refrigerator and mumbling to herself. She didn't stop when I pulled the door shut behind me, and I grinned at the frustration in her voice.

I leaned on the island and peeked around the door to see her collecting cheese cubes from a tray. "Do the Chi Omegas know you're raiding their fancy snacks?"

Blue gave a tiny shriek and slammed the fridge closed hard enough to rattle the glass bottles. Her blue green eyes landed on me—the color of water in paradise, another thing I hadn't noticed about her—and somehow got bigger.

"It's you," she spit out.

My smile widened. "It's me. You want to share some of your pilfered cheese?"

She blinked, then looked down at her handful of food with a frown. "It's not stolen. Courtney said I could help myself to the snacks."

I chuckled. "She probably meant the ones covering the tables outside, but what do I know?"

Blue held out her hand, and I plucked an orange cube from her palm. "No, you're probably right. I just wanted something cold."

"I won't tell if you won't." I popped the cheese in my mouth, and she followed my lead.

We shared her snack while she peered at me with growing suspicion. "Did you follow me here?"

Busted. "To the party? No. Into the kitchen? Yes."

"Why?"

I didn't want to admit she'd been the only thing to capture my attention in weeks—or how much she intrigued me. Sharing my feelings had gotten me into this mess in the first place. To buy myself some time, I came around the island to grab two plastic water bottles from the tub of ice on the counter next to her, handing her one.

She twitched toward the door like she wanted to run. "I'm not having sex with you."

My brows shot up. "Was that an option?"

Blue cleared her throat and took a swig of water. "I don't know, but it felt relevant."

Her eyes caught mine, and the kitchen narrowed to the two of us. I could make a joke and laugh off her knee-jerk response, but the lingering need to burrow under her ever-changing exterior knocked me off guard.

"It's not. Relevant. I don't actually try to get every woman I meet into bed. I mean, the interested ones, yeah, but not for a while. And the whole thing with Eva kind of knocked me out of the game. I couldn't handle a hookup even if I wanted to." My words tumbled over themselves in an awkward tangle, threatening to strangle me if I didn't get a grip on my tongue. I sucked at keeping things to myself.

Blue looked like she'd gladly strangle me too if it would stop this awkward conversation. "I'm sorry your penis isn't working, but that doesn't explain why you followed me."

"My junk works, Sunshine. I just don't have any interest in using it."

She tilted her head, confused. "Then why are you here?"

"I don't know." The truth slipped from me without permission from my brain.

People expected to see me at a party—*I* expected to see me at a party—but none of the scenario felt right, except for her. The world had shifted on its axis at some point, and I needed something genuine.

I shook my head and tried to explain. "I noticed you outside, and it was like seeing you for the first time—like you'd finally come out from behind your cloud. Despite your scowl. I thought I might be looking at the real you for once."

So much for not spilling my guts all over the kitchen. I waited for her to run screaming from the room, but her uneasy expression smoothed away.

"I'm always the real me. Hardcore, unfiltered truth. Whether you want it or not." She didn't sound particularly pleased with the observation, but it was exactly what I hadn't realized I needed until now.

Unfiltered truth. Someone get this girl a lasso.

"The real you sounds perfect. I'm tired of the bullshit."

She took a step closer, examining my face. "I can see why you'd feel that way with the others tiptoeing around you. Why come to a party then?"

It wasn't just my roommates' recent weirdness. This feeling had been building since before Eva, but I hadn't noticed it until she ripped the cover off when she left. Something had to change because I wasn't happy in my life anymore.

I laughed low, without humor. "I don't know. Loneliness. Stupidity. Hope."

"At least the last one is a good reason. Though I doubt it will do you much good if you're hoping for a reunion with Eva."

Blue knew more than I'd anticipated. Had Eva been talking about me? Hurt tried to slice me open before I squashed it flat. Eva and I were done. She'd made it perfectly clear she had no interest in a romantic relationship beyond a good dicking when she felt the urge.

As if she could read my mind, Blue frowned again. "Sorry. I'm not good with sensitive subjects."

Instead of sinking into the defeat and anger and hurt, I found myself coming up with ways to erase the frustration from Blue's face. I hadn't seen her smile yet, and I desperately wanted to make it happen. I wanted to see her full lips curl just for me.

My dick twitched at the thought, and despite the little voice yelling *hallelujah!*, I tried not to stare at her mouth.

Tried and failed. A faint blush lit Blue's cheeks, and she caught her bottom lip with her teeth. The tension ratcheted up, and I went from twitching to rock hard in seconds.

"If you're looking for sympathy, you're better off spending time with anyone outside." Even her voice had gone soft and breathy.

I stepped closer to her, narrowing the distance between us to mere inches, unable to stop myself from testing the reaction. "I don't want to spend time with them—I want to spend time with you."

Her lips parted on an indrawn breath, quick and surprised, and her tropical eyes darkened with hunger. My pulse rocketed to match. Huh. My attraction to Blue wasn't exactly a surprise—smokeshow—but she felt it too.

The slow-spreading heat, the subtle buzz of electricity, the urge to do something supremely stupid.

Blue hauled in a deep breath, and as promised, blurted out the truth. "Friends with benefits seems like a bad idea with Eva between us."

Fuck. Yes, it did. I ordered Big Mac to stand down and scrubbed a hand over my face. She didn't move, as if she hadn't convinced herself either. I could simply turn and walk away. Go back to my sad existence where everyone was afraid to whisper Eva's name in my vicinity and I felt so trapped I couldn't pull in a full breath of air.

A vivid memory of Blue's legs peeking out from under a short black dress at one of my Sunday karaoke deals flashed across my mind, followed by the image of her glaring down at the beanbags like they'd personally offended her.

To hell with walking away. It wasn't about Eva or my miserable ass. I'd gotten a taste of the real Blue, and I wanted more.

"How about friends without benefits? Keep me company this summer. I need to expand my inner circle, and I'm choosing you." I tried not to let the plea sneak into my words, but when her eyes narrowed, I was pretty sure I'd failed.

"If this is a ploy, I want you to know I have no problem using my pepper spray to make a point."

And just like that, my life became interesting again. I smiled at her threat, though I was one hundred percent certain she was serious. Hardcore, unfiltered truth.

"No need for your pepper spray, Sunshine, only your refreshing company." I shoved the benefits to the back of my mind. Blue hit every box for me, but I'd learned my lesson about mixing friendship with pleasure.

She blew out a breath. "Fine. Friends without benefits. At least until Eva comes back."

The major victory I'd just won felt strangely hollow, but I wasn't going to miss my chance to explore something different for a few months.

"Fair warning, I'm a cuddler." With a wicked grin, I pulled her close for a hug. A platonic hug. Purely to see how she'd react. Touching was my love language, after all.

Blue stiffened for a split second, then relaxed in my

arms. We were immediately treading dangerous territory, but my girl came up with the save once again.

She looked up at me and patted my bicep. "Fair warning, when startled, I punch first and ask questions later."

I laughed, a long, loud, unrestrained belly laugh, but I didn't let her go. She was mine for the summer, and I wasn't wasting a second.

2

Blue

It was the laugh that did it. I'd successfully avoided being alone with Adam Mackenzie for months, and he'd managed to corner me in a sorority kitchen at a party I hadn't particularly wanted to attend.

Then he'd managed to get his arms around me in less time than it took me to pick a snack to steal. Impressive, really. I sort of wished I'd timed it.

His chest shook as he laughed, and I fought the urge to melt. Or tuck my hands under his shirt for a feel of the abs he was always showing off. Friends. We were friends. Friends didn't grope each other. No matter how easy it would be to play off the simple touch.

The low rumble made my insides clench, destroying any chance I had at normal thought, so I backed out of his hold. Icy drops of water from the bottle I somehow still held splashed onto my toes, giving me the perfect excuse.

I took a long drink, ignoring the way his face fell slightly at my reaction. Hugging, touching in general, didn't appeal to me, but I still wanted to throw myself back against him.

Part of me wondered if maybe I'd been doing it wrong this whole time.

Despite my retreat, Adam didn't immediately look elsewhere for a more willing target. He leaned back against the marble counter, bracing his hands on either side of him and making the muscles in his upper arms stand out.

"Blue." The quiet comment pulled my gaze back to his face, where a smile flirted across his lips. "I didn't mean to make you uncomfortable."

"I'm not," I lied. He didn't need to know about my sudden curiosity.

"If I ever do, just let me know. Hands off immediately, okay?"

I nodded, afraid my tongue would go rogue again and beg him to touch me. How different would it be if he did it with intent? No. Not going there. I'd been fighting this draw for months, nothing had to change now.

My shoulders threatened to stiffen up again, but I breathed through the reaction. He wasn't making me uncomfortable—*I* was, with my inconvenient attraction and inability to stop picturing him with Eva.

Before I could formulate a verbal response, he pushed away from the counter and circled it to the barstools on the other side.

"How about if we get to know each other better? Right here, right now. I'll tell you anything you want to know, and I promise not to get offended."

I narrowed my eyes at him. "Seriously?"

People generally didn't like when I asked questions. Their preference for my silence didn't stop me from asking anyway, but I wasn't unaware of the awkward pauses that usually followed. For the most part, I'd stopped being embarrassed by it.

He spread his arms. "Yes, seriously. It's our first ask me anything, Sunshine, so make it a good one."

The sarcastic nickname he'd given me sparked an idea for my first question. "Why does everyone call you Mac? Why not Adam?"

A shadow darkened his eyes, but his smile didn't waver. "My first football coach refused to use anyone's first names. Mackenzie was too much of a mouthful for him, so he started calling me Mac. It stuck."

I tilted my head to study him. Body language wasn't my strong suit. I tended to misread any nuance I picked up, but for some reason, I had no trouble reading Mac. His shoulders hunched slightly, like he was bracing himself for disappointment. He didn't like his nickname—or some part of him didn't like it.

The reaction didn't make sense. He *told* people to call him Mac.

"Why does that bother you?" I expected him to offer a platitude, but I should have known better.

"Because that coach was an ass. He saw us as tools instead of little people with feelings and stuff. Our last names were printed on our uniforms, so he never bothered learning our first names. Easier to make a kid run until he pukes if you don't think of him as a person."

"Why do you still use it?"

"Because fuck that guy. I made some good friends on that team, and they liked little Mac. The coach made me faster, but the friends made me the Mac you see before you."

Crap, I wanted to hug him again. What was he doing to me? I circled the island to take the seat next to him. "Eva too?"

"Yeah, her too. She liked the nickname." He rubbed his

jaw, now with several days' worth of scruff instead of smooth like the last time I'd seen him, but he didn't look away. "According to my mom, nicknames are supposed to be a way to forge a connection with someone. She calls me *mijo*—no one else does that, not even my dad or my sisters. It's a special thing between me and Mom. The way you talk to people—what you call them or what they choose to be called—matters."

I tucked away the knowledge that Adam had sisters, right next to the surprising realization he was more perceptive than I'd given him credit for. Eva had warned me, in her own way, but I hadn't completely believed her until now.

The serious moment ended with Adam flashing me a wide grin. "You can call me whatever you want though, Sunshine."

He wanted *me* to pick? The air between us thickened with expectation, and I almost looked behind me to make sure he was talking to me. I'd seen him with Eva, heard of his exploits with the ball bunnies before her. The sane part of my brain assured me he flirted with everyone. The part of me that knew better saw the mask he'd just donned.

The person he'd shown me today didn't mesh with the Mac everyone else knew. Confident, yes, but also sweet and understanding—and sad. Underneath it all, he was sad. I wondered if the others knew how deeply it went.

I felt like he let me see the real person beneath the hotshot football player. With that realization, the decision was easy. I'd always called him Adam in my head anyway. If he was looking for a connection through a nickname, he'd probably be disappointed, but I was who I was.

"Mac is nice, but I like this version of you better, Adam."

He pressed his lips together for a beat, then nodded. "Okay."

My eyes narrowed at his one-word answer. "That's all? No snappy comeback?"

"For you, I can be Adam."

Frustration kicked at me that he was still trying to perform. "I don't need you to be anyone. You said you wanted to be friends with the real me... that goes both ways. I want the real Adam, not a construct you created."

"Ah, so you admit you want me." He wagged his finger at me.

A tiny growl escaped my throat. "I admit no such thing."

"Fair enough. Let's make a deal. We'll both be authentically ourselves, no performing or hiding. We can be real with each other, whatever that ends up looking like."

Adam slid off his stool and offered me his hand with his brows raised. Did he think I was afraid of touching him? With a matching expression, I slapped my palm into his and let him pull me off the stool.

"You aren't what I expected," I told him.

He shrugged at my comment. "I get that a lot. You want another shot at cornhole? My skills extend far beyond the football field."

I blinked at the sudden change in him. "How do you fit your giant head through doorways? I feel like it must be a challenge."

He opened his mouth, and I knew—I *knew*—he was about to make a dick joke. Instead, he nodded toward the backyard. "Let's get your revenge, then you can help me fend off the ball bunnies while we enjoy a nice, relaxing afternoon in the sun."

"Okay, but I can't stay all afternoon. I have dinner plans."

His gaze sharpened. "Big date?"

A short laugh burst out of me, laced with bitterness. "Something like that."

Rob would certainly enjoy forcing the evening in that direction. Though I'd rather light myself on fire than date his son.

Adam eased me closer, his hand tightening on mine. "I don't like that unhappy look on your face. If you need an out, text me. I'll come up with an appropriately dramatic exit strategy. Unless you want me to handle things in person for you. Have muscles, will travel."

His sudden protective streak did things to my equilibrium. I couldn't find my footing with him, so I did what I always did when confronted with an unstable situation. Retreat.

"I don't think that will be necessary, Adam. I can handle myself just fine." I tugged, but he didn't let me go.

Instead, he shifted closer and gripped the back of my neck, holding me in place.

"There is one thing I should probably tell you, in the spirit of realness." He dropped his mouth to my ear, lowering his voice and making my pulse take off again. "I like the way you say my name."

His lips brushed my cheek, then he was gone, somehow already across the room at the doors to the backyard. I forced myself not to cover the spot where my skin tingled. The gesture couldn't even be considered a kiss, and I refused to react while he watched me with dark eyes.

As for his words, there was no denying the sex in his voice, but Adam liked to push boundaries. Eva had told me as much, and I'd seen it for myself over the last few months. Declaring our friendship hands-off probably triggered his baser instincts. He wanted what he couldn't have.

Adam opened the sliding glass door and gestured for me to go first. I held my head high as I walked past, ignoring the pounding of my heart and the urge to drag his mouth down to mine. The tingles were new, but they'd fade soon enough.

I didn't have many friends before Eva, and I wasn't about to screw everything up by giving in to an ill-advised fling. Even if Adam was the only one who'd ever made me burn with a touch.

The Texas heat blanketed me as I crossed onto the patio, and I briefly considered simply leaving. Letting Adam find something—or someone—else to distract him for the summer. Except I couldn't forget the sadness in his eyes.

Eva didn't want to talk about him, but she wouldn't want him to be sad. *I* didn't want him to be sad. A sigh escaped me. How hard could it be to just enjoy his company without making things complicated?

Courtney waved from her spot by the stupid beanbag game, but her gaze flicked to the brooding football star walking close behind me. When her smile turned predatory, my muscles tensed with an unfamiliar surge of protectiveness.

He'd asked me to fend off the ball bunnies, and here I was, leading him straight to a large group of them. I didn't enjoy cornhole, and I had no desire to make up for my poor playing if it meant subjecting Adam to the kind of attention he wanted to avoid.

I switched directions so abruptly he almost ran into me. His large hand caught my waist, and he gave me a tiny smirk as I led him to a deserted seating area around the unlit fire pit. Unlike every other instance in my life, I knew exactly what that look meant.

I'll follow your lead, Sunshine.

I could almost hear his voice in my head. The deep timbre of my imagination making me shiver despite the sweat running down the middle of my back. Annoying.

A quick peek assured me Courtney had gone back to her game. Mission accomplished. I ignored the prick of feminine pride at successfully staking my claim and collapsed into the flimsy patio chair. Adam took the seat next to me, stretching his long legs out to cross his ankles on the edge of the stone circle. With a quirk of his eyebrow, he offered me the water bottle I hadn't seen him carry out here.

I took a long swig, then handed it back. My gaze clashed with his as he tipped the bottle at me in a salute and raised it to his mouth. He watched me watching him, his lips touching the same spot mine had seconds ago.

The stupid tingles started up again, and I dropped my eyes to the column of his throat. "You are stupidly attractive, and it's going to be really annoying if I have to chase away women wherever we go."

He laughed, setting the water on the ground between us. "Good thing you have that pepper spray ready."

I snorted. "I'm not spraying someone just because you can't help flirting."

Adam spread his arms. "Do you see me paying attention to anyone but you?"

No. I'd sat with my back facing the party, and he'd joined me without hesitation. Without sparing a glance toward the gathering of half-naked women on the lawn. The only one seemingly affected by his magnetic presence at the moment was me—and I was struggling under the weight of my own desires.

"What are we supposed to do together this summer?" I asked, surprised by the husky undertone in my voice.

He leaned toward me. "Whatever you want, Sunshine."

Immediately, my traitorous mind conjured up a vision of us twisted together on my pale purple sheets, his body covering mine, his mouth on my neck. I shoved the image away, locking it up with the other fantasies that had no business being in my head.

Friends *without* benefits. Without. Maybe if I repeated the mantra enough times I'd convince myself to follow the path I'd insisted on. Adam winked as if he could read my thoughts. And maybe he could. I'd never spent much time trying to hide what I was thinking.

This relationship was doomed from the beginning if the amusement in his eyes was anything to go by. He wanted a friend, and I couldn't keep my mind out of his pants. Fantastic.

Not complicated at all.

3

Blue

R unning late. Meet you at the restaurant. Mom's text came through as I was trying to put in my contacts, so I squinted to read it with the one eye that could see.

I snorted, careful not to blind myself with my response. Contacts and I had a contentious relationship in that I hated putting them in despite them being easier to deal with than my glasses. My phone buzzed with another message, but I didn't bother checking. Mom always sent a follow up apology.

Hope Caldwell never arrived on time if she could help it, even if she was supposed to be my ride to the dinner she'd guilted me into attending. I blinked the contact into place and added a final swipe of mascara to my dark lashes before shoving my phone in a tiny black clutch. She didn't expect a text back, just like I hadn't expected her to make it home before we had to leave.

I glanced at my outfit in the full-length mirror on the back of the door and grimaced. Mom had laid out the slinky black dress, knowing I'd show up in jeans and a snarky T-shirt if I had my way. The last time I'd worn this dress, I'd managed to make a fool of myself at a karaoke brunch with Eva and her friends.

So, the usual.

I didn't have much higher hopes for tonight. The light in my little bathroom flickered, and I made a mental note to remind Mom to buy bulbs the next time she went to the store. It would probably be faster if I went myself, but she insisted on taking care of the upkeep.

No complaints here since I didn't have a lot of cash on hand to cover when something broke.

We technically didn't live together, but Mom owned the building that housed her dress shop, including the two tiny apartments upstairs. She barely made enough from the shop to cover the taxes and utilities, but when I graduated next year, she was going to sell the whole place so we could move to Dallas full time.

I glanced at her door as I locked up. She spent more time in Dallas than here these days. Not great for the dress shop since I had to run it when she was gone. I was not meant for retail. Maybe if I got paid more, I'd care, but I basically worked there in exchange for free lodging. My paycheck barely covered food and textbooks. I loved my mother and wanted to do what I could to help her, but the job blew.

I'd been living the same life since we moved to Addison when I was fifteen. Go to school, work in the shop, do home-work, spend time with Mom, repeat. My dad was never in the picture, but Mom and I were a cohesive team, which was good because it seemed like no one else was interested in playing.

Except Adam. He'd surprised me by staying glued to my side all day—asking questions and telling me about his family. It was a nice change of pace, but I wasn't holding my breath for it to become a regular thing despite Adam's assurances. People simply didn't stick around when I was involved.

Mom may have been flighty, but I knew I could count on her. She was my constant.

Life had never been lonely with her around, and even though things would change when I graduated, we'd still be together in Dallas. Mom would open her yoga studio, and I'd be her business manager. Thinking about the move dropped a cold lump in my gut, but we couldn't stay in Addison forever.

I jogged down the stairs to the dark street and checked my phone. The Uber was still fifteen minutes out, which meant I'd be late, but I'd probably beat Mom there. I chewed on my lower lip and tried not to let the frustration win.

When Mom had been dating Archer Bolme, he'd always sent a car for me when I joined them for dinner. I probably shouldn't expect the same consideration from every guy she dated, but I couldn't help comparing.

I didn't know how Mom had gone from the sexy, brooding head coach for the Dallas Thunder to Rob Warren, venture capitalist. Athletes had never been a thing for me, but I'd liked Archer. He'd kept the hockey talk to a minimum, and he'd smiled at my jokes.

Rob rubbed me the wrong way, and his son, Shad, was one frat party away from a sexual assault charge. Every time I interacted with Rob, I left feeling bad about myself. Mom seemed happy though, especially once he offered to invest the money for her studio.

I just wished our whole future wasn't tied up with him.

One egregiously expensive Uber ride later, I pulled up in

front of the posh hotel housing the restaurant where I was supposed to meet them. Through the big glass doors, the place looked dim despite boasting several large sparkling chandeliers. If the mood lighting had to be that dark, I seriously questioned the quality of the food. Rob liked places that served tiny portions and had a twenty-page wine list.

At least I wasn't paying. Judging from the people I could see sitting at tables near the front, I wouldn't be able to afford an appetizer here. White tablecloths, candles, glittering jewels on every patron, more silverware than any one person needed.

Mom had been right about the dress. None of the people in there wore jeans.

I sighed as I walked through the door, held open by a guy who probably made more than me per hour to stand there. Icy air coated my moist skin, and goosebumps popped up everywhere. Mom was nowhere in sight, as expected, but I spotted Rob and Shad at a table in the middle of the room.

Rob was good-looking enough for an uptight business type. He wore his navy suit like he'd been born in it, and his light brown hair was perfectly styled with that side swoosh rich guys liked. With his plastic smile, he reminded me of a Ken doll.

Shad wasn't much better, despite being my age. He wore his suit without a tie and with the top button undone. Same dumb haircut, same superior look in his blue eyes. An image of Adam popped up in my mind, as if my subconscious couldn't help comparing the two. Relaxed and playful, his dark eyes locked on me as he ran a hand through his tousled hair—Adam came out ahead in every category.

For a second, I considered waiting outside. The humidity wasn't so bad tonight, and I could finish a chapter

I'd been reading on my phone during the ride. Mom wouldn't be much longer, and I'd rather have her there as a buffer at the table. Before I could turn around, Rob glanced up at the entrance where I stood awkwardly next to the host stand.

He raised an imperious brow, and the host gestured for me to follow him as if he'd only been waiting for Rob's command. I lifted my chin and steeled myself for the inevitable criticism. If Mom had been on time for once, he would have skipped over me entirely to dote on her.

The things I did for love.

Rob and Shad stood to offer me big, creepily white smiles as I approached the table.

"I'm so glad you could join us, Angela." Rob never used my real name once Mom let my very normal middle name slip.

Shad only dragged his gaze over my curves, highlighted in the damn dress. I immediately wanted to go home and shower. Rob's son embodied the stereotype of entitled rich kid—assuming everyone around him existed for the sole purpose of serving him in some capacity.

He'd made my capacity clear on our first meeting months ago when he cornered me in his father's kitchen after brunch and offered to take me upstairs for a quickie. When I'd declined in no uncertain terms and attempted to leave, he'd grabbed my wrist. My mom interrupted him by coming into the room, and I put in a lot of effort to not be alone with him after that. In general, men didn't scare me, but I wasn't stupid.

I tried not to dwell on bad memories, so I buried it back in the dark recesses of my mind where it belonged.

"Mom's running late. She should be here soon."

Rob nodded and resumed his seat. "She let me know."

Shad edged the host away to pull my chair out himself. With no other option besides abruptly leaving, I allowed Shad to help me sit. He pushed my chair closer to the table, then his hand trailed across the bare skin at the back of my neck. My shoulders stiffened, and I leaned forward to grab the already full wine glass in front of me.

I hated red wine, but taking a sip offered me a convenient excuse to avoid any more unwanted touching. The bitter taste coated my mouth, and I had the sudden urge to laugh at the absurdity of my situation. Shad had graduated from Teagan University too, a year before me, with a business degree. These guys were supposed to be professionals, but even my horrible store clerk skills outclassed them.

When I sneaked a glance at Shad, he smirked at me, looking entirely too pleased with himself.

Rob leaned back in his chair, idly swirling his wine in his glass. "Shad, why don't you tell Angela about your summer plans?"

I couldn't care less about Shad's summer, but I didn't want to start this dinner off by sharing my bad mood. Mom would pick up on it immediately, and Rob would be sure to point out, delicately, of course, that I seemed to be having a hard day.

Shad's grin widened. "I'll be working with the business department at TU to set up an internship program with Dad's company, which means spending a lot of time on campus. Maybe we can meet up for coffee or something."

My teeth ground together. I took summer classes every year because my schedule during the fall and spring was always erratic with the added responsibility of managing the dress shop half the time. Now I'd spend my summer sneaking around campus.

"I'd love to see Hope's shop too," he continued.

I opened my mouth to tell him exactly what he could do with his summer plans, but Rob stood as my mom's voice came from behind me.

"That would be lovely." Her sandalwood scent wrapped around me as she leaned down to kiss my cheek. "Hi, baby."

"Hi, Mom."

She patted my shoulder, then circled the table to kiss Rob. The loose skirt and tank top she'd left in this morning had been replaced by a short, vibrant blue, cocktail dress that showed off her toned legs. People often mistook us for sisters because we shared the same sharp features and dark hair, but that was as far as our similarities went.

Hope Caldwell had a savvy businesswoman buried inside her fun-loving yoga personality, and I couldn't even conjure up the fun-loving part. To my surprise, Rob seemed to appreciate both parts of her. He pulled out her chair, much the same way Shad had done for me, but Mom looked a lot happier at the subtle touches.

I drained my glass of wine to keep from making a face. Without missing a beat, Shad refilled it with a generous pour. I growled out a thank you and spared a second to wonder if any drink Shad touched was safe to consume.

Mom smiled at me, the happiness pouring off her. "You look fantastic, Blue. Archer was right. That dress is fabulous on you."

I'd forgotten Archer had found the dress for me. He'd sometimes tagged along when Mom went searching for stock, though he'd sworn us to secrecy. Couldn't have a big, bad hockey coach flipping through racks of second-hand dresses.

Rob's lips thinned at the mention of Archer, but he nodded along. "You look beautiful tonight. It's nice to see the natural color of your hair."

My hand lifted to my updo—the one I'd done specifi-cally because it hid my rainbow streaks—and I tried not to be offended. Rob had a very specific definition of appro-priate beauty. Tonight might be the first time I'd hit his high standards, but I still felt like I'd failed.

Instead of responding to Rob's backhanded insult, I took another swig of wine. Alcohol had never been a coping mechanism for me, but with nothing else in arm's reach, I was relying heavily on the wineglass to keep my face busy.

Mom leaned forward. "I'm so glad you'll have Shad around for the summer, because we have some big news for you." She shared a secret smile with Rob, then lifted her left hand from under the table. "We're getting married."

My chest squeezed like the time I'd knocked the air out of myself falling from an inverted pose. I couldn't tear my eyes away from the enormous gleaming diamond on her finger. Distantly, I heard Rob order champagne and Shad offer his congratulations.

People at nearby tables clapped politely when the cork popped and Rob made a toast to his future bride. I finished off the wine I had in my hand—it got slightly better the more I drank of it—and took a flute of champagne to lift at the appropriate time.

My shock faded in time to hear Rob announce a fall wedding. Fall. As in only a few months away. Everyone else raised their glasses for a small sip, then applauded. I drained mine. The bubbles tickled my nose, but I needed the liquid courage to fortify my facial muscles.

Mom had tears glistening in her eyes as she leaned over to share a chaste kiss with Rob. Happy tears. My impulsive, creative, genius mother was marrying a Ken doll.

I wrenched my gaze away and accidentally clashed with

Shad's. He watched me with a speculative gleam I disliked intensely.

Mom cleared her throat and discreetly wiped her eyes. "I want you to be my maid of honor, Blue, and of course, Shad will be the best man."

I nodded mutely. What else could I say? Mom could ask me to BASE jump off Reunion Tower and I'd strap on a parachute.

She reached out and clasped my hand, squeezing my fingers. "I'm going to be spending even more time here in Dallas to prep for the wedding, so I'm reducing my hours at the dress shop. You'll have more responsibility, but I don't want you overwhelmed trying to pick up my slack, especially in your final summer of college."

A thread of panic tied knots in my intestines. It sounded like she was leaving the dress shop up to me. I didn't like covering when Mom was there, no way did I want to run the thing all on my own. Behind the scenes? Yes. But we didn't have any other employees, which meant if the shop was open, I was all people would get.

My head spun a little, and I swallowed hard. I knew better than to drink on an empty stomach, but those cheese cubes with Adam had been hours ago. If I was going to survive the night, I needed bread or something.

I snagged the waiter's arm as he passed by picking up champagne glasses. "Can I get—"

"We need a few more minutes, please," Rob interrupted.

The waiter didn't give me a second glance as he pulled away and practically bowed at Rob. I frowned at his back, then pressed my lips together when I realized all three of my tablemates were staring at me.

"What?"

Mom fidgeted with her napkin and sent Rob a pleading

glance. What the heck? He usually deferred to her when it came to me.

"The wedding will be an important social event for all of us, but especially for your mother. She'll be launching her yoga studio around that time, and we'll be inviting potential clientele from the upper echelons of Dallas society."

My brows rose as I realized what that meant. "Mom, I thought you were waiting until next year to start the studio."

She gave me a tentative smile, as if she were worried about *my* reaction. "The perfect space came available, and two of the instructors I wanted agreed to come work for me. I'm going to be in Dallas anyway...Everything just fell into place, and Rob and I agreed there was no point in waiting."

There was a point. *I* was the point. The life we'd built together in Addison was the point. I wanted her to be happy, but at the same time, I felt like she was abandoning me right before the finish line. "What about your classes at TU?"

Mom reached across the table toward me. "I'll fulfill my contract with them for the next school year. Don't worry, your tuition will still be covered. You can use the profits from the shop to cover your other expenses. Everything is going to be fine, I promise—"

Rob caught Mom's hand, and she straightened as if he'd pulled a string. "Angela knows how to run the shop. There's another matter we need to discuss. We're concerned about the quality of your acquaintances for the wedding events."

I frowned as I looked back and forth between them. "What do you mean?"

"We can't have you showing up with a drug dealer or someone equally undesirable if you're representing Hope as the maid of honor."

I huffed out a breath. One time. I'd brought a guy around to a family dinner *one time*, and he'd hit on Mom, suggested a threesome, then offered to sell her some of his product. Rob hadn't even been in the picture then.

We'd kicked him out, and I'd blocked his number. It wasn't like I'd chosen him specifically because of his horrible traits. None of that should have anything to do with my mom's wedding. As usual, I couldn't make the connection on my own.

"What are you suggesting?"

"Shad, or someone of his choosing, will accompany you to the events."

"Oh, hell no." The protest exploded out of me without thought, and Rob raised a brow as if to say I was simply proving his point. "If you don't trust my dates, I'll go alone."

Mom winced, and Rob shook his head. "Unacceptable. As a member of the wedding party, you need to present a certain image at each of the events, which will include activities with your date."

"How many events are we talking about here?"

"Several leading up to the wedding itself, all of them prime opportunities to introduce Hope and her yoga studio to the right audience. Your social skills are a little rusty, but we can polish those up nicely with Shad's help."

Shad had remained silent up to then, but his next sentence confirmed my suspicion he'd been in on the wedding plans. "I'll take good care of her this summer."

The urge to punch his smug little face rose so suddenly and violently I had to clench my hands together under the table. I turned to my mom, expecting her to be equally offended on my behalf, but her sad smile dropped a brick in my gut.

"He's not wrong, baby. You have trouble finding dates, and this could be a chance for you to come out of your shell. Please just give it a chance."

"I can get a date," I ground out.

The clear pity on her face cut me open. "There's no shame in admitting when you're not good at something. Shad has a lot of connections, and who knows, maybe you'll meet someone you like."

"I can get a date," I repeated. My stomach churned with the urge to puke. Heat suffused my body despite the chill in the restaurant, and all I could think about was escaping this hellish nightmare. "I'm sorry, but I think I'm going to head home. My stomach is bothering me. Probably something I ate earlier." Or the fact that my own mother had tossed me to the wolves.

Mom frowned. "Do you want me to come with you?"

I waved her off as I stood and dropped my napkin on the table. "No, I'll be fine. I just need to rest. Congratulations. Love you, Mom."

"Love you too, Blue," she called to my back. Neither of the men said anything, but I could feel Shad's gaze on me as I slalomed between tables.

I couldn't get out of there fast enough. One too many glasses of wine paired with a sharp slice of betrayal. Mom was supposed to be on my side. We were supposed to be a team against the jerks in the world.

The heat smacked me in the face when I emerged onto the street, but I sucked in a deep breath of the warm air. Car exhaust and someone's overly floral perfume made me cough, and I suddenly missed the pine scent in Addison. An acute pang had me laying my hand over my chest as I struggled to hold myself together.

Mom was getting married. To Rob. I dreaded the day, but she'd looked so happy I'd do anything in my power to help. Despite Shad's *kind* offer, I'd find a way to show up with a respectable date as requested.

A couple entering the restaurant gave me a strange look as they passed, and I remembered the entire front wall was glass. The idea of Rob—or worse Shad—seeing me freak out made me start walking. I should call an Uber, but something else niggled at me.

They weren't entirely wrong. I sucked at talking to people, especially male people. I liked to think I didn't have many friends because I hadn't had time to fritter away while taking classes and running the shop, but the truth was I didn't know how to make a friend. If not for Eva, I wouldn't have any experience at all.

Then again, I'd spent all afternoon next to Adam, mixing heavier topics with jokes and increasingly bad suggestions for summer activities. Before I'd left, he'd stolen my phone to add his number. *In case you need me.* Not the actions of someone who planned to forget my existence after I left his immediate vicinity.

A horrible idea circled my mind, encouraged by the wine in my system.

Adam could make friends with a lawn chair, and he had no problem finding dates. His charisma was as natural as breathing. I stopped on the corner and pulled up the contacts list on my phone.

He wanted something to do this summer...well, I had a project for him.

4

Mac

I knew she'd call—I just hadn't expected it to be a few hours after I dropped her off at her mom's dress shop. The apartment was dark when I got home, thank god, so I'd brought my stuff in and collapsed on my unmade bed. If Shaw or RJ—or Noah, though I didn't expect him to spend much time here with Chloe in the apartment right across the landing—knocked on my door, I'd pretend to be asleep.

Sleep didn't come, but I put in a solid four hours of intense moping before the phone rang. Blue's name flashed on my screen above the picture I'd taken of her frowning at me.

Her dark brows pulled together over those blue green eyes, staring straight into me, seeing way more than anyone else did. The ringtone started over, and I realized I'd been laying on my bed in our dark apartment staring at her picture like an idiot.

I swiped the screen and tried to clear the cobwebs from my brain. "Hey, Sunshine. Miss me already?"

She huffed. "No, but I do need your help."

My lethargy faded instantly, and I sat up. "Are you okay?"

"Yes. I drank a little too much at dinner and then didn't eat dinner. Will you come get me?"

I hit speakerphone so I could get dressed, pulling on the first pair of shorts I grabbed. "Where are you?"

Blue hesitated, sending my pulse skyrocketing. "I'm at the corner of Wood and Main...in Dallas."

A quick search told me I was forty-five minutes away. "Is there somewhere nearby you can wait?"

"There's a coffee place on the corner."

"Perfect. Go inside. I'll be there as soon as I can." I was already grabbing my keys and hustling out the door.

"Thanks, Adam."

She hung up before I could ask what had happened or why she didn't just call an Uber. I'd find out soon enough.

———

I PULLED up to the coffee shop on the corner of Wood and Main forty-two minutes later, and Blue was exactly where she said she'd be. She sat by the front window staring into space, her sharp features highlighted by the bright interior of the building.

When I opened the door and stuck my head out to whistle, she blinked, focusing on me instead of whatever was haunting her. She wasted no time climbing into my Jeep, and I waited until she buckled up before I reversed out of the parking spot.

I kept my eyes on the road despite the tiny dress riding up her thighs as she tucked her legs under her. "Want to talk about it?"

Blue pressed her lips together for a second, then reached up to pull the pins from her updo. "It's a long story."

"I have time."

Her hair fell around her shoulders in wild waves, and I squeezed the wheel to keep my hands on my side of the vehicle. The rainbow streaks hidden under layers of dark chocolate brown made me a little grabby. I loved the surprise pop of fun mixed with her natural color, or what I assumed was her natural color.

Blue shook her head and ran her fingers through the tresses a couple of times before she slumped back against the seat. "My mom is getting married."

"You don't look happy, so it must not be to Archer Bolme."

Her gaze cut my direction.

"What? I can't know things? He's on SportsCenter all the time, and he's a local legend. Add in Eva is a little bit in love with your mom, and I know way more than I want to about hockey's bad boy coach."

"I didn't realize college football stars followed professional hockey."

"I have many skills, which I will gladly talk about for hours on end, but we're not discussing me. What's wrong with your mom getting married to not-Archer?"

She rubbed her temples, and I made a mental note to get some water in her as soon as possible. "Rob, my mom's boyfr—fiancé—is sad gooey white bread when she could have had a delicious crusty sourdough. Who she dates or marries isn't my choice though. Which is apparently a good thing because according to them I am incapable of finding a date to the wedding festivities on my own."

At that moment, I decided I'd never call him Rob. Not-Archer would live on in infamy. "So you got shit-faced and walked out on dinner?"

"I did not get shit-faced. I had too much wine in a short

period of time...then I walked out on dinner." A giggle escaped from her, and I revised her level of drunk. Not sloppy, but definitely tipsy.

"Okay, first, food. We're stopping at Papi's. Second, why do you care what white bread not-Archer thinks?"

The smile faded, and she turned to stare out the window at the passing darkness. "It's not important."

"Bullshit. If it wasn't important, you'd be eating steak right now instead of frowning at the trees."

"Maybe I'd rather spend time with you than Rob and Shad."

I ignored the little ball of warmth growing in my chest to make sure I'd heard her right. "Shad?"

"Rob's son. He graduated from TU last year. Business major. Finance, I think. He's working for his dad's company, and he's exactly as pompous as all that makes him sound."

"Who voluntarily calls their kid Shad? His name sounds like it's in past tense."

Blue snorted. "You'll probably get to meet him since he'll be spending time on campus this summer."

"Yay," I deadpanned. "I've always wanted to meet someone named Shad."

"Stop it."

"I Shad you not," I muttered.

Blue dissolved into laughter. "This is definitely worth a missed steak."

Making her laugh filled a part of me I hadn't realized was empty. "I'm not surprised you chose me over Shad, but you're not getting off that easily. Tell Daddy Mac what's bothering you."

She shuddered. "Please don't refer to yourself as Daddy Mac. I have enough parental issues without adding you into the mix."

"We're getting closer. What parental issues?"

Blue angled herself toward me and studied my face. "You don't give up, do you?"

"Never. Persistence is my finest trait...after my abs."

Her gaze flicked south, then back up. "I'll take your word for it. My mom raised me all on her own. Her parents wrote her off when she got pregnant as a teenager, and my dad wasn't in the picture. Having me made her life infinitely harder, but she never treated me like a burden. She's always been my best friend, always been there for me, and now she's leaving Addison to pursue her dream of a fancy yoga studio."

"Why is that bad?"

"Because I'm still here."

Her quiet comment sucked all the joy out of the space between us. I drove in silence for a few miles trying to imagine what it would feel like to only have one family member. The ever-present chaos was a hallmark at my mom's house, despite none of us kids living there anymore.

As the favorite, I'd never thought about what it meant to be left behind. I'd bet it hurt like hell if she thought her mom was choosing not-Archer—or even Dallas—over her.

Kind of like being told by your best friend that you're good enough for a quick fuck, but not a proper date.

I shoved the comparison away. Blue didn't need me moping all over her when she was already dealing with shit. Change was hard, good or bad, and it sounded like a major change had just upended her life. Technically, I was a change too, but I was sure as hell going to be a good one.

My headlights hit the Welcome to Addison sign, and I realized I'd let the quiet go on for too long when I should have asked the obvious question. "Do you *want* to go with her?"

Blue spared me a frustrated glance. "Not if it means living with Rob and Shad."

"Why am I not surprised he still lives at home," I mumbled.

She smacked me in the arm with an open palm. "Do you want an answer or not?"

"Damn, girl. No need for violence." I was hoping for another smile, maybe a giggle, but Blue remained solemn. At least she was facing me again.

"Please. That probably hurt my hand more than your bulging muscles."

"I prefer sculpted, but I'll accept bulging since you're obviously distraught. Is your mom's marriage going to affect your last year of school?"

Blue shook her head, pulling her hair over one shoulder. "No. Nothing should change other than my hours at the shop."

"Are we angry with Yoga Mom? I can call Shaw for some afterhours shenanigans if necessary. He just stocked up on toilet paper."

She sent me an incredulous look. "You're a senior in college and you still pull pranks like that? Nevermind. No shenanigans necessary. I'm not mad at her. I feel guilty because I was looking forward to graduating and getting out of the dress shop, but I wasn't ready for Mom to start the process early."

"Maybe you should talk to her about it."

Blue crossed her arms and tilted her head. "Have you talked to your roommates yet?"

I narrowed my eyes at her, then returned my attention to the road. "Are you asking because you want to change the subject?"

"Yes, but it also directly affects me. You wanted to spend

time with me this summer so you could avoid them. I was interested to know if that was still the case."

I winced. When she put it that way, I sounded like a dick. "I wasn't *only* doing it to avoid them. Really, avoidance was a tiny perk compared to spending time with you."

"Flattery doesn't work on me."

"You just haven't experienced my flattery yet."

Interest lit her eyes, but she stayed doggedly on topic. "I'm assuming your attempts to distract me mean you haven't seen them."

"Everyone was gone when I got home," I relented.

Her expression softened, lips curling up into a tiny smile. "That must have been a relief for you."

"It's only a minor reprieve. Shaw's going to kick my ass tomorrow when he finds out I skipped training today to go to a party. Then RJ will give him shit, and I'll have to spend the rest of the session watching them eye-fuck each other."

Just the idea of showing up and laughing off Eva's absence made me exhausted. A week of enchiladas and smothering at my mom's house helped create some distance, but I wasn't stupid. The rest of the crew knew Eva had fled town rather than date me.

They weren't here though. Blue was.

"What about Noah and Chloe?" she asked.

I shook my head as I turned into the parking lot for Papi's. "With Eva gone, I figure Noah will spend most of the summer across the landing. Hell, even if Eva were here, he'd be over there every night. Did you know he bought her a bed?"

The Jeep lurched to a stop, and Blue glanced around at the other two cars taking up half the available spaces. "What is this place?"

I stopped staring at her long enough to make sure the

building wasn't on fire or something. Nope. Papi's barely qualified as a restaurant on a good day. It was a converted gas station with two little tables inside, but it had air conditioning.

"Papi's isn't fancy dining, but they know how to make a damn fine taco. Come on, I'm buying."

A couple of people sat at the picnic tables scattered around the grass outside, lit by the bright fluorescent lights inside the shop. They ignored us as I ushered Blue through the doors. The small space was clean and smelled like my mom's kitchen.

The last bits of my annoying misery cloud lifted, and I made a note to come back here the next time it hit me hard. Food therapy.

Blue followed me to the counter and stared at the menu written directly onto the wall. In the three years I'd been coming here, it had never changed. The system worked great for Papi's, college kids loved cheap Mexican food and a late-night tequila fix, but Blue wasn't part of the usual college crowd.

She squinted at the scripty handwriting, then sent me a quick glance. "I'm glad you brought me here."

"I'm glad you called." Between her and the tacos, my night looked infinitely better than it had a few hours ago.

5

Mac

The tender moment lulled me into a false sense of security. I should have known better.

Blue leaned onto the counter and tried to smile at the cashier who was completely ignoring us. "I'll have a margarita, extra—"

I covered her face with my hand, muffling the rest of her order. "She'll have water and the big mama taco plate."

Blue swatted at me, but she only landed a glancing blow against my side. Her mumbles got more aggressive though.

Three people showed up behind us, and I didn't want to hold up the line, so I went with the quickest solution. I wrapped my arm around her waist, effectively flattening her flailing limbs at her sides.

"I'll have the same thing. Thanks."

The cashier wrote down our order and handed the ticket back to the kitchen without looking directly at us. I'd been coming to Papi's Taco Stand at least once a week for the last three years, same middle-aged lady behind the counter, and I still didn't know what color her eyes were.

I tapped my phone to the white square while holding

Blue back with one hand. The cashier slapped two large paper cups in front of us before moving on to the next people in line. I used to have a running bet with myself to get her to laugh, but tonight I had another grumpy lady to deal with.

Blue tried to juke around me, but I wrapped an arm around her middle and hauled her away from the counter.

"Should have taken you to Whataburger," I muttered.

Her dress rode up, and I got a delicious glimpse of toned thigh before I tugged it down for her. I may have let my thumb linger against her warm skin a little longer than necessary. Blue finally realized she wasn't going to overpower me and huffed in my direction.

"What's the matter, Sunshine? Forget your pepper spray?" The tiny clutch she'd carried might have changed the power dynamic—I wasn't going to discount the possibility of being pepper sprayed—but she'd left it in my Jeep.

Blue glared at me as I filled the cups at the water station. "I don't appreciate you deciding what I want here."

"Trust me, you don't want a margarita here. Besides, I just drove two hours to pick up your sloshed ass, and I didn't hear a thank you."

"I'm not sloshed anymore," she insisted, then quietly added, "I'd like to be before starting this conversation."

I shot a glance at her, but she wouldn't meet my eyes. "What conversation?"

She snatched her cup out of my hand and chugged half of it on the way to a table. "Thank you."

I pinched the bridge of my nose, unsure if she was grateful for the drink or the ride. Maybe both? Blue was hard enough to follow when she was sober and relaxed. In that dress, keeping up was a lost cause. I couldn't stop staring at her legs long enough to pay attention.

For a stupid second, I considered dumping the cold water over my shorts to send Big Mac a clear message. Off. Limits. Instead, I joined her at the spot she'd chosen, grateful she hadn't bothered to look down.

"What conversation?"

She sat up in the squeaky chair and squared her shoulders. "I want you to teach me how to get a date."

Suddenly, I wished *I* had a margarita—or at least a double shot of tequila. She held my gaze while a million scenarios flew through my mind, the tropical color tempting me to dive right into a bad decision.

When I didn't answer, she plowed on. "You wanted something to keep you busy this summer, and I need to find an appropriate escort. I'm not willing to ask my mom or Rob for help—"

I held up a hand to stop the flow of words. "This has to do with the wedding?"

She nodded, nearly strangling her cup. It was on the tip of my tongue to offer myself up as tribute, but a broken part of me deep inside kept the words from escaping. She hadn't asked me to escort her—she'd asked me to teach her. I couldn't handle another friend deciding I wasn't good enough to date.

That didn't mean I was going to let anyone else tutor Blue.

"What exactly are you asking for? A little help with a meet cute? Ways to keep a conversation going? Blow job pointers?"

Pink tinted her cheeks. "Everything. I thought you could tutor me, maybe practice flirting, and you could help me figure out what I'm doing wrong when I go out."

"How?"

She tilted her head and her brow furrowed as if she was confused by my question. "By coming with me?"

I frowned. "That's a lot of expectations for a couple of dates and a wedding. Are you sure you want to let these people dictate how you feel about yourself? I like you the way you are, awkward hottie and all."

Her lips pursed at the words, and I reminded myself I wasn't repeating past mistakes. I could be friends with a woman without getting my dick involved.

Blue echoed my thoughts. "No offense, but you don't count. Friends without benefits, remember?" She released her death grip on the cup and flattened her hands on the table. "Honestly, the wedding ultimatum was only the catalyst. I don't want to disappoint my mom, true, but I also want to prove to myself I don't *have* to be a social outcast. I may not want a relationship now, but I don't want to be alone forever."

The way she said it—like stating a fact but with a determined tip of her chin—pulled me all the way in. My mom used to threaten to tattoo *I can do it myself* on my forehead. I was intimately familiar with the concept. And with the loneliness.

I tapped my thumb on the table. "If I agree, I have a few demands."

Her eyes narrowed. "Like what?"

I held up a finger. "Tutoring only. We're not doing some bullshit fake dating thing. I'm not going to pretend to be your boyfriend if you get embarrassed about this." She opened her mouth to interrupt, but I powered through. "I'm done being someone's dirty little secret."

She winced. "No fake anything."

"While we're on the subject, no secrets. I don't want to

find out three months from now I was grooming you for a cult or something."

Blue gave a decisive nod. "No secrets."

I leaned back in my chair, crossing my arms as I studied her before I presented my final demand. "You have to be willing."

She scoffed. "I came to you. How is that not willing?"

"You came to me after shotgunning a bottle of wine during a high stress period with a lot of emotional fallout. Tomorrow Blue might wake up and regret everything about this conversation. In which case, I have no problem forgetting this ever happened. Even if you're one hundred percent on board, you might not like me pushing you out of your comfort zone. I'm not going to drag your grumpy ass around if you don't want it."

Blue studied me. "Are you a psychology major?"

I chuckled. "No. Business management with a minor in music."

"The best I can do is promise to try, but you can't give up when I mess everything up either."

"I'm not the giving up type. Unless there are spiders involved. In that case, I'm fucking out." I shuddered. "So many legs."

Her nose wrinkled. "I certainly hope there won't be any spiders involved in my dating life. Will you teach me or not?"

Before I could give her a final answer, the cashier called our number, so I hopped up to grab the food. I was going to say yes—no doubt in my mind—but one aspect of her request still bothered me.

The need for her to date other guys while I watched. I'd never considered myself possessive until the last twenty-four hours or so. Even my relationship with Eva had been low-

key. Some might even say hidden. I might have been bitter
—was still bitter—about the end result, but I'd had no
problem sharing her with the world. Eva demanded attention wherever she went, including mine.

Blue only needed herself, utterly confident doing her
own thing even if it meant she was alone doing it. Except for
now, apparently.

Pressure built in my chest when I pictured Blue smiling
at another guy, with another guy's hands on her. My fingers
curled into claws around the plastic tray holding our food. I
thanked the apathetic cashier and yanked napkins from the
holder to give myself a few more seconds before turning
back to the table.

Violent urges weren't usually my thing, but I couldn't
deny the savage response heating my blood. I didn't
examine the reaction too closely. Blue was a friend asking
me for help. I'd provide whatever help I could. My dick
twitched at the possibilities, and I frowned down at my
crotch.

Big Mac had his own ideas of how to help, which I
intended to ignore. He always got me in trouble anyway.

I set the tray of tacos and sides on the table between us
and met her questioning gaze. "Okay."

A smile slowly emerged, like the sun coming from
behind the clouds. "Okay?"

We stared at each other, letting the reality of my agreement settle. I'd probably regret this in the morning, and I'd
definitely regret it when we got to the post-date scenarios. I
wasn't actually sure I could give her pointers on blow job
etiquette without a mutiny from Big Mac.

Blue broke the moment by grabbing a napkin from the
pile. "Great, we can start right away."

I pointed a taco at her. "Slow down, speed racer. I don't

have a seminar prepared for teaching socially awkward hotties how to people."

"Fine. We can start tomorrow."

I snorted. "I have class tomorrow, then training, and..." I trailed off when I realized I didn't have anything to add after training. It was my week to get groceries, so I should probably go shopping, but I didn't have cheer practice or movie night or a fashion show. Eva had slowly taken over my life. Without her, there was suddenly room for something new.

Hopefully, Blue's crazy request would be good for both of us.

"I'm going to need a couple of days to come up with ideas," I finished lamely.

"Maybe step one could be talking to your roommates."

The mouthful of taco I'd just bitten into threatened to get stuck in my throat. This time, the choking feeling wasn't from any possessive caveman urges—it was pure, unfiltered dread. Eva and I had kept our ill-fated relationship a secret from my roommates, and they'd all had front row seats to watching it crash and burn.

They kept asking if I was okay, and I didn't know how to answer. I wasn't. I was shook. I caught my feelings at random times, but the sharpest bits were from her up and leaving without talking to me rather than losing the love of my life. I was starting to suspect I'd fooled myself into wanting a future with Eva. How was I supposed to explain I'd fucked up my friendship for nothing? And that I was upset because she'd ghosted me when she should have had my back?

I swallowed hard and wiped my mouth with a napkin before covering with a joke. "That seems unnecessary, and frankly, borderline hostile on your part."

A flash of unease crossed her features, but then she

studied my face and smiled. "You can't avoid them all summer."

"Who said anything about avoiding them? I just don't plan to introduce the topic of my doomed relationship with Eva. Or the aftermath. Or what happened to my favorite running shorts. You know what, avoiding them might be the way to go. Can I move in with you?"

Blue laughed quietly, and I smiled to myself. Her laughs weren't easy to come by, but I was proud as hell when I could bring her a little happiness.

"Careful, Sunshine, I'm not hearing a no."

"Adam, I live in a tiny efficiency. You're bigger than every piece of furniture I own."

"Ah, well I guess you'll have to stay at my place to save me."

She twisted her lips. "Save you from what? Your strong, supportive relationships with your friends?"

I pouted and grabbed another taco. "Your logic is ruining my avoidance tactics."

"Good, because I'm not moving in with you."

I gave her my best hurt look. "Harsh."

She rolled her eyes. "But you can come over when you need a break. You could always sit on the floor."

"Okay, now that my issues are settled—"

"Avoidance isn't a recommended method of settling your issues," she interrupted.

I ignored her. "Let's talk about what *you* want."

"I already told you."

"What about after the wedding? What's your bigger picture?"

She sighed. "All I want is to make it through my last year of college without firebombing the relationship with my mom or being betrothed to one of Rob's underlings."

I cocked my head. "I wasn't aware a betrothal might be part of the deal."

She crunched into her taco, and it crumbled in her hands. The furrow between her brows deepened as she stared at the mess on her plate. I waited for her to put her thoughts together, and when her tongue swiped across her bottom lip to catch a dollop of sour cream, my thoughts plummeted to my dick.

"Did you know I've never had a boyfriend?"

My eyes shot to hers. "How is that possible?"

Blue chewed carefully and swallowed before answering. "Because while most guys like the way I look, they don't like anything else about me. I seem to be missing the filter that everyone else puts to great use, and the way my mind works doesn't always make sense to them. Add in that I very rarely feel attracted to the people interested and..." She shrugged. "Dating just doesn't seem worth it."

Shitballs. I'd known this path would be tricky, but dating lessons for someone who doesn't really want to date but doesn't want to be alone—and taking myself out of the running while I'm at it? Hell. Pure hell.

I already knew I'd be spending a lot of time with her this summer, but now I was making it my mission to give her the companionship she'd clearly been missing. I was going to be the best damn friend she ever had. Maybe she'd realize she doesn't need to do this to herself. Or maybe she'd get sick of me, and I'd be back where I started.

My chest tightened with a hint of pain, but I ignored the warning. Blue wasn't Eva. I wasn't trying to force a misguided relationship out of affection and a shared history. Still, I should figure out how screwed I was.

"Do you think dating would ever be worth it?" I didn't

hold my breath while she considered her answer, but it was close.

"For the right person, yes." She pushed the last taco toward me. "What happens if this whole thing is a disaster too? What if I'm destined to be alone?"

I let out the lungful of air I'd been hoarding. "First, that's a little dark, even for you. Second, you'll just have to marry me. We can be crotchety old people together collecting spoons and yelling at kids to get off our lawn. Boom, problem solved."

"Do you always propose to girls you've known for a day?"

"Aw come on now, we're old friends. And I've only made that offer to one other person. She wasn't interested."

Blue rested her chin on her hand and waited until I took a big bite to respond. "Maybe it was the sex."

I damn near choked on my taco. "Okay, time to head home."

6

Blue

Six days later and I still hadn't stopped replaying the conversation with Adam in my head. Sweat trickled down my back and between my breasts as I walked across campus to my first class of the summer, but my discomfort went bone deep.

He was right. After he'd dropped me off and I'd slept for twelve hours, I'd regretted my drunken proposal. So much that I'd mostly avoided his texts and pretended not to be home the one time he stopped by. I wasn't going to call the whole thing off, but I needed some time to get used to my own idea.

Adam's persistence was working though. My sparse responses hadn't dulled his enthusiasm in the least. Once he'd pried my schedule out of me and realized the end of his first class lined up with the beginning of mine, he'd gleefully planned a route between campus, my apartment, and back to TU which would almost guarantee he'd be late for his second class.

When I pointed out his error, he'd countered by claiming one of the perks of being a star football player included unlimited late passes. There was no dissuading him when he wanted something, and he wanted to drive me to class. I had no idea why, but I wasn't letting him win this one. He needed to focus on his own schedule.

I'd been forced to resort to drastic measures and leave early. He should still be in his class as I hiked to the Anderson Business College, or ABC as everyone called it. The sleek new building made almost entirely of chrome and glass glinted in the afternoon sun. Modern wasn't really my aesthetic, but I could appreciate the icy blast of the air conditioning as I pulled the doors open.

My courses were almost an afterthought at college. Considering I had a ready-made job with my mom after graduation, the generic business degree Mom had talked me into seemed as good as anything else.

I'd figured out early I learned best reading the textbooks on my own, and I despised the participation part of my grade. It's not that I was afraid to talk in class, but I always somehow managed to say the exact wrong thing while simultaneously missing the point entirely.

I preferred online courses because the participation component was usually limited to commenting on a post. That I could do. This summer, I'd elected to take two courses so I could take the minimum credits in the fall and spring semesters before graduation. Now that I was the de facto manager of the shop, reduced hours or not, I'd need all that extra time.

One of my classes was online. The other, unfortunately, was not. I didn't realize how unfortunate until I made it through the second set of doors and found Shad loitering in the lobby. My steps faltered, and I slid to an abrupt stop on the smooth tile.

He was talking to a small group of guys wearing the

uniform of self-important finance bros stuck in the Texas heat—brightly colored cargo shorts, a short sleeve button down, and an expensive-looking haircut topped off with too much gel to make it look artfully tousled. I snorted, then covered my mouth. The last thing I wanted was for him to hear me.

If I believed in karma, I might have wondered what I'd done in a former life. As it was, I felt like I was being punished for something. Maybe the universe had heard my dirty thoughts about my best friend's ex.

I winced as I realized I hadn't returned Eva's text from the night before. A good friend, I was not.

Shad hadn't spotted me yet, so maybe I had time to atone first. Just as I was debating the shortest distance out of the lobby, Shad clapped one of the bros on the back and shifted my direction. I considered diving behind the couch next to me, but it was too late.

Damn my squirrel brain.

He smiled, giving me a slow appraisal. "Angela, always a pleasure. You look good enough to eat."

I frowned and glanced down at my overall shorts and sneakers, unsure how to respond to his creepy cannibalistic compliment. I'd told Adam last week flattery didn't work on me, then he'd promptly proved me wrong. All he had to do was send me an appreciative glance and I suspected my panties would burst into flame.

Shad's flattery went so far in the other direction I wanted to take a shower. Alone. He sauntered toward me, and I managed to put the couch between us.

"What are you doing here?" I asked him.

The edges of his smile twitched for a second at my brusque tone, and I hoped he'd finally decide I wasn't worth his efforts. I didn't have a lot of time to waste indulging him, but I didn't want to burn bridges before the wedding. If not for my mom, I'd have simply walked past him without acknowledging his greeting.

No such luck.

Shad spread his hands to encompass the lobby. "This is where I'm working over the summer. Are your classes in this building too?"

His innocent tone threw me for a second. I'd assumed he was here because of me, but maybe it was just bad luck after all?

I glanced at the stairs leading to the classrooms, noting the lack of other students in the lobby. "I have one class here. Business ethics with Professor Conrad."

"How lucky for me. My office is right next door to his. Why don't you come up and check it out?"

The offer sounded harmless, but his sleazy smile made goosebumps rise on my arms. I should have let Adam walk me to class like he'd suggested. At least then I could follow his lead on how to extricate myself without making a scene.

As if I'd summoned him, Adam appeared next to me and slung an arm around my shoulders, pulling me against his side—away from Shad. "Miss me?"

I'd been nervous about seeing him again, but all I felt was relief. I couldn't contain my smile at his ridiculously good timing. "Don't you have a class right now?"

"Got out early and wanted to see my girl."

Shad's brows rose at Adam's word choice, and I winced as I imagined him regaling Rob with the newest drama.

Before I could correct Shad's mistaken assumption, Adam held out an iced coffee. "Thought you might want this."

Ugh, no wonder people loved him. He was effortlessly *nice*. I snatched the chilled plastic cup from him and took a long, satisfying drink. Salted caramel slid across my tongue in a cold wave, cementing his rise to the top of my friend list.

"How did you know I liked salted caramel?"

"I asked Chloe to look at her secret spreadsheet of friend info."

My gaze jerked to his. "She has a spreadsheet?"

He shrugged, but the teasing gleam in his eyes said he was messing with me. "I haven't seen it myself, but I've heard rumors. Mostly from Noah."

I snorted, but I wouldn't put it past Chloe to have a collection of knowledge about the group hidden away somewhere. The girl could be scarily organized.

Shad cleared his throat, and I realized I'd forgotten him completely. Adam glanced between us for a second, then extended his hand.

"I'm Mac, Blue's summer bestie."

Shad's smirk faded as he shook Adam's hand. "Shad Warren, I'm doing some work for the business school."

Understanding lit Adam's face. "The future step-bro. Nice to meet you."

I couldn't tell if Adam was lying or not, but his smile looked distinctly predatory. Momentary concern for Shad twisted my stomach.

Then Shad opened his mouth. "Angela was about to come on a private tour of my office." The emphasis he put on "private" made it clear his offer hadn't been harmless. All my concern vanished, replaced by my usual urge to strangle him.

Adam's fingers pressed into my arm, dragging me closer. "Looks like she's busy now."

Shad gave him an easy smile. "So it seems. Maybe next time, Angela." He gave us a head nod and headed toward the double doors. Both of us watched him through the glass wall until he disappeared from sight.

As soon as he turned the corner, Adam gave me a little space. "Angela?"

"It's my middle name. The only thing I got from my father, and I hate it. Rob insists that Bluebonnet isn't a real name, so he calls me Angela. Shad picked it up from him."

"Have you told him you prefer Blue?"

"Yes. He hasn't listened, and I decided it wasn't a battle worth fighting."

Adam jerked his chin in the direction Shad had left. "He knows it bothers you."

I tilted my head at him. "How can you tell?"

"The way he watches you when he says Angela."

This. This was the reason I'd asked Adam to help me. Not just to get a date, but because he saw what I didn't in people. I knew Shad used my middle name to poke at me, but it had taken me a few weeks to figure it out. Adam picked up on it in less than five minutes.

I wanted that skill. Especially now that Shad would be a permanent fixture in my life.

Adam wasn't done though. "And what happened to not keeping anything important from me?"

My frown deepened. "I wasn't keeping anything from you."

He crossed his arms. "How about the fact that your future step-bro wants to fuck you?"

"How does that have anything to do with me? My possession of a vagina does not put me at fault when someone else decides they want to use it."

I wasn't completely oblivious—I knew Shad was hitting on me—but after the disastrous first meeting at his dad's house, I'd hoped he was only doing it out of habit. Now that our parents were engaged, I assumed he was doing it out of spite.

Adam's gaze traced my face, then his shoulders relaxed. "I never said it was your fault, but that asshole was seconds from putting his hands on you. If I'd known what was going down, I would have been here earlier."

I let out a huffy breath. "I didn't know he was going to be here today."

"We know now. You're not coming into this building by yourself again."

"You're not being practical," I tried to reason with him.

"Fuck practical. I'm not letting that walking red flag manipulate you into being alone with him."

My hackles rose at Adam's commanding tone. "I wasn't aware my request for your services came with bodyguard privileges as well. Do I pay extra for that?"

A growl escaped him, and he shoved his hand into his hair. "No wonder you and Eva get along. Your tongue is just as sharp as hers."

I lifted my chin, surprised by how much this frustrated side of him struck me as sexy. "I'll take that as a compliment."

"You should." He shook his head, staring at the stairs over my shoulder. "I'd do the same for her. For anyone I thought might be in an unsafe situation. Let me walk you to and from class, please?"

His eyes caught me, dark with need, and the world shifted under my feet. Frustrated Adam made me hot, but pleading Adam broke down all my defenses. Under no circumstances could I let him know the power he had over me.

"Okay, but I can't imagine Eva ever needing you to protect her from an unsafe situation."

"She didn't need me at all," he muttered.

"Is that why your relationship didn't work out? Because you wanted her to need you and she didn't?"

Adam shifted from foot to foot, and I wondered if this was another one of those questions I wasn't supposed to ask. He'd claimed to like my style of unvarnished truth, but he wouldn't be the first to change his mind.

Instead of making an excuse and leaving, he let out a dry laugh. "I don't know. We didn't discuss it."

"Not even when she left?"

His jaw tightened. "No. She told me we were done, then took off without telling me. Didn't even say goodbye."

"Maybe..." I trailed off, for once thinking about my words before I spoke them aloud.

Maybe it was the sex...

My last comment over tacos filled the space between us. Adam heard it as well as I did even though nothing broke the silence, and strangely, my awkward analysis brought him out of his sadness.

He waved his hand, dismissing the idea. "Definitely wasn't the sex."

"How do you know if you haven't talked to her since she left?"

"Because I'm good at sex, Sunshine." The easy confidence in his words made my breath catch.

"That's what they all say," I teased, but truthfully, I had no idea what anyone else said about their bedroom skills.

Adam's lips curled in a slow smile as he moved toward me, deliberate and unhurried. I had plenty of opportunity to evade him, but the burning curiosity inside me whispered *what if...* He stalked forward, and I retreated until my back hit the cool wall.

I shuddered out a breath when he stopped with mere

inches between us. His gaze stayed locked on mine as he lowered his voice.

"You sound concerned, so let me put your mind at ease. Sex should be fun for all parties, and I make sure everyone leaves satisfied."

"How?" I breathed.

"I ask what the lady wants, then I listen and deliver. It isn't rocket science."

My brain helpfully provided an image of him spread out on my sheets wearing only a cocky grin. With some effort, I shoved the vision aside. "I know. It's biology—a subject some might consider just as challenging."

He squinted at me for a long moment. "Am I imagining things, or are you implying sex is a challenge?"

Dread slithered down my spine. "Clearly, not everyone is as skilled as you claim you are."

"Of course they're not. Being good at sex takes a dedicated effort, and I'm trying to not be offended by your lack of faith."

I leaned closer, not interested in sharing my boring sex life with the other students starting to trickle through the room. "I'm sure you're very talented, but not everyone strives for your level of thoroughness."

His brows rose. "Hold on. I want to be super clear here. You've never had an orgasm?"

Heat rushed up my neck, but I refused to look away. "Not with another person."

He scrubbed his hand down his face, the subtle rasp of his stubble shooting wet heat straight to my core. "You can't tell me shit like that and not expect me to take it as a personal challenge."

"My orgasms, or lack thereof, have nothing to do with

you," I lied. The last few had definitely featured him heavily. "I have to go to class. Thank you for the save. Again."

He didn't move as I slid away. "Anytime, Sunshine."

I felt his gaze on me like warm honey as I climbed the stairs, and deep down, I knew his last comment wasn't referring to his well-timed arrival. It was an offer.

7

Mac

After yesterday's showdown with Blue and her stalker, it was almost a relief to reenter football society. I stood in the hallway outside the weight room and psyched myself up for the return to my normal life. The one that still felt like the time I'd shrunk my favorite taco boxers. I could get them on, but nothing fit right and there wasn't enough ball room.

The big metal doors clanged shut behind me as I showed up late for training. Shaw had decreed "voluntary" workouts, but everyone knew we were gearing up for a second championship run. Voluntary, my fantastic ass.

I'd considered sleeping in, but by now my roommates knew I was home. They'd surprised me by giving me space the last week—a courtesy I would not have extended—but someone, probably Shaw, had set my alarm for five a.m. sometime in the last twenty-four hours.

Fuckers better appreciate my presence. The next time I went grocery shopping, I was getting wasabi powder to put in his green smoothie mix.

RJ saw me first from where she stood grinning at Shaw's

ass as he used the squat rack. She nodded in my direction, and Shaw's gaze locked on me in the mirror.

"About time you showed up," he grunted.

I joined them and dropped my bag as he re-racked. "Why? You need some pointers?"

RJ snorted and poked my stomach. "From you? Is that a pooch I see?"

"Nah girl, that's all muscle. I know you just want a peek." I grabbed the hem of my shirt and lifted the material far enough for me to smack my abs.

She laughed, and Shaw threw his sweaty towel at me. "Stop hitting on my girlfriend."

"She was mine first."

I didn't know why I let the thought slip out. Usually, I was better about filtering myself. Shaw sent RJ a quick look then jerked his chin toward the locker room doors.

"He's not wrong," she muttered as she gathered her stuff to leave.

The rest of the room had already emptied out, or maybe it had never filled. I wouldn't put it past Shaw to set up a training session with just the three of us to fuck with me. Our captain was wily, one of the reasons I loved him.

RJ waved as she sauntered through the door, leaving me and Shaw alone. I braced myself for a lecture, but he did the thing where he stayed quiet until I talked. I hated it when he pulled the Yoda shit, but it worked one hundred percent of the time.

Silence made me jittery.

"I'm fine," I blurted out, skirting him to reach for the dumbbells.

I wasn't entirely lying. Sometimes, I felt fine. If I wasn't thinking about Eva's face when she walked out, or all the times I went to text her and had to stop myself, or the tender spot in my chest where my best friend used to be.

Or how I'd used her to try to fix my dissatisfaction with my life. Turned out, she wasn't what was missing before, but she sure as hell was now.

To be fair, I hadn't had those moments nearly as much since getting involved with Blue. I absently did a few bicep curls, focusing way more than I needed to on my form in the mirror.

I didn't need to see Shaw's face to feel the disbelief coming off him.

"I'm over it." I made the mistake of glancing his way to see if the second time had been any more convincing.

Shaw raised a brow. "No, you're not. Are you going to talk to me, or do I need to sick Noah on your ass?"

I racked the dumbbells I'd barely used. "Why isn't he here, anyway?"

"I wanted to start off easy. Thought you might be more willing to open up if it was just me."

"You brought RJ," I pointed out.

Shaw sighed and ran a hand through his hair. "Yeah, that was an accident. She woke up early and saw me getting my gym bag. You know she'd rather eat glass than miss a chance to get her hands on some weights."

I snickered. "That's what you get for trying to corner me by hiding it from her."

"I don't hide shit from her. As soon as she started pulling on her leggings, I told her I was going to corner you. She agreed to leave early if I asked. That's how much she loves you."

Emotion clogged my throat for a second as I wiped down the bench. I loved her too. Like a sister. The same way I'd sworn I loved Eva for years, until she showed up at the apartment after the championship with a bottle of tequila and a proposition. Seemed like a good idea at the time.

And now I was thinking about Eva again. Fuck.

Shaw shook my shoulder, halting my attempts to clean the vinyl. "It's okay to be sad or whatever, but talking about it might help."

I sank down onto the bench and gave up on trying to get around the conversation. Shaw would back off if I refused to talk, but he wouldn't give up. He'd slowly wear me down until I wanted to pay RJ to smother him in his sleep. Better to get all the bullshit out of the way now.

Besides, I was tired of avoiding my friends.

"Thinking about what happened with Eva sucks. I figured talking about it would suck more, so I haven't. Mostly I want you guys to stop treating me like I'm ten seconds from buying a pillow with her face on it."

Shaw sat next to me on the bench. "Aren't you?"

I shoved him sideways. "Prick. I'm not making voodoo dolls with her hair or anything. I thought at first she broke my heart, but this feels like a different kind of hurt. Like despite everything we've been through together, I didn't measure up in the end."

He sighed with a heavy frown. "It wasn't about you. Eva wasn't meant for any of us—a fact I thought you knew until you let your dick do the thinking. She'd walk all over you if you guys stayed together, and that would only annoy her."

I narrowed my eyes at his reflection in the mirror. "You sound like you have inside knowledge."

"I have eyeballs and a functioning brain. Plus, a girl-friend with inside knowledge who's way smarter than me. Eva wasn't abandoning you—she was trying to give you both space to deal with the new dynamic."

"Would have been easier to deal if I had my best friend here," I grumbled.

"The rest of us are still here, asshole. We missed you at karaoke last week, by the way. How'd your mom react to having her second favorite son home?"

I barked out a laugh. Shaw had met her a few times over the years, and Graciela Mackenzie hadn't met a friend of mine she didn't immediately adopt. She regularly referred to him as her favorite son because he made her breakfast once then cleaned up after himself.

"I spent a week watching House Hunters with her and letting her stuff me with enchiladas. What do you think?"

"Sounds like she was in heaven, and you were moping."

I pointed at him. "Hey, House Hunters is compelling. I saved the moping for after she went to bed."

"I take it you didn't tell her what happened with you and Eva?"

"Nah, man. That'd break her heart for real, and I'm not in the business of hurting the people I love. She's been planning our wedding since the second grade."

Shaw twisted his fingers together in front of him, then tilted his head to look at me directly. "What's really bothering you about this?"

I hadn't tried to put the feelings into words until now and having an audience didn't make the effort any easier. "She left. She's never given up on me before, and I'm afraid I fucked this up bad enough that I won't get her back."

"You still want a shot with her?"

"Nah, that ship sailed." An image of Blue, tropical eyes twinkling as she teased me, busted into my head. It wasn't the same, not even close. Loving Eva was comfortable and easy—I'd been doing it my whole life—and making things physical felt like a natural next step.

The way I felt with Blue was *not* comfortable. It was vibrant and thrilling and electric, like breathing in the air before a thunderstorm. Dangerous and exhilarating all at once. She saw me in a way no one else did, not even Eva, and I could feel myself shifting closer to that version of me every time we were together.

I wasn't sure I was ready to let go of the Mac I'd built, and I wasn't sure I had a choice.

Shaw watched me grapple with all the deep shit in my head. "It's not Eva, is it?"

"Fuck, man," I groaned. "It's everything. School, football, girls—everything. Doesn't the endless, unknowable void of the future terrify you?"

He glanced toward the door where RJ disappeared. "Not anymore."

"Oh say less. Please. I can't handle another relationship truth bomb."

Shaw stood and stretched his arms above his head. "Eva will be back at the end of the summer, ordering us all around to her satisfaction. Change is inevitable, but she's not going anywhere, no matter how bad you are with your dick."

I threw my hands in the air, though I *did* feel better. "Why is everyone suddenly down on Big Mac? Is this because your girl can't stop looking at my abs?"

He propped his hands on his hips and sent me a pitying look. "Riley may have been yours first, but she's mine last."

"That's what I told you when she first got here," I reminded him.

Despite his questionable methods, some of the weight on me had lifted. Shaw and RJ, Noah, Soren, D—all of them were as close as my family. They'd give me shit, but they loved me. I'd throw down for any of those assholes.

"You can come back in," Shaw yelled toward the door.

Seconds later, RJ was stacking plates on the squat bar like a boss. "Finally. I couldn't hear shit out there. Get it all settled or do I need to get involved?"

Shaw hooked a hand behind her neck and pulled her in for a quick kiss. "It's as sorted as it's going to get for now."

I leaned down to grab my bag, sure now the "mandatory" training had been only for me. "Thanks for being nosy bitches. At least there were only two of you."

RJ patted Shaw's ass then sent me a cheeky grin. "Chloe and Noah wanted to come too, but Parker had seniority."

"If you're all here harassing me, who's checking on Eva?"

She scoffed. "You think Eva would let us check on her?"

Eva may have hurt me, potentially more than I realized if Shaw's head wasn't up his ass, but she was still my best friend—still part of our crew—and they needed to step up where I couldn't.

"I think this isn't a decision she gets to make."

They shared a look, and Shaw shrugged. "Riley talks to her pretty regularly. She's as fine as you are."

"Fantastic," I muttered under my breath. I didn't want her hurting.

RJ glanced at the bag in my hand. "What are you going to do now that the cheerleaders have banned you from practice?"

She didn't mean to score a hit, but RJ had good aim. I usually spent my time doubling up on workouts with the football team and the cheerleaders. Some of those ladies could probably bench more than me. I was built for speed, but I didn't slouch with my strength training.

Until the last few weeks.

Cheer practice had already started for the summer, and Lizzy, one of Eva's squadmates, had straight up uninvited me from attending. Honestly, I wasn't even mad. While I enjoyed the focus on different skills they offered, without Eva there, I didn't feel the draw I did before. Unlike with my new summer bestie. Maybe I could convince Blue to start her dating lessons at the gym.

Better yet, Johnny's would be open in a few hours. Alex was on sound tonight, so I knew the music would be good. We could grab a pizza, practice some flirting, and hopefully, I'd get her to laugh again.

I hefted my bag over my shoulder and sent RJ a lazy grin. "I have other pursuits."

8

Blue

Got a great idea.

I dropped my phone back on the nightstand with a groan. Adam had no concept of appropriate texting times. The sun was barely peeking through my curtain, and my alarm wasn't set to go off for another two hours.

The shop was closed on Tuesdays, and I didn't have any work to do for school. I'd planned to sleep in and indulge in a big serving of biscuits and gravy from the Pancake Shack, a local, poorly disguised knock-off of Waffle House with *wayyy* better food.

My phone dinged again, signaling the first of what would be many, many more. Adam didn't believe in moderation when he wanted attention.

You're not going to ask what it is?

It's okay. I'll tell you.

Johnny's tonight.

Just you and me.

The texts came in fast and furious, and I shook my head.

So far, I'd found responding only encouraged him, but ignoring him never stopped the flood of messages.

We can work on your mate finding skills.

Unless you've decided to marry me after all.

I smothered a laugh. Adam's confidence was awe-inspiring.

I know you're reading these.

Answer the door.

I sat up in bed, frowning at his last message. He wouldn't...

A knock echoed in my tiny apartment, and I groaned. Maybe if I closed my eyes he'd go away. Despite the absurd hope, I stayed where I was, staring down at my phone.

Answer the door, Sunshine.

Dammit. His stupid nickname made me all squooshy on the inside. Why was I still reading these texts? Guilt for ignoring him slowly crept into my fuzzy morning brain.

Adam had never been inside my apartment. He'd dropped me off a bunch of times now, but he stayed at the curb until I went in the side door next to the shop. How did he know which apartment was mine?

The question—and my need for coffee—had me lurching out of bed. I made it halfway across my living room before I realized my sleep shorts were still in a pile on the floor in my bedroom. Answering the door in my underwear would definitely send the wrong message.

The newly discovered sexy part of my brain insisted it was the right message, but I went back for my shorts anyway. A quick glance down assured me my boobs hadn't gone rogue in the night through an armhole of my tank. My nipples were clearly visible poking against the fabric, but I shrugged.

Good enough.

Another knock sounded, and I padded back to the living room on bare feet. Adam could deal with my pajamas if he was going to show up at my place unannounced.

I eased the door open a crack. "Yes?"

Adam pressed a shoulder against the jamb and leaned forward into the tiny space. "Morning, Sunshine. Miss me?"

"In the last fifteen hours? No. I was sleeping."

He held up a coffee cup, paper this time, and the sweet scent of warm caramel made my stomach growl. "How about now?"

My eyes narrowed. "Is this going to be a regular thing?"

"Probably." He lifted the coffee above my head when I reached for it. "Invite me in and you can have your reward."

"You mean bribe."

He grinned at my disgruntled tone. "Whatever works."

I moved back and swung the door open. He wasn't leaving anyway, might as well get a free drink out of it. Adam stepped inside, examining my sparse furnishings and bare walls. I closed the door and leaned against it as his gaze came to rest on me.

"Do you work out?"

My brows rose at the non-sequitur. "Not really. I run occasionally, when I have time, but it's not a habit."

His face lit up. "Yes, girl. Time to get you on a schedule. You and me, we're going to be the jogging power couple."

I gestured between us. "We're not a couple."

"Couple as in two people doing something together. Like Johnny's tonight." He waggled his eyebrows and held out the coffee.

I took my prize, cupping my hands around the warmth to give them something to do. "Does *anyone* tell you no?"

"It doesn't happen often. Want to go running now? I skipped out on training since Shaw used it to ambush me."

Questions clogged up my mind, but I didn't have enough caffeine in me to sort through them. "Stay here."

I didn't expect to him actually listen, but it was worth a try. To my surprise, he only followed me to the bedroom door, which I promptly closed in his face. Before anything else, I took a long pull from the cup in my hand.

Blessed caffeine and sugar shot into my system, and I let out a happy sigh.

"I heard that." Adam's muffled voice came through the thin wood as if he were standing next to me. "You're welcome, by the way."

I set the coffee on my dresser to pull out a pair of athletic shorts, a clean tank, and a sports bra. Even if Adam didn't convince me to go running, I tended to wear athleisure stuff while lazing around the apartment.

It didn't take long for me to brush my teeth and change, but when I emerged, Adam had abandoned his post to poke through my single bookshelf.

"Lucy Score. Nice choice. Great banter."

I squinted at him. "You read romance novels?"

He straightened to flip through the brightly colored book in his hands. "I have three older sisters and no respect for personal space. I read everything they tried to hide, then I realized I liked the happy endings. And the smut."

"How much older are they?"

"One year, three years, and four years. My mom likes to say she kept trying until she had me." He set the book down and clapped his hands. "Ready to get active?"

I held up my mostly full cup. "I'm not clear on why you think I'd want to go running before I've finished my coffee. Actually, I'm not clear why you're here in the first place."

"To convince you to go to Johnny's with me tonight."

"Again, why did that require an early morning wake-up call?"

Adam rolled onto his toes and bounced a couple of times as if he simply couldn't stand still. "Because I thought you might ignore my messages and stay in. Also because I finally talked to Shaw and I wanted to tell you."

A curious warmth filled my belly. Probably the coffee. "Do you feel better?"

"Yeah. Not one hundred percent, but better. Drink your bribe coffee. The day is wasting."

"The day has barely started. This is a crazy idea, but you could go running with your athlete friends instead." I regretted the cranky words as soon as they passed my lips.

Running didn't sound bad, and I enjoyed Adam's company. I just didn't respond well to surprises.

Instead of leaving me to wallow in my pissy attitude, he grinned. "I could, but I want to run with you."

My cheeks heated, along with the rest of me, and I admitted his undivided attention was a dangerous thing. Especially in the tiny confines of my apartment.

With a grumble, I drained the last of my coffee and tossed the cup in the trash. "Fine. I'll go running with you, but I want to stop at the Pancake Shack for breakfast."

"No. Absolutely not. If we're getting breakfast, we're going to Whataburger."

"I'm not running to Whataburger. It's halfway across town."

"It's barely two miles from here."

"Which is halfway across town."

Adam grabbed the sneakers I kept by the door and cornered me in the kitchen to press them into my hands. "You can make it. We'll walk if we have to, and I'll pay for breakfast. No more excuses."

I hadn't had Whataburger in years, but a free breakfast was a free breakfast. The Pancake Shack wasn't going anywhere. Still, I didn't want to give him the impression he could barge into my life and order me around.

My chin lifted. "These aren't excuses. I'm not some ball bunny waiting on your beck and call."

"I'm aware of that, Sunshine. Otherwise, we'd be naked and working up a sweat in a much more satisfying activity."

"That's a terrible idea," I mumbled. "Like running to Whataburger."

He gripped the counter on either side of my hips, caging me in as he leaned into my space. "Might as well give in. You know you're going to anyway."

My traitorous heart took off in a galloping rhythm. Normally, I take the words people say at face value. Easier that way than trying to intuit whatever hidden message they intended. In this case, I felt the double meaning all the way to my toes.

Adam's eyes flicked to my lips for a split second, and I nearly dropped my shoes. Heavy tension pressed down on me, making it hard to pull in a full breath. Goosebumps rose on my arms, and the sensible part of me knew I needed to de-escalate the situation before either of us did something stupid. The dangerous part of me wanted to see what would happen if I pushed him a little further.

"Sometimes the struggle is the fun part," I whispered.

Heat flashed in his eyes. "I'll keep that in mind when you're begging me for rest later."

I was in over my head. Sexy banter was so far outside my comfort zone I needed a passport, and all I could think about was grabbing a handful of his shirt and hauling him against me. Not a move I'd ever considered before.

With a surprising amount of regret, I shook my head.

"You win. Whataburger for breakfast—but I get to pick the next time."

"Good girl." He tapped my nose and backed away to wait by the door.

The bubble burst, and a wave of unfulfilled longing threatened to take me to my knees. No wonder people screwed up their lives for sex. I hadn't understood it before, but Adam was giving me a new appreciation for the dictates of my body.

I glared at him as I laced up my shoes. "You can be incredibly frustrating."

He chuckled, completely unfazed by my criticism. "I know, but you're going to get the rock star of breakfasts. I promise not to gloat when you thank me later."

Adam shifted seamlessly into friendly teasing, and I struggled to keep up, reminding myself of all the reasons I shouldn't get involved with him. Eva. The wedding. My sanity.

I straightened and tried for the same carefree tone. "That was a lie, wasn't it?"

"Yes. I'm absolutely going to gloat." Adam opened the door and ushered me outside, barely waiting for me to lock up before taking off down the steps.

9

Blue

"You're doing *what*?" I collapsed onto the velvet sofa in my mom's apartment. One of the few pieces of furniture left among the chaos of boxes. She settled next to me on the worn cushions. "Selling the building. Rob found a buyer who offered more than it's worth if I sold now. The guy wants to turn it into a bar."

My mouth opened and closed a couple of times as I uttered a series of nonsensical noises. I'd napped after getting back from my run with Adam, then come over here to see if Mom wanted to get a late lunch before she headed to Dallas. How long had she been planning this? More importantly, why didn't she tell me?

Mom patted my arm, waiting patiently for my brain to catch up to her second bout of big news this month. "I know this is sudden, but my instincts say it's the right move—the right time. I can get the studio started early since Rob's assistant, Laura, offered to help run the business side."

I tried really hard not to hate Laura in that moment. Mom needed a business manager, and I wasn't available. I didn't want to stand in the way of her dreams, but the solution hurt. Was I so easily replaced?

"Where will we live?" I finally stammered out.

A smile lit her features. "With Rob and Shad. We decided it would be easier on wedding planning if I just moved in now, and he's happy to give you a room too until you're ready to blaze your own trail. Shad offered to take you to school and back since he'll be there for the summer anyway. The commute isn't too far, and I know the business department offers online hybrid options for your Fall classes. You probably wouldn't have to be on campus at all until you graduate, and if you do, Shad said he'd take care of you."

She squeezed me into her side, pride rolling off every syllable, but my stomach seized at the thought of living in the same house with Shad, who'd texted me several times since our run-in at the ABC yesterday. Nothing too obviously offensive, but with clear sexual innuendo if I looked for it. Sometimes also if I didn't look for it.

I shuddered. I'd thought Adam's pouting when I refused to join him at Johnny's tonight would be the high point of the drama today. If I'd known it was only going to get worse, I might not have sent Adam away so fast.

Mom leaned down to get a better look at my face and a furrow formed between her brows. "You don't seem as excited about this as I thought you'd be. No more afternoons spent at the store when you should be studying or spending time with your friends." She clasped my hand gingerly between hers. "I want you to enjoy your last year of college. Selling the building will help you do that."

I took a deep breath and forced my mind to engage. "How will I pay for my living expenses?"

She smiled. "I'm giving you some of the money from the sale. Rob helped me set up a trust, so it'll last all year."

Of course he did. Free lodging, a consistent ride, some spending money—I'd bet none of these generous gifts came without stipulations.

"What do I have to do?"

"Well, he asked that you take the color out of your hair and let his personal shopper pick out some pieces for you."

I glanced at her flowy skirt and tank top, then at my own running gear. "What's wrong with the clothes I have now?"

"Nothing, sweetie, but there's a certain image he wants to present to his business partners, and we'll be seeing them often. He just wants you to be prepared. You'll have final say in anything you wear."

I nodded, not at all surprised. Rob was vocal about my shortcomings, at least when Mom wasn't around. Phantom walls squeezed my shoulders as I imagined living with Rob and his idealized vision of a family. Molded into a presentable stepdaughter and paraded around like a prize dog.

Mom loved him, but that version of the future seemed horrible. Even if I was willing, I wasn't sure I was capable.

What was my alternative though? Without the building —the shop, our apartments—I had nowhere to live and no money coming in. Mom was right. Under normal circum-stances, I should love the opportunity to focus on myself for a while without worrying about how I'd pay for my books next semester.

But with Rob and *Shad*? No.

"How long do we have?"

"The contract is already signed. Closing is in two weeks."

Two weeks. My chest tightened, but I straightened my shoulders. I had two weeks to find an alternative because I was definitely not on the market for Rob's brand of helpful critiques or Shad's daily sexual harassment. I also wasn't going to ruin this for her by making it about me. She'd always put me first, created a safe, stable, happy life when the rest of the world sucked, and I'd sure as hell make her the priority now.

Mom bounced a little in her seat, and her grin widened. "I'm so happy, Blue. The studio already has a waitlist for the classes, and I can see the future we wanted right in front of us."

The future *she* wanted, with Rob's assistant instead of me. I tried to exorcize the ungrateful thought, but it refused to budge. We'd made plans together—start a yoga studio where she'd teach while I ran the office. People weren't my forte, but I understood numbers. She was the reason I was getting a business degree.

I didn't dream of that future the way she did though. For the most part, I didn't think about what *I* wanted at all, other than stability and maybe the chance to see Adam naked.

The last thought drew my mind to a screeching halt. No. I would *not* be seeing Adam naked because we were friends without benefits. A status I'd insisted on in a knee-jerk reaction to my visceral attraction to him and my loyalty to Eva.

My mind was starting to spin out of control, and I could feel the icy touch of panic at the edges of my thoughts. I needed to leave before I said something I'd regret.

"I'm glad, Mom. Are you okay here? I'm supposed to meet a friend later, and I really need a shower first." I squeezed Mom's hand, hoping she wouldn't push me to start packing now.

"Of course, baby. I'm almost done anyway." She sent me her best *mom* look. "You should start too. I put some boxes for you in the back room of the shop."

So much for escaping. "I'll start tomorrow. Do you still want me to open or are we done with that completely?"

She brushed her hands together. "Done. The new buyer wants in as soon as possible. I'm donating the stock to a women's shelter in Dallas, and the fixtures are going to Sally over at Wildcat Boutique. You can relax until the move, minus all the packing of course."

"Of course," I muttered.

Mom hugged me again. "It'll all be worth it in the end."

I highly doubted things would work out as well for me, but I wasn't going to spoil this moment for her. "It's going to be great."

———

I DIDN'T MAKE the conscious choice to join Adam at Johnny's. Most of the day was spent alternating between making a packing spreadsheet and looking at rooms for rent in Addison, with the occasional break to stare hopelessly out my tiny window.

Without a car, I was at the mercy of places to live within walking distance of TU, and none of them were in my price range of zero. My small savings wouldn't last more than a few months, even with Mom's stipend.

In the end, I grabbed my wallet and went for a walk in the evening heat.

Twenty minutes later, I regretted my snap decision when I got to the bar with sweat slicked between my thighs and the beginnings of a blister on my foot. Johnny's was a squat building with posters and beer signs filling the front windows. The half-full parking lot lined up with a section of trees which offered some privacy from the rest of town only a few blocks over.

Adam might not even be inside. I hesitated, but I didn't feel like walking back to an apartment that wouldn't be mine much longer. Getting sweaty hadn't magically produced a solution, might as well try to take my mind off the situation instead.

The last time I'd been at Johnny's, the place had been packed and covered in glitter for an event. On a normal Tuesday night, only half the tables were taken, and the dim light didn't penetrate the shadowy corners.

I had no trouble finding Adam, surrounded by a group of women wearing short dresses and heels. The whole star athlete situation hadn't really hit me, mostly because we spent time together away from the hype. A quick scan of the room assured me none of his close friends had shown up.

The discrepancy felt weird until I remembered his early morning text. *Just you and me.* Maybe he hadn't invited anyone else even after I'd turned him down. Of course, showing up alone didn't stop him from being surrounded by people.

The air conditioning made my shirt feel clammy where it stuck to my back, but Adam spotted me almost immediately. His smile widened as he dragged his gaze over my torso. I glanced down, unsure what shirt I'd thrown on with my shorts after my shower. A dark red TU football logo stretched across the heather gray background.

Not my shirt, after all. Eva must have left it at my place one of the nights she stayed over. We were almost the same size, so I hadn't noticed. Honestly, the material was super soft, and I didn't hate repping for the football team now that I'd gotten to know some of them.

When I glanced up again, he raised a brow in question. I had no trouble interpreting the expression. *What are you doing here?*

Good question. I braved the circle of women and planted myself next to him.

His attention returned to my face, and I realized his smile before had been polite and distant, but right now, his eyes lit with mischief. "I thought you weren't coming tonight."

"I promised not to hide, no matter how much I regret my request, so here I am." It was at least partially the truth. Hitting bottom apparently made me desperate for a distraction. Might as well go with the one I'd already set up.

"Come on." He laced his fingers with mine and tugged me across the room to the bar where the music was slightly quieter.

I stroked the cracked pleather of a barstool as we passed, trying to think of a non-offensive way to ask my next question. "Why do you come here?"

"Lars, the owner, lets me and Alex use the sound system to do our own thing. Usually karaoke events, though Alex has to go solo on the End of Summer Cosplay Karaoke because I'll be too busy being a football god."

I didn't comment on his football god status. "Why is this place called Johnny's if the owner's name is Lars?"

"Have you tried to say Lars's? Plus, the sign was already there. No point buying a new one."

Finally, logic I could understand. We found a spot next to a group of women surrounding a single guy in a backward cap. Adam sent him a short nod, and the guy shifted his harem over a little to let us have a second seat.

"You know him?" I asked.

Adam took the chair closest to them. "That's Holbrook, our former running back. He just graduated, but he's hanging around for the summer."

The bartender greeted Adam and started setting up a

series of shots in front of the group, mixing with one hand while lining up glasses on the bar with the other. I stared for a long moment, impressed despite myself.

Adam gave him a friendly smile. "Can I get a water? And put whatever she wants on my tab."

I hadn't planned to drink, but I didn't have a lot of opportunities to drown my sorrows without resorting to eating ramen for a week.

"I'll have whatever that is." I pointed to the pale blue liquid in the shot glasses next to us.

The bartender winked and slid one of the drinks over to me before turning his back to make another. I knocked back the shot that smelled like suntan lotion and gasped at the heat trailing down my throat.

Adam chuckled. "You really want to try this tonight?"

"Yes. Educate me."

His lips twisted as he scanned the room. "Let's start with finding a good subject."

I hailed the bartender again and held up the shot glass. "Another please."

In seconds, I had a refill. "What are you looking for?"

"My buddy, Taco Truck. Defensive lineman. Looks like he'd eat quarterbacks for breakfast. He's the perfect beginner target for your flirting lessons."

I choked on my second shot. "You want me to flirt with a guy named Taco Truck?"

"Yeah, don't mind the nickname—it's from his sister. He's the shyest guy I've ever met. I think his brain turns off when he's within ten feet of a woman."

The bartender stopped by to grab my empties and raised a brow. I nodded at him. "Shouldn't we start with the lecture portion before jumping into the lab?"

Adam gave up his search and relaxed onto his stool.

"Nah, I want to see what you can do before I start giving pointers. He's not here though."

Relief shot through me, but I tried to play along anyway. "What about someone else?"

"I don't see anyone else who would work for this. We need to ease you into flirting, not toss you in the deep end with the sharks. Lecture, it is." Adam winked at me, and unlike with the bartender, a coil of heat unfurled in my chest. "Any place in particular you want me to start?"

My clit.

I scrubbed the thought from my brain, and blurted out the first non-sexual thing that crossed my mind. "Is there a uniform requirement here? What do I wear to give off the 'I'm looking for a good time' vibe?"

Adam choked on his water. "You *do not* want to give off that vibe. Unless you're just in it for a hookup."

I frowned. "Why not? I *am* looking for a good time, though I don't think a hookup would qualify."

He scrubbed a hand down his face. "Please don't start talking about your disappointing sexual experiences again. 'A good time' means sex. Straight up. *You* want a relationship. For that purpose, your clothes are perfect."

"I need a better explanation." The bartender left another shot in front of me, so I braced myself and swallowed. The liquor went down smoother the third time.

"Women looking for a good time usually don't come to a bar dressed like the sexy girl next door. You look like you're here to relax and have a few drinks. No ulterior motives or drama."

I was stuck on the 'sexy girl next door' comment. "Can you be more specific?"

"It takes a lot of confidence to be comfortable in your skin, and a lot of people use clothes or makeup to boost that confidence. Especially since chatting up some dude puts you in the danger zone of rejection." He eyed the new shot the bartender left in front of me. "And some people drink too much to ease the anxiety."

My eyes narrowed. "Careful, summer bestie. You're getting awfully close to sounding judgy."

"And you should consider slowing down on the shots."

Pass. The dread churning in my gut had finally abated, and I felt good for the first time all day. With Adam next to me, I wasn't worried about anything.

"No, thank you. If I'm going to be living in my own personal hell soon, I might as well enjoy myself now." I downed the shot, and Adam shook his head at the bartender. He wasn't even subtle.

I shoved his arm. Or, I tried to shove his arm, but I only grazed him. The room spun a little, and my momentum tipped me face first into his lap. I caught myself on his jean-clad leg, forcing air through my nose slowly the way my mom taught me.

Adam's arm curled around my back, and he helped me straighten. "No wonder you were tipsy the other night. You're a lightweight, Sunshine."

"I don't drink much," I muttered, trying to will the bar to stop shimmying.

"Okay, I'm not sending you out into the dating trenches while you're trashed. Why don't you drink some of this water and tell me what's wrong?"

He slid his glass closer to me, but I didn't want to be responsible, sober Blue for a little bit. I wanted to make dumb decisions without overthinking everything. Ignoring the water, I scanned the bar until my gaze fell on the circle of girls he'd been with when I arrived.

I jerked my chin at them. "How about you tell me what a girl does to get your attention?"

Adam didn't even glance over. "There's not much a girl can do to get my attention if she doesn't already have it. Either I'm interested or I'm not. The key is to figure out who's interested."

His explanation didn't bode well for my future in flirting. "How am I supposed to know if someone is interested?"

"Sometimes you just feel it."

"Give me an example," I demanded.

Adam's hand curled around my hip, and he pulled me closer, almost into his lap. His stubble brushed my hair as he whispered in my ear. "Did you wear this for me?"

I let out a laugh to cover the full body shiver he elicited. "I did not. This shirt was an accident, just like my presence here." Somehow, I refrained from mentioning Eva. Something in me didn't want to share this moment with her, despite wearing her shirt.

He eased away a few inches, but his hand stayed locked in place. "That was your example, Sunshine."

The shiver should have clued me in, but my brain felt slow. Melty. Like honey in the sun. Suddenly, I couldn't remember why I was trying so hard to find someone else. Adam was *right here* and touching me and he smelled so good.

I braced a hand on his chest and turned toward him, leaning in until I could feel his rapid exhale on my lips. "Is this how I was supposed to respond?"

10

Mac

She was going to kill me. The headlines wrote themselves. *College football star dies from massive erection.* How was I supposed to function when all my blood was rushing to my cock?

My fingers twitched on her hip with the need to haul her all the way into my lap. I wanted her wild, writhing on top of me. With one tiny shift, I could taste those coconut drinks she'd been downing on her tongue.

The reminder of her shots pulled me back from the edge of stupidity. Even if I wanted to toss out the lessons I'd learned about mixing friendship with sex, I didn't take advantage of women who'd been drinking. Another point I should probably mention.

Later.

I gave her a little nod and eased away. "Yeah. That response would definitely get a reaction."

Disappointment flashed on her face for a brief second, then she reached for my water and drained the rest of the glass. When Scott, asshole bartender and former friend, came back from delivering drinks to Holbrook's group with his smirk firmly in place, I stood and held up my credit card.

"We need to close out."

"You're welcome, man," he said quietly as he took my card.

I shook my head, keeping a firm grip on Blue. He'd never fed drinks to any of the girls I brought here before, but then again, I never paid for their drinks. Yes, Blue had asked for each shot, but he acted like he was doing me a favor by helping her get drunk.

Blue leaned against my side, propping her head on my shoulder. It was difficult to tell how hard the alcohol was hitting her, but her body was loose and curled around me. Compared to how tense she'd been when she walked in, I'd say she was flying with a solid buzz.

Not to mention the whole *personal hell* comment. She hadn't shown up here for me and our dating lessons.

Lars needed to know about Scott's version of help, but not now—I'd send him a message tomorrow. Blue walked with me to the door, watching Holbrook and his ball bunnies.

"I don't understand what they hope to get out of hanging all over the football players."

Honestly, I didn't either, but I'd enjoyed the hell out of the attention. "Not your style?"

"I don't think so. I'd feel weird standing around touching someone without a goal. Despite my current location, I mean. Touching you feels right."

"Naturally," I said, steering her toward my Jeep and trying to rationalize her words. She didn't mean them the way Big Mac insisted on taking them.

Blue frowned as I opened the door for her. "Where are we going?"

"Back to my place," I responded without thinking.

Her brows shot up and the excitement in her eyes nearly took me out a second time.

I hoped future generations recognized my heroic restraint when presented with Blue, tousled and playful, offering herself up on a silver platter. Maybe a plaque or a commemorative inscription on the bar.

"Get your mind out of the gutter," I teased. "We're going to watch movies until you're sober again. On the way, you can tell me what happened between breakfast and now to convince you getting liquored up was the best plan for tonight."

She pulled up straight and poked my stomach. "I'm only a little inebriated, and I'm perfectly capable of handling myself. You could just take me home."

"I don't want to. Now get in."

———

SHE DIDN'T TALK on the drive, but she didn't get tense again either. I spent the ten minutes poking the sore spot in my chest by thinking of Eva and the way I'd fucked everything up. I could have said no when she came to me. I could have laughed it off and kept things the same as they'd always been.

I'd spent years—decades—with Eva. Touching her all over to help with stunts, sleeping next to her on camping trips, hell, we went to prom together. Not once did I have to tell myself not to kiss her.

The urge simply never occurred to me.

I loved the Eva I'd known all these years, and I missed her. My best friend. I didn't miss the sex, didn't sit around fantasizing about her, unlike another female friend who I couldn't stop thinking about.

If I intended to maintain my relationship with Blue, I absolutely needed to keep my dick in my pants. Treat her like everyone else, and stop pushing just a little farther toward the line between friends and something more. The self-preservation part of my brain warned me to turn around and drop her off like she'd suggested. Stop the slow roll toward hunger and need.

But I didn't want to.

I also didn't consider my roommates might be home and might question Blue's presence. Not until I opened the door to our apartment and nearly ran into RJ coming the opposite direction. Anyone else I would have trampled, but RJ was almost as tall as I was, and she could definitely bench press more than me.

Blue giggled from her spot plastered to my side, and RJ's brows rose.

"So that's where you disappeared to."

I maneuvered us out of the doorway, so RJ could leave. "I didn't disappear. I told you I was going out. You said you were meeting Shaw at the camper for what I can only assume was his dumbass idea of privacy. The mosquitos are going to eat you alive if you get naked out there in the woods."

"Wouldn't be the first time," she muttered.

"His country ass grew up in the woods. You know if you keep encouraging him he's only going to get worse."

She sighed. "I know—I'm a sucker." Her eyes landed on Blue. "Haven't seen you in a while. I thought you might have left with—"

RJ stopped and let out a quiet curse. "Right. I'm going to go before things get more awkward. Nice seeing you again, Blue. Better be at training tomorrow, Mac."

I ignored her judgy stare and closed the door after her. Blue pulled away as the silence settled around us. She circled the living room brushing her hand over the giant couches and lone recliner.

"That's two. Where's the third?"

I followed her, close enough to catch her if she lost her balance. "At Chloe's. Where else?"

"Did you know this is only the second time I've been in here?"

"Is that so?" I didn't really care, but the longer we dawdled out here the more I could focus on non-sexy things like whether I'd left my laundry out and what the hell that rancid smell was coming from the kitchen.

Blue didn't seem to notice. She peeked into the galley space and headed for the hallway. "I came over once for movie night. Before you and Eva imploded, and she stopped inviting me here."

I winced. Nothing like the consequences of my actions to get my head on straight and my mind out of my pants. "You're here now."

"I'm here now," she repeated slowly as if considering some deeper meaning of the words.

This was a new experience for me. I didn't have a quick comeback or a joke. The moment didn't feel right, and I wasn't entirely sure how to act. I wanted to get her into my room, but I was also apprehensive of being alone with her.

I'd never doubted my ability to make the right decision before, and the hesitation was wreaking havoc on my nervous system.

Blue wobbled to the hallway and looked over her shoulder. "You coming?"

I pressed my lips together to keep my first thought inside my head and simply nodded. When she didn't go any farther, I realized she didn't know which room was mine. Was I always this much of an idiot?

"First door on the left. Across from the llama."

Her gaze skimmed the door and landed on the llama picture Soren had given us years ago. "There's no glass in the frame."

I joined her in the hallway to gaze at the smirking animal. "Yeah, Chloe broke it. We just cleaned out the shattered glass and hung it back up."

She tilted her head. "None of you seem like llama enthusiasts. Why did you keep it?"

A smile played at my lips as I remembered the day Soren had presented it to us. Back then, D had lived with us too, and he'd had a strict policy about...well, everything. Soren'd said he couldn't find a picture of an ass, so the llama would have to do.

"It's sort of become a reminder to keep working hard, even when no one's watching." When D and Soren left to play pro ball, Shaw insisted on putting it in the hallway where we couldn't miss it.

Blue flashed me a smile. "That's a good motto, except I'm tired of working hard. Let's watch a movie before I have to go home and finish packing."

She crooked a finger at me while opening the door behind her. I'd bet every cent I owned she had no idea how alluring she looked—wild rainbow hair falling over her shoulders, tropical eyes gleaming with trouble—but her words finally caught up to my sluggish brain.

"Why are you packing?"

Blue collapsed back on my bed, giggling, and I went from half-mast to rock hard in an instant. I'd had fantasies

—very detailed fantasies—about the scene in front of me, and no amount of logic was going to convince Big Mac to calm the fuck down.

"Mom's selling the building."

I closed my door and leaned against it, flattening my hands against the cool wood. "Wasn't that the plan? Sell the building after you graduate and start a yoga studio in Dallas?"

"She's selling it now. We're supposed to move in with Rob, and Shad can drive me to and from school. One big happy family." She smirked at me. "Guess I don't need your bodyguarding anymore."

I tensed. "Is that what you want?"

"Heck no. I want to live in Addison—far away from Shad —and finish out school. Mom may not need me to help her start up the studio, but the job is still waiting for me when I get my degree." She scooted up to sit against the headboard. "Are you going to join me or watch from the doorway like a voyeur?"

Against my better judgement, I grabbed the remote from my nightstand and climbed onto the bed. "We'll find a way to keep you here, and as long as Shad is going to show up at your class, so am I."

A possessive streak had me wrapping an arm around her as I searched for something with zero sex scenes.

Blue tucked herself along my side like we'd been doing this for years, twining her leg with mine. "It's not your responsibility to help me find a place to live."

"No, but I'm going to help anyway." I realized I needed a heavy hitter to distract from the subtle scent of her, so I switched away from the movies to my favorite show of all time. Ted Lasso.

Her head dropped down onto my shoulder as the opening scene played. "Thanks," she whispered.

Torture. Straight torture.

I focused on the TV, absently stroking her arm with my thumb. She smelled like a garden—not flowery, but fresh and clean, like green things after a rain—and her skin was really soft. Was it a lotion thing or was she soft everywhere? My mind wandered to all the other places we were touching, and I wrenched my attention back to the screen.

For once, the show wasn't doing it. I kept imagining Shad's smug face in the ABC, and my insides clenched at the thought of Blue leaving with him, riding with him, sharing a living space with him. Shad would have all the power as long as Blue had no reliable transportation of her own.

Some quick calculations told me unless I dropped my classes I wouldn't be able to give her a ride from Dallas. If she were in town? Yes. Easily.

I didn't know what Blue's money situation looked like, but generally, not having a job made it hard to lease an apartment. She could rent a room, but at this point in the summer, most of the spots would be filled with dorm kids taking summer classes.

I knew a lot of people. I could ask around.

The thought of setting Blue up with some rando I met at a party rubbed me the wrong way. Eva's room was free, but Chloe had already started transforming it into her dream office. Every time I saw her, she whipped out her phone to show me progress pictures. I could ask her to switch it all back for Blue, and she'd most likely do it.

Or...

The idea dawned on me slowly. We had an empty room too. Sort of. Noah spent all his free time with Chloe, usually over at her place because he was a hermit on his best days. He'd let it slip he was getting Chloe a bigger bed, so I doubted he'd be back here all summer.

Blue would have to be okay with storing her stuff, or maybe sending it to not-Archer's place with her mom. I could probably even convince Noah to let her stay here for free. Now all I had to do was convince myself to keep things friendly when I had twenty-four-hour access to a woman I couldn't seem to stop thinking about.

"I think I have a plan," I blurted out, but she didn't respond.

I craned my head to peek at her face, and sure enough, Blue had fallen asleep against me. The show played on quietly while I lay there struggling to find the right course of action. As if she could sense my dilemma, Blue's hand slipped under the hem of my shirt and rested against bare skin.

My entire focus narrowed to the flutter of her touch, the warmth of her breath wafting across my chest. If I stayed here with her, woke up with her curled up next to me, the line might blur too much to hold me back—if I could sleep at all.

I skimmed my fingers over her waist, the curve of her hip, then yanked them away. Touching women while they slept was a no-no, even if she'd crawled into my lap herself. I blew out a silent breath and slowly eased away.

If Blue woke up, I'd take her home as promised. If not, I'd spend the night on the couch. Wouldn't be the first time I'd slept out there, though it *would* be the first time I'd wake up alone.

11

Mac

The bed jostled a little as I scooted off it backward, but Blue didn't wake up. She curled around my pillow in her sleep, burrowing in with a sigh. I tossed the edge of the blanket over her, then nearly tripped on her shoes. I hadn't noticed her take them off when she came in, but of course, I'd noticed her tuck her sock-covered feet under my calves.

I shook my head and remembered at the last second to turn off the TV. None of my previous encounters had ended with me tucking a woman into bed and *leaving*. When Eva and I had been only friends, we'd slept in the same bed with no weirdness. She didn't enjoy cuddling, and she'd kick in her sleep if anyone got too close.

Once we'd added sex to the mix, she mostly stopped staying over. I snorted as I gathered a throw pillow and one of the tiny blankets we somehow ended up collecting. It wouldn't cover my crotch and my feet at the same time, but at least I could pretend to be decent.

In the dark living room, I gripped the hem of my shirt and hesitated. None of my roomies were home, and besides, they'd all seen me naked. Even RJ, though that was a horrible accident I promised never to bring up again.

Blue, though, hadn't. She'd also never had a roommate. Never had to share her space with football players who often forgot to clean or go to the grocery store. I grinned. My plan would definitely be an eye-opening experience for her, and I kind of loved she couldn't just move out if we annoyed her.

She'd have to learn to interact with people, just like she'd asked me to teach her. Hell yes. Professor Mac was in session.

I tugged off my shirt as I congratulated myself, but I left my shorts on. No point in giving Big Mac an introduction. I emptied my pockets next to me on the floor and spread out across the couch, stupidly glad we'd splurged on XXL furniture.

Before I could do more than close my eyes, my phone chimed with an incoming text. I sighed. Ignoring it wasn't an option, but it was probably a party invite rather than an emergency. The urge to disappear from the world for a few hours hit me like Duke on his fourth Red Bull.

The phone went off again, and I grabbed it from the floor. Two messages from Alex, my music buddy.

Hey man. Check this out.

Then a link to what looked like a singing competition. It wasn't the first time he'd sent me vocal stuff. Alex thought I was wasting my talents with football, but I had a good shot at the NFL and no one in the music business knew who I was. Even I didn't have enough energy to focus on both at the same time.

I had to pick one—rake in money playing football, buy my parents a new place, set my sisters up for retirement, then see where my voice could take me.

Another message came through while I was dismissing the first two. *Don't sleep on this. If you talked to someone besides me, they'd tell you to get your ass in gear.*

I scrubbed a hand down my face, surprised by how much the competition tempted me. Lyrics weren't my strong suit—I preferred the raw emotion of the music—but Alex could take the notes I wrote and turn them into something beautiful for me to sing.

We'd been working the last year on an album, though he took it way more seriously than I did. No one else knew. Alex wanted to keep things under wraps until we had a final product, and I agreed with him. I didn't need anyone thinking I was slacking off with my other responsibilities.

Of course, the secret didn't stop Alex from pestering me to sing every chance I got. I knew the deal. Practice made perfect. Hell, I spent most of my time working on my football skills with the team or with the cheerleaders. Except I wasn't this summer. With Eva gone, I only had the team responsibilities, and my schedule had opened up.

My lips twisted and I clicked on the link. A competition for singers/songwriters. Original work only. Open registration with a reasonable fee. We'd have to submit a sample which would go through several levels of judging, and the final group would perform at a live show.

I was about to close the tab until I saw the prize. Enough money to cover school costs for Alex and a one-on-one internship thing with producer Lacey Duvall. She was a visionary, and well known for developing up and coming artists. We'd just talked about her last week, actually. Alex was probably shitting himself at the opportunity.

Dammit. I couldn't ruin this for him. The dates were tight with football camp and the start of the season, but not impossible since it was based in Dallas.

I switched back to his messages. *I'll think about it.*

He sent back a series of increasingly weird emojis, ending with an alien. I didn't even try to interpret them. When Alex got excited, his mind moved at lightspeed. It made him a little hard to follow, but the brilliance couldn't be denied.

For the second time in twenty minutes, I dropped my phone to the floor and tried to relax. I wanted to tell Blue about the competition—see what she thought of the opportunity, if it was worth the sacrifice—but first I'd need to tell her about my music. Honestly, I just wanted to talk to her. Her mind was fascinating, and she helped me sort through all the packaging to get at the heart of things.

Going back into my bedroom was a no-go. My willpower only went so far, and I wouldn't come back out a second time. After her little stunt at the bar, I was certain I wasn't alone in wanting to blur the lines of our friendship.

In the back of my mind, I wondered what would have happened if I'd spent time with Blue before getting involved with Eva. Would I have been in the same frustrating, friends-without-benefits situation, or would her adamant refusal have encouraged me to pursue her? I wasn't pursuing her now...was I?

Shit. Was I? Staring at the slightly darker parts of the popcorn ceiling didn't offer much in the way of answers.

A snippet of the song I'd been working on with Alex floated across my mind—one I'd attempted to write lyrics for. The music wasn't quite right yet for the chorus, and we were missing the drama. A big wow factor moment that would reach down and tug on someone's soul.

I let the notes twist and turn in the back of my thoughts, and though I knew better, I pictured Blue lying in my bed. Only in this version, she was naked and panting for me.

Talk about wow factor. I groaned as Big Mac perked right up.

He wouldn't be denied this time. I unbuttoned my shorts, giving him some space. None of my roommates would be home until morning, and Blue was passed the fuck out in my room. True, she'd recovered pretty fast after the night with the wine, but she hadn't been nearly as gone as tonight.

The imaginary version of Blue moaned my name—my real name—and I rubbed my cock through my boxer briefs. Fuck, I was in deep. Dream Blue spread her pretty thighs for me and dropped a hand between them.

She didn't close her eyes though. Those blue-green depths stared up at me in challenge, daring me to match her rhythm.

No problem. I hooked the waistband of my undies and let Big Mac free. Dream Blue's lips curved into a satisfied smile as I gripped him tight. I wanted her hands on me, her mouth, her anything as long as she kept grinning like that.

The illicit chance of being caught by her made everything hotter. In my mind, I joined her on the bed, taking her mouth like I'd almost done earlier. Taking her hand and adding my own fingers to hers. Taking her up, up, up as her nails dug into my shoulders.

Her tits bounced slightly with the roll of her hips, and I wrapped my lips around the rosy tip. Sucked until she begged and pulled my hair. Uttered words into her ear as she tightened around me.

Yes, baby.

Fuck your hand and pretend it's me.

Come for me, Sunshine.

Flames licked at the base of my spine and my balls tightened. I grabbed my shirt from the floor just in time.

Fuck. I hadn't come that hard in months. Years. Maybe ever.

I'd thought my fantasies before were harmless, but having her in my room, in my bed, brought reality into stark contrast. Blue deserved a friend who wasn't looking for a chance to see her naked. Bad enough her future stepbrother was rolling on her. I collapsed back against the cushions with my shirt balled in my fist.

Frustration mixed with the lethargy spreading through my muscles. I had other female friends. Plenty of women would be willing to take care of Big Mac without getting emotionally involved. All I had to do was ask.

I hadn't, but maybe I should. If I had another outlet, maybe Blue wouldn't hold the same forbidden attraction.

Deep down, I knew the logic was bullshit. None of the ball bunnies held my attention the way she did. None of the cheerleaders made me want to spend all my time with them. No one else could take Blue's spot in my mind, not even Eva.

I dropped the shirt next to my phone and pulled the stupid throw blanket over my chest. None of this chaos was necessary. I'd convince Blue to move in here—for her own good—spend the summer keeping my hands off her, and when Eva came back in the fall, I'd be back to my old self who didn't question everything.

12

Blue

I woke suddenly and without mercy. My body knew I wasn't at home before my head, which was decidedly fuzzy. Sunlight streamed through a big window, falling across the messy bed, and I remembered with sudden clarity cuddling with Adam last night until I'd fallen asleep.

Previous data suggested I didn't like cuddling—in general, I didn't like people touching me—but curling up next to Adam had felt so good. Had I ever done anything simply because it felt good?

I rubbed my eyes and finally took stock of my surroundings. The giant bed I was lying in took up most of the room with a dresser opposite holding the TV and a desk positioned near the window. A guitar sat in a stand within arm's reach of the chair, and the rest of the room was surprisingly tidy.

Adam didn't seem like the cleaning type, but he clearly put in some effort. I eyed the second door, and hoped he had his own bathroom. When I slid my legs over the side of the bed, I had to sit with my head between my knees for a second. My stomach wasn't pleased with me, probably because I'd skipped dinner in favor of those suntan drinks.

I focused on the swirling gray pattern in Adam's comforter until the urge to puke passed. He'd probably forgive me, but I didn't want to risk it. It already looked like I'd kicked him out of his own room.

My experience might be limited, but only half his bed was mussed. Unless I'd spent the night on top of him, he'd left after I fell asleep. Not a great sign after I'd made a pass at him. I probably shouldn't have done that since I was the one who'd insisted on friends without benefits, but I had a hard time regretting the decision. The shots themselves I regretted. Deeply.

Being hungover sucked.

Once I could stand like a normal human, I hobbled to the mystery door, then let out a breath when it revealed a compact room containing a toilet, sink, and shower stall. The whole place smelled like him, and my stomach gave a different kind of jolt.

I distinctly remembered throwing caution to the wind and hitting on him last night. In the mirror, I watched my face slowly turn pink. Fantastic. I was only a little embarrassed by my actions, but I'd feel a lot better if Adam had been here when I woke up.

What did it mean that I spent the night alone in his bed?

Part of me, the part that sounded disturbingly like Rob, tried to claim he'd left out of disgust. I knew from Eva he had no problem sleeping next to his friends, male or female. If we were friends, he'd have simply claimed his side of the bed.

We *were* friends. Yet he wasn't here.

I shook my head at my disheveled reflection and did what I could with the limited supplies. Once I'd relieved myself and rinsed my mouth out with water, I felt better. RJ had mentioned training in the morning, and Adam had skipped enough time with the team I knew his friends would make sure he attended.

My first concern was getting home, but with the store permanently closed, I suddenly didn't have anywhere to be. Walking the several miles to my building sounded horrible, and I'd only spend the time depressed and packing. The boxes could wait.

When I returned to the bedroom, I noticed the note sitting on the nightstand next to my wallet and phone. A simple piece of lined paper ripped from a notebook and folded in half. "Sunshine" was written on the outside in a messy scrawl, hopefully Adam's.

I tilted my head as I picked it up, riding the wave of excitement heating my belly.

Morning, beautiful. Had to go to training. Be back at 8. Don't go anywhere.

I glanced at my watch. 7:38. Wow, I'd really slept in. Adam's terse order should have annoyed me, but it calmed the desperate little voice half-expecting him to ask me to go. Besides, it would be stupid for me to leave now just to make a point.

Fatigue pulled at me, but I wasn't quite ready to find out what Adam would do if he came home and I was still in his bed. Coffee would handle the exhaustion, if I could find some in his kitchen.

My shoes weren't where I left them by the door. No doubt I could walk around in my socks without issue, but I wanted all my things accounted for when Adam got back. Just in case.

I did a cursory search under the bed and in the corners. Nothing. Adam had probably moved them into the living room. I found myself next to his desk, staring down at a computer and a beat-up Wonder Woman notebook.

The image of him studiously taking notes made me smile, but Adam wasn't the studious type. Maybe he used it for football plays? Curiosity got the better of me, and I opened it to a random page.

Music. Pages and pages of notes, some with lyrics, some without.

Adam wrote music. I had no frame of reference for the skill level, but the effort alone was impressive. I spun in a slow circle, looking around the room again, this time surprised to find very few references to football. A TU duffel bag in the corner, a framed picture of Adam in his uniform standing with a bunch of women and one harried looking man, a football on the dresser.

Eva's room was plastered with cheer paraphernalia, which made sense considering how big a role cheerleading played in her life. My mom's apartment could double for a tiny yoga studio. At least, it could before she'd packed away everything. Adam's room didn't share the same level of passion.

A kernel of knowledge solidified in my gut. Adam was a lot more than a smooth-talking, top-ranked receiver. He played into the role, letting everyone believe there wasn't any more to him, to Mac. No wonder he liked it when I called him Adam.

I wondered why no one else bothered to look beyond the surface.

The sound of the front door opening snapped me out of my introspection. Adam and his roommates were home, and I needed to decide if I was going to come out of his bedroom disheveled and wearing the same clothes RJ had seen me in the night before.

Adam didn't give me the choice to hide.

"Blue, get your fine ass out here," he yelled from the living room.

Snickers followed his bellow, and I winced. Social situations weren't easy for me, but I knew these people. Albeit, not as well as I knew Eva. Worst case scenario, they'd think Adam and I had hooked up. Hopefully, they wouldn't care.

I ran my fingers through my hair one more time, then walked out of the bedroom.

Shaw and Noah turned to me as I appeared at the end of the hallway, and I could hear RJ rummaging in the kitchen. Adam leaned against the wall with a big grin on his face.

"Sleep well?" he asked with innuendo thick in his voice.

He knew very well how I'd slept since he'd clearly come into the room to change before leaving for his football thing. Shaw grabbed a pillow off the couch and threw it at Adam's face.

"Don't worry," he assured me. "We know he slept on the couch last night."

Now, so did I. "I'm not worried. Do you have coffee?"

Shaw scoffed. "Eva would never forgive us if we didn't keep a stock for her."

"She's not in town," I pointed out.

Adam pushed away from the wall and beckoned me forward. "I'll show you. Feel free to grab whatever you want. We probably have breakfast stuff too."

RJ snorted from her spot in front of the refrigerator. "Oh? Did you finally go grocery shopping?"

He rolled his eyes. "I don't know why you guys insist on physically going to the store. We could get all our shit delivered."

She sent him a sweet smile. "Then we wouldn't be able to tease you when you forget. Every. Time."

I swallowed a laugh, but Adam didn't bother. He chuckled and shoved her out of the way so he could open the fridge. "We don't have any caramel, but you can have Eva's fancy cold coffees. Want some eggs?"

RJ eyed me with interest as Adam handed me a premade chilled latte. Not my usual, but I'd take it. "Thank you."

He'd already started pulling out pans and breakfast foods, so I didn't bother answering his question. I was getting fed whether I wanted it or not.

RJ sidled up next to me, leaning against the counter and stretching her long legs out in front of her. "So... what's going on with you and Mac?"

He tossed a hand towel over his shoulder as he adjusted the heat on the stove. "I can hear you."

"You chose not to answer my question earlier. Now it's her turn." RJ softened her words with a smile, but I didn't feel entirely placated.

Normally, I'd blurt out the truth, probably too much of it, but Adam's back stiffened slightly when she wasn't looking. He cared what I said. For once, I chose my words deliberately.

"We're friends—summer besties—but hopefully, also fall besties and all the rest of the season besties too." From the corner of my vision, I watched him relax.

RJ's smile widened. "It's hard not to be besties with Mac."

"It is. He's helping me through some challenges, and I hope I'm doing the same."

"About freaking time," she muttered, taking a big bite of her banana. "Let me know if I can help too. Eva collects people like it's her damn job, but she has impeccable taste. Mac, don't eat my breakfast while I'm in the shower."

"No promises. I'm not saving food while you and Shaw take your sweet time."

RJ sent me a knowing look that I think was supposed to be a message about shower sex, so I nodded back even though I had no idea what in particular I was nodding about. Body language was hard.

"We'll make it a quickie then," she quipped and disappeared into the living room.

I joined Adam next to the stove. He cracked at least a dozen eggs into a bowl, and my brows shot up. "How many people are you feeding?"

"One normal person and four football players." The front door slammed shut, and Adam leaned over to glance into the living room. "Three football players."

The scent of bacon hit my nose and my stomach growled. "Is this a regular thing around here?"

He laughed. "Me cooking? No. I can do it under duress though. In this case, I lost a bet with RJ this morning so I'm on breakfast. Normally, I'd order in from somewhere, but she wanted homemade bacon and eggs. Weirdo."

"Not quite Whataburger, is it?" I mused.

"See," he pointed the spatula at me. "I knew you'd understand."

Adam started humming a familiar tune under his breath, and I wanted to broach the subject of his music, the notebook. Eva never talked about Mac's music other than his insistence on dragging everyone to karaoke. Why not?

In the end, I nudged his side and went with something simpler. "Thanks. For last night."

He grinned. "Anytime, Sunshine."

"Are you always this happy in the morning?"

"Nah, but I had a good workout, and my girl is here having breakfast with me."

I shook my head. "Your girl needs a shower and a ride home."

Adam handed me a plate with eggs, bacon, and toast, nodding his head at the counter seats. "Breakfast first. I want to talk to you about something."

My gut clenched as I shoved steaming food in my mouth. Adam didn't usually preface conversations—he simply started talking. Maybe breakfast was a pity meal meant to make me feel better when he explained how he wouldn't have time to help me after all this summer.

I swallowed and took a bite of bacon in an attempt to hide my hurt feelings. "About what?"

Adam snapped the burner off then propped his hands on his hips as he met my eyes. "Moving in with me."

13

Blue

I inhaled at the wrong time and sucked bacon shrapnel into my lungs. After an embarrassingly long coughing fit, I croaked out, "What?"

"Move in here. In Noah's room. At least for the summer. He said it was fine. Do you need me to help you carry stuff?" He punctuated his impromptu speech by flexing, as if I wasn't already acutely aware of his muscles.

I glanced toward the hallway where RJ had retreated. "You told them about my personal problems?"

His expression sobered. "No. I told them you needed help, and everyone was on board."

The quick hit of panic softened to confusion. "Why?"

"Why what?"

"Why would they help? They barely know me."

"Because we take care of each other. That's what friends do. Plus, Noah owes me for not blabbing about his 'secret' love affair with Chloe to her brother."

My brows rose. "He thought it was a secret?"

Adam shook his head in disgust. "For a quiet guy, Noah is shit at keeping things on the down low."

I remembered Chloe's smitten face when she described Noah the first time we'd met. He wasn't the only one unable to hide his feelings. Eva had told me how their crew rallied around Chloe and Noah when they needed help, and I'd seen for myself how tight-knit the group was—I hadn't expected to be included.

No wonder RJ had given me the contemplative look. She was probably wondering why Adam would insist I needed to live here, and I had no doubts he'd insisted. In the back of my mind, I wondered the same thing myself.

"Couldn't be any worse than Rob's house," I muttered.

Adam heard me and rubbed his hands together. "Excellent. That's not a no. Let's talk details."

I pushed my food away, not capable of eating and making major life decisions at the same time. "You already have details?"

"Of course. We have it all worked out. Noah said you can use his room free of charge. He got the okay from Chloe to stay with her for the summer. You can use his bed and stuff. Don't worry, we'll get you clean sheets."

"What about *my* furniture?"

Some of his excitement faded, and he sat down facing me on the other stool. "Okay, we had *most* of the details worked out. I assume you would have moved it all into not-Archer's place. Can you still do that?"

I took a slow sip of my coffee and considered the situation. Rob would probably prefer if I stayed at his house where he could control me better, but he couldn't force the matter if I refused. Mom would expect him to do what Adam and his friends were doing—help.

Mom's stipend would stretch a lot farther if I didn't have to pay rent. The slow swirl of panic I'd been ignoring since yesterday dissipated, and excitement tingled at the base of my spine. Adam was offering me the perfect solution, as long as I could stand living with three roommates. And they could stand living with me.

I'd make nice with any number of roommates as long as one of them wasn't Shad.

"Yes," I mused. "I think I can do that. There's still time for them to take my furniture with all Mom's things, and I can store anything I won't need for the summer."

If Noah's room was even close to the size of Adam's, I'd have no problem fitting what was left in there. Then there was Adam. He watched me think, not interrupting or rushing me. Could I live in the same apartment as him and keep things platonic?

I groaned inwardly. Evidence suggested I wouldn't need to worry about it because he'd take care of maintaining the distance of friendship himself.

Decision made, I finished off my coffee. "When can I move in?"

Adam let out a whoop. "Now, if you want. Well, not now. I have a study session today, but after that. I can bring my Jeep over and load it up."

I held up a hand. "Just to be clear, this doesn't change our previous agreement. I still want to learn how to pick up a date, and I only have about a month and a half left before the first event."

"Understood. Step one, get you settled in your new digs. Step two, lessons in love. Let me finish this up and we can go pester Noah about moving his shit."

Despite his warning to RJ, he put the rest of the food in a casserole dish, covered it with foil, and stuck it in the oven. I was shocked they even owned a casserole dish, let alone that Adam knew how to keep food warm.

I narrowed my eyes at him as he put the foil away. "You're hustling them, aren't you."

He winked. "Don't tell them. If they think I'm incapable of basic domestic chores, I don't have to do any."

"I hope you don't plan to keep getting away with that while I'm living here."

"Never, Sunshine. For you, I'll cook and clean. I might even get groceries."

I chuckled as I handed him my half-empty plate—I'd believe it when I saw it. We cleaned up to the sound of Adam humming something low and soulful. He found my shoes for me, and with nothing left stopping me from taking a chance, I followed Adam outside.

Across the landing, Noah cracked open the door, revealing a strip of his bare chest. He declined help moving, but I heard Chloe squeal from inside a few seconds after he went back inside. Margarita nights would be a lot easier if all I had to do was stumble fifteen feet from her place to ours.

Ours. The word sounded almost foreign to me when referring to an apartment. I sneaked a glance at Adam and tried to squash the warm feeling spreading in my gut. He'd come through for me, and not in a small way.

My attraction was becoming dangerously close to a crush.

Adam caught my arm before we left the landing. "Is now a good time to call your mom? I can cancel my study session if you need me to help you move immediately."

I pressed my lips together and pulled my phone from my back pocket. "Sure." No going back now.

Adam leaned against the wall as we both listened to the ringing on the other end. "How do you think she'll respond to you moving in with a bunch of highly attractive football players?"

I couldn't imagine it. "She'll be happy I'm making friends."

Her voicemail picked up, and Mom accepted the call halfway through, as usual. "Hey, sweetie. What's up?"

I met Adam's eyes and hesitated. Mom and I had always been on the same page—same dreams, same goals, same future—but somewhere along the way we'd veered into different books. How was I supposed to tell her I didn't want the life she was setting up for me? He held out his hand, as if he fully expected I'd hand over my phone and let him handle this for me too.

Determination tightened my jaw, but I forced the words out.

"I'm not moving in with you." I chewed on my lower lip as Adam's shoulders shook in silent laughter.

Not the most auspicious start, but Mom was used to me. "Okay, you sound like you have an alternate plan."

I took a breath to organize my thoughts, then laid it out. "Thank you for setting up a system for me, but I want to stay closer to campus. I'll be moving in with a friend..." My eyes flashed to Adam, and the heat there made me feel like I was lying. "A couple of friends."

"Do I know any of them?"

I knew her question was rooted in curiosity, but it still bounced around inside me, setting off all kinds of guilty feelings. "Do you remember Eva?"

She laughed. "No one could forget Eva."

"These are her friends, mine now too, I guess. They offered me a room in their apartment."

"Do you mean Mac and his football buddies?" The sheer

glee in her voice knocked me sideways for a second. Did *everyone* love him?

"Yes, Mac and the others. Would Rob be able to store my furniture and a few things at his place even if I don't stay there?"

"Of course, honey. It's my home now too, you know."

Oh, I knew. She'd never called the apartment home, and the slip hit me harder than I expected. Things really were about to change. Adam pushed away from the wall and wrapped an arm around my shoulder. He didn't say anything or try to take over, and I was grateful for his support.

"Great." Now for the part I was dreading. "I'd still like the stipend you set up for me. My expenses are low but not zero."

"The money is yours, Blue. You more than earned it helping me keep the shop running, but I would have given it to you anyway."

Emotion clogged my throat. Regret, gratitude, love. I was going to miss her so much. Why couldn't she have married Archer instead of Rob?

She continued as if she knew I needed a second. "The movers for my apartment will be here tomorrow. We thought we'd set you up with a slightly later date, but now we can just have them take everything at once. Will that be too soon?"

I laughed, blinking away the sheen of tears. "No, it's fine. Adam will appreciate your quick timeline."

"Adam?"

"Mac. I'll explain later. Will you be at the apartment?"

She sighed. "No, honey. I finished packing last night, and Rob set up this dinner thing with some potential investors. I can come back if you need help though."

Her offer was genuine, but even if I said yes, she'd be late for one reason or another and spend more time reminiscing than packing. She deserved to put the studio first, and I'd be faster without her.

"I'll be fine. Enjoy your dinner."

Adam squeezed my shoulder and walked me in a circle between the two apartments, somehow knowing I needed to move.

"You're going to have so much fun living with those guys." Her wistful tone didn't surprise me. Mom loved the atmosphere of a college town—it was why we'd settled here in the first place. Well, that and the dirt-cheap building.

"Okay, I have to go call the movers. Remember to breathe, baby. Change can be scary, but worth it if you embrace the adventure. Love you."

As I'd expected, she didn't offer any warnings. Mom's style had always been to offer unwavering support and let me learn my own lessons.

She hung up as I responded with a muttered, "Love you too."

Adam bent to meet my eyes. "Well?"

The whole situation had a surreal sleepover quality I'd only experienced once before. I could push everything back a full twelve hours if I wanted to and stay at my place until the very last minute. Considering I'd spent the *last* twelve hours avoiding my apartment, I decided to do as Mom suggested—embrace the adventure. In moderation.

I let my lips tilt up as excitement replaced the trepidation from earlier. "I can move in tonight, as long as Noah is ready."

"Hell, yeah, roomie." Adam spun me around once, then set me on my feet to holler at Chloe's apartment. "You hear that, Noah. Time to get your ass in gear."

Adam's phone pinged with a message, and he pulled it out to show me. *Faster than your slow ass. Half my stuff is already here. I'll move the rest before you get back.*

My body burned from all the innocent touching, and I was sure my face reflected my inflamed state. Still, I surreptitiously inhaled Adam's scent when he tucked me against him.

"We're moving her in tonight. Bring your giant muscles. I'll get the pizza." He didn't wait for a response before he ushered me to his car. "Come on. I'll drive you home. You have packing to do, and I have to do this study thing. I'll swing by after to help."

Help. It seemed Adam was always helping me. His Wonder Woman notebook flashed across my mind, and I realized he hadn't stopped moving since he got home, probably since he woke up. Adam didn't have a lot of down time. No wonder he didn't talk about his music. When did he have time to work on it?

I let him lead me to his Jeep and tried not to think about how quickly my life was changing. Change usually meant I wouldn't know how to respond or what steps to take or even what direction to orient myself. The sheer weight of those decisions made me freeze up. Without something to ground me, I couldn't move at all.

The shop, my apartment, Mom, all the things I'd assumed were solid had turned into quicksand, and Adam, despite his fast pace, was giving me the stability to find a new path. I just hoped I could keep up.

14

Blue

At the end of the day, my new roommates and across the landing neighbors moved all my stuff into Noah's room. An entire apartment—a tiny one bedroom, but still—condensed down to a couple of boxes.

Noah was true to his word and had cleared out the closet and dresser for me to use. I didn't know where he put his stuff, and I didn't ask. Shaw got me new sheets as a welcome home present—his words—since I certainly didn't have any that would fit Noah's king-size bed.

Adam ordered pizza from Johnny's, and everyone stayed to watch a movie. My first official movie night with the group. The entire experience felt surreal for being so normal. When everyone piled onto the couches and Adam hooked an arm around me, I didn't even need to be on the end.

I couldn't help missing Eva a little, but for the first night at least, I didn't regret my decision one bit.

By morning, my brain had helpfully supplied several reasons why I should be wary. The first of which was realizing I needed to tell Eva I'd moved in across the hall. She may have been gone for the summer, but no one doubted she'd be back by fall to resume her spot as the queen of campus.

I had no idea where I'd be at that point. Hopefully, in a place nearby I could afford with my mom's stipend, but I had no promising avenues. My last year of college was turning out to be surprisingly haphazard.

Noah's room was darker than mine in the morning, so it was tempting to go back to sleep and pretend I wasn't gearing up for a potentially dramatic phone call. I'd never been the type to hide from adversity though.

I grabbed my phone and my glasses, wondering if anyone was still in the apartment besides me. How much more awkward would the conversation be if Shaw or Adam walked into my room while I was explaining my entirely platonic presence?

Were random bedroom visits from super attractive athletes something I'd have to steel myself against? I squinted at the door, relieved to see a flimsy lock on the knob.

Most likely, I wouldn't have to worry about privacy, and I knew from experience Adam liked to run in the morning. I listened for a few seconds, only hearing silence. They probably had training too, and I had class, eventually.

The one where Shad and Adam squared off outside my classroom several times a week in a barely disguised show of dominance. I didn't understand men. Eva would probably have some insight. I sighed. Enough procrastinating. She deserved to know, and I didn't have a good reason for putting off the call any longer.

Eva picked up right away, which meant she wasn't busy.

"Hey there, new bestie. Changed your mind and decided to join me on the beach yet?"

I chuckled and relaxed immediately. "No, but I have some news from Addison."

"If you're talking about your new living arrangements, I already know."

My mouth dropped open and my mind whirled. "How? I just moved in last night. Everything happened in one day."

She tsked. "Chloe called me literally the second she heard. I could hear Mac bellowing outside her apartment."

I pulled my glasses down and rubbed the spot between my eyes. "I should have realized."

"Yes, you should have, but I'll forgive you if you tell me how Mac's doing."

Adam was exactly the topic I *didn't* want to discuss. "Can't you use your spy network to ascertain his emotional wellbeing?"

"Ooo, I hit a nerve about something. You always start using thesaurus words when you're uncomfortable. Did Mac make an ass of himself?"

I made note of the habit and frowned at her intrigued tone. Time for a distraction unless I wanted her to suss out all the issues I wasn't ready to discuss yet.

"How about if I tell you about my mom's big news?"

"Oh yes, spill the tea on Mama Caldwell. I heard there are wedding bells in the future, but Archer Bolme is still considered single. What am I missing?"

"She's marrying the guy she started seeing after Archer."

"The one with the asshole son?"

If I rubbed my forehead any harder, I was going to leave bruises. I'd told her about the experience of meeting Shad for the first time, and apparently, it had made an impression.

"Yes. Her fiancé, Rob, is a prominent businessman in Dallas, and his son works at his company. I'm in the wedding, and they want me to show up for several high-profile events."

In true Eva form, she figured out the cause of my anxiety before I had to explain it. "Oh honey, are you nervous about your social skills?"

"I wasn't until they sat me down and told me Shad would be picking my date."

"Oh, hell no." I could hear the temper in her tone, and I wondered how much it would take to get her to come back and defend my honor herself. "I know you didn't take that shit lying down. If you didn't advocate for yourself, I'm happy to come up there and do it for you."

Not much, apparently. Eva was a born protector.

"That's not necessary, but I appreciate the offer. I told them I could find my own date. The problem is I'm having trouble executing. If I show up with someone Rob doesn't approve of, I may end up having to choose between being there for Mom or avoiding Shad, and you know I'll always choose Mom."

"What does Hope have to say about all this?"

"She was there for the conversation, Eva."

The silence on the other end stretched out longer than I was comfortable with. "I know I'm not good with people, but she's never suggested I should be any other way but myself. In fact, I'm not sure she'd have said anything at all if not for Rob and their guest list."

Eva blew out a raspberry on her end. "Not good enough. Their guest list shouldn't be more important than her daughter. I know you feel like you have to always choose her because it's only been the two of you forever, but honey, she's not choosing you now. I'm really disappointed in her."

I flopped back on the bed, glad she understood the root of my hurt feelings. "You're right, but—"

"No buts, Blue. You have two choices. Well, three, but I know you won't pick option three. One, go alone and face Rob's wrath. You're not required to spend time with people, period. Two, produce a date by...when's the first event?"

I laughed dryly. "Three weeks."

"Okay, produce a date in the next three weeks. I suggest one of the lovely men you find yourself living with. Any one of them would go as your date in a second. Hell, take RJ as your date. You guys would make a beautiful couple. If Rob is willing to pimp you out to Shad's friends, he's not expecting you to show up with your soul mate anyway."

I frowned. She was right. I'd gone straight to a date with romantic interests, but pairing me off with one of Shad's friends would be purely for image purposes. Of course, I'd heard Rob's disdain for professional athletes thanks to Mom's previous relationship with Archer, so I wasn't sure taking one of my football playing roommates would hit even that low bar.

Still, the idea was worth testing while I tried to find a 'suitable' date.

Clearly, I should have gotten out of my head and called Eva earlier. "Thank you. I might do that."

"You know, you're the easiest to convince out of all of them. Everyone else lets their emotions call the shots, but you're refreshingly reasonable."

I grimaced, not entirely thrilled with the description. If only she knew about my recent swan dive into the emotional waters. "Making a logical decision isn't hard when there are only two choices."

Eva stayed silent, waiting.

I couldn't help myself, and I knew *she* knew I'd ask. "What was option three?"

"Don't go at all. You'd be making a vivid point, but you'd probably hurt Hope's feelings."

"No," I spoke without a second's hesitation, and Eva laughed.

"See? I knew you wouldn't take option three. You may be utterly reasonable, but there's a deep well of compassion inside you."

My heart warmed as her explanation replaced my earlier hurt.

It felt good to have someone believe in me so completely. I'd thought I had that with my mom, but recent events had made me reevaluate my perceptions. We'd never had any major disagreements because she'd postponed her dream in order to raise me, and I'd spent my life trying to make her decision worth it. Even with the sudden distance in our relationship, I wasn't willing to abandon my mother on her wedding day.

I squeezed my eyes shut for a second to regain control of my burning tear ducts. Crying would get me nowhere. Another subject change was in order.

"Enough about my problems. What are you doing out there on the beach?" I asked.

"According to my parents, getting the perfect golden-brown tan to highlight my blonde hair."

I didn't miss the bitter undertone for once. Adam must be rubbing off on me. "What are you actually doing?"

"Meditating, or trying to. I think I'm terrible at it. There's a cheer facility here that runs workshops over the summer, and I've been helping out in exchange for use of the floor. Some of the kids here are really good. I've learned a lot."

Her answer didn't surprise me in the least. Eva was dedicated to her squad, which was nationally ranked. I'd looked it up. She wouldn't miss her summer commitments without finding an alternative way to improve.

"You're going to be an even bigger asset to your team when you come back."

She laughed. "Thanks, girl. Seriously though, is Mac okay?"

I couldn't put her off again. She really cared about him, and it was cruel to keep the information from her because I was afraid I'd reveal too much. "Yes. He's working through his feelings, but he's getting better."

"I'm glad," she said softly. "Look, I have to go. I have a shift at the center, but call me anytime you need to explore your feelings. Spoiler alert though, I'm never going to be okay with your mom marrying anyone other than Archer Bolme."

"I understand." We said goodbye, and I hung up the phone with a smile on my face.

Eva tended to have that effect on me, which was why I'd continued to spend time with her after our first meeting at the shop. A weight lifted from my shoulders knowing she wasn't upset about me moving in with Adam and the others.

Right on time, the front door to the apartment opened and closed. Adam's voice reached me through the walls, too muffled to make out specific words. Other voices mixed in, all with the same happy, energetic tone. My roommates were home.

With no warning, Adam burst into my room holding a grease-stained white paper sack. "Time to wake up, Sunshine. We brought breakfast."

I sat up, thankful I'd worn my full pajamas to bed and equally thankful Adam hadn't bothered to put on a shirt after his run. Sweat glistened on the ridges of his muscles.

One drop trailed down his abs to the low-slung gray shorts he wore.

It took me an embarrassingly long time to focus on the food in his hand.

"Did you bring me something from the Pancake Shack?"

"Biscuits and gravy, but you only get them if you come out here and eat with me."

He was being careful not to actually enter the room, and I remembered Eva's words about being reasonable, which had felt a lot like being boring. I could be spontaneous. Fun.

"What if you came in here instead?"

His brows rose, and he gave me a quick nod. "Be right back."

To my disappointment, he was wearing a shirt when he returned with a second bag, plates, utensils, and napkins. Everything we'd need for breakfast in bed.

Except he didn't join me on the bed. He set my food next to me, then took the chair at the desk. It didn't matter. I repeated the mantra a few times until I started to believe it. Instead of pouting, I opened up my bag and dug in.

He'd brought me my favorite meal. Unasked. Who cared if he sat next to me on the bed to eat it?

The soft squishy part of me whispered *I do*, but there was nothing I could do about it short of making a fuss. I didn't do fusses.

Instead, I broached a subject I'd been curious about from the beginning—Mac and Eva's origin story.

"Tell me how you ended up coming here with Eva."

He didn't hesitate. "We grew up together in the Austin suburbs. She's...she *was*...my best friend for a long time. The football player and the cheerleader, right? But it was never like that before. She was just Eva. A force of nature with a fierce need to protect the world."

How interesting, I'd classified her the same way. "Did she protect you?"

"Yeah. Private school kids can be pricks. Everyone there had money except my family. My dad worked in the administration, so I got to go for free. Eva didn't give a shit that we weren't rich. Her family fit right in, but her parents treated her like a possession to be passed back and forth. She spent all her time at our house. That's how she got into cheerleading. My sisters used to practice tossing her in the air when we were little."

I imagined a tinier version of Eva laughing uncontrollably on top of a pyramid made of Adam's family. "That sounds dangerous."

He snorted. "Oh, it was. They used to practice on me too until I got too big. Then I had to do the throwing. When it came time to pick a college, Eva didn't care where she went as long as they had a good cheer program. Her family was funding her, but they expected her to finish early with an MRS degree."

My nose scrunched as I tried to sort out what those letters could mean. "I don't understand."

"M-R-S as in a married woman. They sent her to college to find a husband."

My shock kept me silent for several seconds while I chewed. "Wow. I'm not sure how to respond since she doesn't seem to have the same aspirations."

He laughed. "No. She does not. Anyway, we never even considered applying to different schools. TU was my top choice, and they offered me a football scholarship. No brainer. Eva was ecstatic. We came here and just kept doing what we were doing in high school. Until the championship game earlier this year."

I finished off the last bite of my breakfast and laid back,

stuffed. "I thought you and Eva had been involved for longer than a few months."

"Sexually, no. Emotionally, all my life. She's always been a constant, like my mom making enchiladas when I come home and the guarantee that at least one guy on any team is going to be a narrow-minded piece of shit."

"An interesting list," I mused.

"The world is the world, and I try to focus on the good parts. Eva is a good part."

"Even now?"

"Even now."

I stared up at the ceiling, not ready to meet his gaze yet. "Have you ever felt trapped with all these constants, yet scared of change? Like you made certain choices—ones you don't regret—and they locked you onto a path, but you don't know how to do anything else?"

The bed jostled as Adam lay down next to me. He was close enough I could feel the heat from his body, but we weren't touching. The silence lengthened, and I assumed he was trying to find a nice way to tell me he never felt that way.

"Yes."

I sucked in a shocked breath, but he wasn't done.

"I've always been good at football. My parents worked hard to make sure I had every chance to succeed in school. No one in my mom's family went to college. The obvious choice was to do the thing I was good at—play football for a scholarship, kick ass, get into the NFL, buy my parents a new life. One where they don't have to work their asses off just to have the people they work for look down on them."

He took a deep breath. "I've always been good at football, but I don't feel it in my soul."

"What *do* you feel in your soul?"

"Music. The way it sucks you in." His eyes cut to me. "Sex and love and hunger—need—all wrapped up in a series of beats, a sensuous rhythm, a sound that pulls on everything inside me. I'm good at that too, but football is my life."

"Why haven't you told anyone this?"

Adam shrugged, brushing my arm and setting off ripples of sensation that coalesced in my chest. "No one's ever asked —except you."

I nodded as the urge to ask him more things, all the things, washed over me. We had time now. In between responsibilities and wounds and want versus need. Caught in a space where the real world hadn't intruded yet, neither of us made an effort to move away.

"I have more questions."

He studied my face and smiled. "Ask away, Sunshine."

15

Mac

I scowled at the lone towel on my rack as the water running down my body slowly cooled. The last two weeks living with Blue had tested the limits of our apartment's hot water heater. She liked long, scalding showers after our runs in the morning. I knew because the thought of Blue naked, warm, and wet sent me to my own shower to handle Big Mac's incessant need for the woman.

Nothing like a spray of cold water to convince my dick to focus elsewhere. If only it worked on my mind too.

I couldn't stop thinking about her. Without the shop to run, she had actual free time around her classes, and she spent them quizzing me on the best way to approach people in a social setting. Talking about finding a date was fine—it was the hands-on practice I couldn't handle.

Blue would come out of her room, ask me a bunch of questions I tried my best to answer honestly, then flirt with me mercilessly until Big Mac begged me to put him out of his misery. She'd smile and touch and inch herself closer to crossing the line we'd both drawn.

I never even considered stopping her, and she always

pulled back at the last second with a quiet thanks. Fuck. I liked it even better when she dropped the act.

Hence my presence in the shower despite our break from training this morning. I considered circling back around to the fantasy of Blue joining me under the water when the door crashed open in real life, making me jump.

RJ waltzed in and frowned at my mirror. "That's what I thought."

I lowered the loofah to cover as much of my junk as possible. "Girl, I told you from day one you were cut. You're going to get the same answer at every mirror in this apartment."

She pursed her lips, carefully not looking in my direction. "Your bathroom is clean."

"Yes. Shocker. I clean. Sometimes. Is this conversation necessary to have while I'm naked?"

RJ dropped her attempts at modesty to glare at my face. "Oh? Does it bother you to have someone barge in during your shower?"

"That was for your own good, and Eva sent me in there."

"Twice?" She shook her head, resuming her examination of the wall next to the door. "It doesn't matter. Shaw and I just got back from campus, and the kitchen is clean."

"So you had to run in here to tell me?"

"Did you clean it?"

"Not today..." I didn't want to admit I couldn't remember the last time I'd cleaned it, but we'd definitely made a mess this morning when Shaw insisted he knew how to make homemade waffles.

He did not, in fact, know.

"Exactly," she shot back. "I think we have our very own Cinderella."

"Blue?"

"Yes. Keep up. When was the last time you did the dishes?"

"Why?"

"I think Blue cleaned up around here."

The water was distinctly lukewarm and edging toward chilly, but I tried my best to follow the conversation. "I thought you guys did it."

"Not us. I'm assuming from you sidestepping my question it wasn't you either. What about your laundry?"

Laundry was one of my least favorite household tasks because I tended to get distracted and forget to switch the clothes from the washer to the dryer. I'd shared my little secret about chores and expectations with Blue the day she moved in, but laundry was the exception. Washing clothes sucked.

Now that RJ brought it up, my hamper hadn't gotten full in a while. "Suspiciously clean."

RJ sent me a triumphant grin and pulled the bathroom door open. "I knew it."

"Let me talk to her," I shouted to her retreating back.

She waved in my direction as she disappeared into my bedroom. "That was always the plan."

I shut off the cold water and grabbed my towel. The one I hadn't washed in at least a week. With some concern, I held the material up to my face and took a test sniff. Dryer sheets. The good ones Shaw bought because RJ liked the smell.

Guess I wouldn't need to steal one of Shaw's clean towels after all.

Now that RJ had pointed out the cleaning discrepancy, I noticed the evidence everywhere. I'd done a half-assed shave last night, and I definitely hadn't been neat about it.

Yet my countertop was sparkling. Literally. I hadn't even been aware there were sparkly bits in the stone.

The more I thought about it, the more I realized it wasn't just cleaning. Last week, I forgot to hit the grocery store, but when I got home from watching film, the fridge was full of vegetables and my frozen pizzas were restocked.

I got dressed and went in search of my sexy, sneaky roommate.

Blue wasn't hard to find. She was sitting in the living room with a textbook spread out in front of her while a cartoon played on the TV. Her eyes flicked up for a second when I came in, then went back to her studying.

Well, that wouldn't do.

I sat next to her, jostling the book, and tugged on a magenta strand of hair. "I know your secret."

Her slumped posture straightened, and she closed her book, gathering up the rest of her stuff. "Which one? I have a lot of secrets."

"Not from me, you don't."

"Yes, I do."

I gripped my chest with as much drama as I could muster. For real, Shakespeare would be proud. "You mean you don't tell me everything. That's it. I demand my bestie bracelet back."

Blue's lips twitched, but I didn't get the laugh I was hoping for. "You've never given me a bestie bracelet. No one has."

I made a note to immediately go out and buy her a damn bracelet.

"What secret do you think you know?" she asked in an exasperated tone.

"When you put it that way, I'm forced to question my certainty. Did you clean my bathroom?"

She shot up off the couch and brushed past me. "I don't want to talk about it."

Her reaction was extreme even for the teasing I'd been dishing out. I thought back to the last time I'd needed to clean anything, and it was a solid two weeks ago—before she'd moved in. RJ had made it sound like a one-time thing, but my Spidey sense went off.

"Have you been cleaning my bathroom *this whole time*?"

Blue spun around, rainbow hair flying, and poked me in the chest. "What part of 'I don't want to talk about it' did you misunderstand?"

Her finger drilled into my pec again, so I caught her hand as a safety measure. "Why are you cleaning my bathroom? You have your own bathroom." I narrowed my eyes at her. "Are you installing cameras or something? Because trust me, people don't like when you have secret camera access."

She stopped trying to free her hand and tilted her head. "Why would you know that?"

"Personal experience involving a slight misunderstanding with Eva and some door cams."

Her brows shot up. "No. I'm not installing cameras, you pervert. I wanted to thank you for giving me an alternative to Shad, so I've been doing some stuff around the apartment. It's not a big deal, just a little cleaning and a few other chores."

It felt like a little bit of a big deal. No one had ever cleaned for me before. "Did you do Shaw and RJ's bathroom?"

She blushed a pretty pink, but her chin came up. "No. I offered, but RJ laughed at me."

Out of nowhere, my protective instincts engaged. RJ had left that little tidbit out of our conversation. I loved her like a fourth sister—fifth sister? It was hard to keep track these days—but I wasn't going to let her hurt Blue's feelings. "Why the fuck would she laugh at you trying to do something nice?"

Blue patted my chest where she'd poked it a minute ago. "Not like that. She loved the thought of finally having a clean bathroom, but she claimed Shaw would hate the idea."

My hackles settled, and I snaked an arm around her for a hug. Blue relaxed immediately. She circled my waist and let her head rest against my chest, a huge improvement from when we first talked and she threatened to Tase me.

"He would. Shaw doesn't like to feel beholden to his friends. Thank you for doing it, but please stop with the ninja cleaning."

She looked up at me, eyes pleading. "What if I only do it every other day?"

"Is this a compulsion or are you just incapable of accepting help without repaying?" Either way I was going to start cleaning my own shit before she could get to it.

Blue wiggled her head back and forth with a shrug. "Probably the second, but I'm not discounting the first."

"Fine. You can clean the shared areas, but no hiding it. Own it. Be proud of your new compulsion."

Her nose wrinkled, and she pulled back until I caught her hand, preventing her from going any farther. "If you want me to let you bathe in your own filth, so be it."

"Nah, I take my baths at the facility. None of our bathrooms have a tub, and let's be honest, me using a regular sized tub would be like trying to squeeze a watermelon through a cat door. Wait, that's childbirth. And maybe it wasn't a cat door." My favorite part of the day was watching the humor bloom in her tropical eyes. Followed closely by any chance I got to touch her.

I stroked my thumb across her palm, and she let me get away with it once before gently breaking the connection. This was our dynamic now. Casual touching, snuggling during the reinstituted movie night, heated looks we both ignored. A little push here, a tug there, easing us closer to the edge of friendship.

She walked backward slowly toward her room. I hoped it was because she didn't really want to leave. "I'll make note of your bath fetish. Right next to the camera thing."

"I like baths. They relax me."

Her steps slowed. "I like showers, but especially when the showerhead is oversized. More hot water coverage."

I followed her, keeping a safe distance between us. Just far enough I wouldn't be tempted to give in to desperation and reach for her again. If she came back on her own, though, I wouldn't look as desperate. There were other things I was supposed to be doing on my day off—it was my week to get groceries—but I'd much rather spend time discussing plumbing with her.

"I have a fancy rain showerhead. One of the best splurges I've ever made. It's fantastic for making sure your front side and your back side are warm at the same time." Not my best conversational gambit for convincing a girl to spend time with me.

"Noah's shower is one of those handheld ones that connects to a holder." She dashed my hopes by crossing the threshold.

"I can honestly say I've never thought about Noah's showerhead, but that makes sense. These apartments aren't equipped to handle tall, dark, and handsome football players. Noah's a redhead, but it's a dark red, so he counts. Don't tell him I said that though." I stopped at the line of Noah's door, toe to toe with Blue as she stared up at me. "For the record, you're welcome to join me any time. You'd fit perfectly."

She rolled her eyes and closed the door in my face. Denied. I probably should have left off the last part, but I couldn't help myself. My primary form of communication was flirting. Most of the time, I was kidding. In this case, I meant every word.

I took a deep breath to get my racing pulse under control and turned toward the kitchen to make a grocery list. At the top, I added cleaning supplies and a new showerhead. The rational part of my brain tried to insist I'd do this for any of my friends, but I'd lived with Shaw for over a year and I'd never volunteered to clean.

Blue was smart to put some distance between us. I kept trying and failing to think of her only as a friend and roommate. Every day I spent with her made me wish I hadn't agreed so easily to friends without benefits.

Maybe I was incapable of learning from my past mistakes, but the longer we danced around each other, the more I wanted. I was tired of talking myself down.

Eva's words flashed through my mind like they always did when I felt like giving in. *I don't want a relationship, Mac, I just wanted some fun.*

This time, they didn't jolt me with pain. This time, I saw the difference. Eva wasn't looking for me, she was looking for a distraction. I should have told her about my feelings before we got involved—the itch to make a change, the stretch for something different—but I didn't. Somewhere along the way, I'd stopped sharing.

Eva hurt me when she left, but maybe I'd been pulling away for a lot longer. Maybe Eva had too.

As much as the thought of losing Blue's company scared me, I wasn't making the same mistake again. Blue knew parts of me Eva had never touched. She understood my restlessness, she wanted Adam, not Mac.

And I wanted Blue. I wanted every prickly, confident, beautiful inch of her, and I was done holding myself back.

16

Blue

I knew I was tempting fate the second I chose to brave the kitchen in my sleep shirt and undies. Earlier in the day, Adam had stalked me all the way to the border of my room, but I'd managed to scrape together enough wits to leave him in the hallway instead of inviting him inside.

Then I'd hidden like the coward I apparently was. So much for not hiding from adversity.

When I came out to scrounge for dinner, I found a brand-new rain showerhead sitting on the counter decorated with a big purple bow. My heart lurched—not a reaction I usually got from plumbing equipment—and my resistance crumbled.

Thank goodness Adam hadn't been in the room. I'd grabbed the present and a box of Cheez-Its before retreating again. They'd lasted me until after midnight, but I needed real food.

The cold tile felt good under my bare feet while the rest of me overheated. Stress always made me hot. With an upcoming project and the approaching deadline of my mom's first wedding event, for which I was still dateless, pressure threatened to crush me.

I'd spent the evening trying to study instead of fantasizing about Adam, and I only put myself at a forty-seven percent success rate. The living room was dark, and the kitchen was lit only by the stove light. Footballs players trained *a lot*, so my roommates tended to go to bed early unless Adam pushed them to go out. Even so, it wasn't early.

The hem of my vintage Rainbow Brite shirt brushed my thighs, but I didn't care if one of them caught me. Shaw and RJ didn't make me nervous like they had at the beginning. They were what I thought it might be like if I had siblings. Real siblings, not the pervy version Shad insisted on manifesting.

Cooking anything seemed like too much work to my tired brain, but for once, the fridge was full of healthy food I hadn't bought. Healthy food that required some kind of preparation unless I planned to eat raw carrots. Screw the veggies—I wanted carbs. Toast would have to do.

This was my life now. Toast at midnight because I was too much of a coward to face my roommate. At least I was an equal opportunity coward—I'd been avoiding Eva too. Chloe talked to her regularly, and the lack of any news meant nothing much had changed on her end. A lot had changed on mine.

I sighed and rested my forearms on the counter, waiting for my meal to pop up. Mom had texted earlier to make sure I remembered her engagement luncheon was next week. I remembered. I'd simply planned to ignore it until I had a solid strategy for finding a date.

My grand plan of having Adam teach me to be fun and sexy was backfiring spectacularly. He nailed the fun and sexy part, but every time I tried to mimic him, I either felt like an obvious fraud or I fell headfirst under Adam's spell.

Admittedly, he hadn't been as much of a player as I expected. Football players were stereotyped as promiscuous for a reason, right? Not this group. With RJ and Chloe, even Eva to some extent, all the men were on lockdown. I should probably appreciate their very taken status since I haven't had to deal with any groupies or late-night visitors, but I felt a little bad about originally assuming Adam only paid attention to women he wanted to sleep with.

He paid attention to everyone, and now I was avoiding him. Not a great way to learn.

None of my evolving feelings toward Adam would help me show up to Mom's luncheon properly paired off with a respectable date, and I hadn't suddenly developed the ability to make small talk without mentioning my menstrual cycle.

This first event was a small, intimate gathering of mostly family and friends. Rob's family and friends. She'd even given me an out because she wanted me to have time to settle into my new place. I only intended to use it in case of emergency.

The toast popped up, but my appetite had disappeared. Sleep sounded better than eating, but I'd regret it when I hoovered up a trash breakfast in the morning. Tomorrow was one of the three days a week I went running with Adam in the evening. Which brought me full circle to the stupidity of hiding from him.

Along with the stupidity of skipping dinner and the stupidity of thinking I had any idea how to be friends with someone who starred in my dirtier fantasies.

As if he could sense my swirling thoughts, I heard a door close quietly in the hallway. Shaw and RJ's door squeaked, so it had to be Adam. For a second, I considered running back to my room, but the questions circling quietly in the back of my mind surged to the front in a deafening roar.

What if I didn't run this time?

I felt him first—his warmth on my back. His arms brushed mine as he caged me against the counter, flattening his hands on either side of me. I didn't move.

He leaned down, and his breath tickled my ear. "Miss me?"

Goosebumps exploded across my skin and my nipples hardened to peaks against the soft cotton of my sleep shirt. I was suddenly very awake.

"Were you gone?" I tried for a teasing tone, but it came out a little more needy than I wanted.

HE CHUCKLED, and the throaty noise made my inner muscles clench. "Can't sleep? You seem stressed."

"Nothing a little alone time in my room can't fix." Ten seconds of spending time with him, and I'd already mentioned sex. That had to be a new record.

"I wasn't going to mention it, but now that you brought it up..." I could hear the smile in his voice. Inside, I was burning up, embarrassment and need tangled together in a confusing mess.

"See, this is why I get shunned in polite company. I always say the wrong thing or wear the wrong outfit or stick out a little too much."

His hands twitched on the counter like he wanted to reach for me, but they stayed planted. I wasn't sure if I was grateful or disappointed.

"Blue, you might be too much for polite company, but you're just right for me. Polite company sucks anyway. Too much truth left unsaid and too many lies spread around with smiles."

The world around me slowed for a long beat as I tried to process what he was saying.

Adam lowered his head to nuzzle my neck. "I love the way I see a different color in your hair every time I look at you. Hidden pieces of a rainbow, waiting for me to find them. Like you."

My heart sped up, and my insides did the goo thing again. He was catapulting us well past friendship, and I didn't hate it. I wasn't sure what had happened in the last twelve hours, but Adam wasn't the patient teacher he'd been the last few weeks while I practiced on him. Playing pretend while secretly enjoying the attention.

"I thought we weren't doing this," I said.

His lips brushed the sensitive spot under my ear, making me shiver. "I changed my mind."

"When?" I asked breathlessly.

"About ten seconds after we made the agreement."

I turned toward him slightly. "Why wait until now?"

Adam skimmed a kiss across my jaw, and his stubble started a ripple of tingles down my neck to the deepest part of me. "Didn't want to fuck things up again."

"Aren't you worried that's how it will end?"

"I'm more worried you'll spend the rest of your life believing you can't have an orgasm with another person, and I won't get the chance to prove you wrong."

"Adam," I groaned.

His hand slid over my waist and flattened on my stomach, pulling me in until the hard length of him pressed against my butt.

"Think of it as another lesson in what your body is

capable of. It doesn't have to change anything. If I need to back off, I will, but Sunshine, I'm dying for a taste of you."

I chuckled low. "I'm still not having sex with you, Adam."

His hand on my stomach slowly closed, gathering the fabric in his fist. "We don't need to have sex for me to give you an orgasm—if you'll let me."

My body was on fire, being consumed from the inside out with wet heat.

"The choice is yours. Are you going to tell me to go back to my room, or are you going to let me show you how much better it can be?"

One time—to satisfy my curiosity. Tomorrow, we could go back to practicing, to convincing myself I didn't imagine him every time I closed my eyes alone in my room and slid my hand between my legs.

I gathered my courage and turned. "Show me."

A slow, wicked smile curved his lips. "Good choice. Now spread your legs, Sunshine."

Before I could say a word, he lifted me onto the counter. When I didn't immediately obey his order, he palmed my thighs and separated them for me. My shirt rode up to my hips, and his thumb stroked a line of fire outside the boundary of my panties.

I sucked in a breath as he shifted his big hands to my hips and eased me forward until my butt hit the edge of the counter. He kissed my neck, teasing me with a hot swipe of his tongue.

"If you want me to stop at any time, you just tell me, okay?"

I nodded, but he pulled back slightly to meet my eyes.

"I need you to say the words."

"If I want you to stop, I'll tell you." I meant what I said, but I also knew nothing short of a zombie apocalypse would make me tell him to stop.

Adam sank to his knees, holding my gaze. "Good girl."

Why was that phrase so hot coming out of his mouth? Coming from anyone else, it would sound patronizing. But Adam so clearly knew what he was doing, and it was a pleasure to have him teach me, have him praise me.

His fingers hooked under the waistband of my panties, and he drew them down until the counter got in the way. "Lift," he ordered.

This time I obeyed right away. He slid them down my legs and off, then stuffed them in his pocket.

I raised a brow. "I want those back."

"And you'll get them. Later."

Adam lowered his head, and a short montage of the other times I'd tried this flashed in my mind. I recognized the point where I usually stiffened up and couldn't escape the prison in my head. A lock of his hair tickled my skin as he kissed a trail from one hipbone to the other.

"Look at you, already soaked," he breathed against my core.

The sheer delight in his tone erased any nervousness. This was Adam, not some random encounter where I needed to perform. The tension left my muscles, and I let out a long, low hum.

"That's it, baby. Relax for me."

His quiet words sent a spike through my system, and he followed them up with a swipe of his tongue I felt all the way to my toes. He may have been a goofball, a human golden retriever, but the man knew how to use his mouth. And his fingers.

I dropped my head back against the cabinets with a thud and muttered prayers, obscenities, anything except stop. I moaned his name, and his hold on me tightened. He made a rough sound of satisfaction when my fingers gripped in his hair. Sharp bolts of pleasure sped through my blood, sending me tumbling head over feet into an abyss of shared sensation I had no idea I could feel.

In no time, I was close. So close. I arched my hips, begging for more.

He grinned up at me. "Having fun yet?"

In response, I used his hair to yank him back down. Adam obliged my unspoken demand and stayed right where he was while I writhed against his face.

The orgasm hit me like a truck. A shudder wracked my body, and I might have blacked out for a second. I blinked up at the dark ceiling, only then considering our roommates were only a short distance away. How loud had I been?

My pulse pounded in my ears, but not from the prospect of being caught. I was still trembling, and I already wanted more. Adam kissed my inner thigh and trailed his fingers over my calves as he stood.

He helped me off the counter and steadied me when my legs wobbled dangerously. "Have I proved my point, or should I try again? Just to be sure."

My first instinct was to dive headfirst into the second round he was offering. I wanted it so badly I had to roll my lips together to keep the words in. One time to prove a point. That was all it was supposed to be. A tryst in the dark not to be mentioned in the morning. I couldn't afford to fall into the trap of thinking Adam wanted more simply because he was the first person to ever give me an orgasm.

"Thank you, but I'm good." I cringed at the weirdly polite way my answer sounded. I needed to leave the room before I accidentally said something worse. "I think I can sleep now."

Adam nodded his head and took a step back, shoving his hands into the pockets of his sweats. "Don't forget your toast."

For once, I couldn't read his voice, but I didn't dare look directly at him. My willpower was shredded enough. In one quick swipe, I tossed my now cold toast onto the plate we'd shoved out of the way at some point.

"Goodnight, Adam." I chanced a peek at him, but his hooded eyes didn't reveal anything in the dark kitchen.

"Goodnight, Blue." His gaze stayed on me until I shut my bedroom door between us, and I realized a disturbing truth. One time probably wouldn't be enough.

17

Blue

A persistent, annoying beeping brought me to consciousness right as dream me was running my tongue along the grooves of Adam's abs. Sunlight filled the room, and I glared blearily at my phone as I swiped at the alarm. After a fitful night of dreams where Adam showed off his real prowess, I woke feeling horny, frustrated, and hungry. The dry toast hadn't made it past my desk, so I'd fully skipped dinner.

I shouldn't have gone out for the stupid toast. Shouldn't have let him lift me onto the counter. *Definitely* shouldn't have let him show me what I was missing.

The sneaky voice in the back of my mind added *shouldn't have left him out there alone.*

I burrowed under my pillow on the giant bed and grabbed two handfuls of comforter. Tremors still occasionally shook my leg muscles, and I couldn't squeeze them together hard enough to relieve the ache.

This was Adam's fault.

My stomach growled in a demand for real food, and I released my death grip on the bedding. Logically, I shouldn't blame Adam for my own reaction to him, but for once, I didn't feel like being logical. I wanted to throw all the consequences out the window and indulge.

Instead, I listened for any sounds of movement in the hallway. Theoretically, all the football players should be at training now, but Adam had skipped several times since I'd moved in. No one said anything about his absences, so I kept my mouth shut too. Shaw was the captain. He'd know better than me about Adam's team responsibilities.

Usually when he skipped, Adam waited until Shaw, RJ, and Noah left, then went out himself shortly after. I was extremely curious about where he spent his alone time, but the secretive vibe made me hold my tongue. If he wanted me to know, he'd tell me.

I didn't have any say over where he went or what he was doing—or who he was doing it to. Despite the contradictory evidence of last night, Adam and I were only friends. Friends who didn't kiss. Friends who delivered on promised orgasms. Friends who would never work as anything more because Adam was Adam—funny, sweet, massively hot, surrounded by friends—and I couldn't even keep my Mom around.

The constant need to remind myself of that fact was getting on my nerves. I'd never had a real relationship, never really wanted one until now. The thought of putting faith in someone to hold up their end of the deal, to stick, to want me enough to stay even when a better offer came along... What was I supposed to do with the clammy palms and the churning in my stomach?

Easier to wait for the inevitable. Or it had been. Now, I'm wondering if the all or nothing mentality might not be the way to go. I'd asked Adam to teach me, maybe I should pay attention to *all* his lessons.

With a huff, I tossed the covers aside, slapped on my glasses, and threw my hair into a messy ponytail. If I were back in my apartment, would I be lazing about in bed? No. I'd be prepping for a job I hated.

My movements slowed with the elastic only half wrapped around my hair. I didn't hate working at the dress shop. Did I?

I mean, I didn't enjoy it, especially when I had to deal with people. Half of the time I couldn't identify the front side of the dress, and people tended to expect someone who could give them advice on fashion.

My arms lowered, and I sank onto the side of the bed. It wasn't just the clients. I hated having my time tied to the hours of the shop and having to rush to make my classes when Mom inevitably showed up late once again. The utterly useless attempts to modernize the computer system. The constant struggle to cover expenses. Helga, the temperamental mannequin who refused to keep her left leg attached unless we bribed her with the good spot in the window.

Huh. I hated my job—and I didn't have to go back. Ever.

I waited for the rush of excitement, but none came. The dress shop was gone. Mom had hired someone to clear out the last of the merchandise, and construction had already begun on the new cowboy-themed bar going in. The version of me who had worked there wasn't the same person who spent her free time pretending not to want to sneak into her roommate's bed every night.

And who now had a very good reason to actually try it. I didn't hate the idea. I didn't hate the person I was now. Change freaked me out, but after last night, I realized I might have been selling myself short. I could do hard things. Like take a chance with my roommate.

I squeezed my eyes—and my legs—shut for a second, willing myself to think about anything except Adam. Food. I should get food. I could satisfy at least one hunger. Besides, the counter needed to be cleaned, preferably before Shaw and RJ got back from training and did their morning smoothie routine.

The hallway was quiet, the apartment, the whole world maybe, but when I entered the kitchen, I found Adam there in a pair of basketball shorts and nothing else. He leaned against the counter eating a bowl of sugary kid cereal, and his eyes lifted to me before I could reverse course.

I rooted to the spot, one leg extended like I'd intended to keep walking. His gaze trailed over me in a lazy perusal that I felt *everywhere*. A few hours ago, the phantom touch had been his real hands and mouth.

He hadn't said anything—hadn't even moved—and I was on the verge of begging him for a repeat.

Adam's lips curved into a sexy grin. "Morning, Sunshine. Sleep well?"

"What are you doing here?" I blurted out.

"I live here. Want some breakfast?"

I shook my head and started past him to make coffee before I realized there was already some made. Adam followed my gaze.

"I thought you might be tired after your long night," he said.

"I thought we were going to pretend it never happened?"

He snorted. "I never agreed to that. I said I changed my mind—and I meant it—but if you need us to keep classifying ourselves as friends without benefits, I can do that. For now."

At least I wouldn't spend any time trying to figure out where last night left us. Without looking directly at him, I poured myself a cup of coffee and headed for the fridge to drown it in salted caramel creamer.

The air conditioning dried the fine sheen of sweat on my neck, and I took a big drink before I attempted to engage Adam in conversation again. Hopefully, this time without the undertone of accusation.

"Good morning. Yes. I slept well." I sounded like I had a stick up my butt, but I succeeded in answering his question like a normal person.

He laughed and put his bowl in the sink. "Good to hear, but I don't need the vanilla version. Go ahead and say what you're thinking."

"You have a very talented tongue."

Adam grinned. "I'm up for more anytime, Sunshine." When he took a step toward me, I flinched back. He stopped immediately and frowned. "If something is wrong, you need to tell me. No keeping secrets, remember."

"Nothing is wrong," I lied, but Adam raised a brow.

"You're all stiff again, and that's not the face of a well-satisfied woman."

I tried to judge my current expression, but without a mirror, I was lost. My face was my face. He was wrong about my satisfaction level though. "I'm uncomfortable right now because I'm not sure how to act in this situation. You were supposed to be at training, and I wasn't ready to see you yet."

He tilted his head and studied me for a long moment, then extended his palm. "I know how to fix this."

I instinctively put my hand in his, though I was suspicious about his intentions. If he tried for another round, I wasn't sure I had the willpower to say no, but I *was* sure it would be a mistake. Once was a fluke, twice made a pattern.

Adam tugged me gently, pulling until I stood between

his spread legs staring up at him. He tucked a loose strand of hair behind my ear and traced my jaw on the way down.

"My mom always says communication is key. I'll stay away as long as you need me to, until you're comfortable, but I'm not going to promise I won't be spending every second thinking about last night. I've been thinking about you since the beginning, so nothing has changed other than the accuracy of my fantasies. Any time you want to pull my hair, I'm game."

The memory of Adam's thick hair between my fingers last night made my hand twitch. He fantasized about me?

My lips parted, and his gaze shot to my mouth. We hadn't kissed last night. Another surreal aspect of the situation I didn't know how to address. What if he was a horrible kisser? Considering the skill of his tongue, I highly doubted it, but unlikely things happened every day.

What happened now? Were we supposed to be touchy feely friends? How long before Eva found out and murdered me in my sleep? The questions built in my mind until one escaped.

"Why didn't you kiss me last night?"

His fingers curled around the back of my neck, and he tilted my chin up. "Last night was for you. Kissing you will be for me."

Everything about this situation was new to me, but I understood one thing for certain. I wanted to kiss him— wanted his mouth on me in every way possible. No amount of bad friend voodoo or common-sense restraint slowed the growing urge.

"Why can't it be for both of us?" I knew I was pushing where I shouldn't, but I couldn't seem to help myself.

Adam let out a possessive growl and gave in, lowering his mouth to mine. I'd thought I was prepared, but he pushed away from the counter to flip our positions. My head spun as he pinned me in place.

His thumb pressed down on my chin, parting my lips to deepen the kiss. I let out a quiet whimper and ran my hand down his bare chest, tracing the curves and edges of muscle and bone. Adam devoured me, leading me down a hungry path and demanding I follow.

Gladly.

I'd waited my whole life to feel this rush of need, the desperation and pure unfiltered lust. Like he promised, Adam showed me what I'd been missing in my previous shallow relationships.

I sank into the kiss, testing, teasing, giving and taking with a sigh. The hands cupping my face trembled, and he groaned. Adam shifted forward, and I felt his hard length against my stomach. No doubts there—he wanted me—but he didn't push.

A heady feeling of power shook me. I could have what I wanted. Right now. I slid my palm lower over warm skin, tracing the deep V of his abs.

Adam flattened his hand over mine when I reached the waistband of his shorts. "Not here, Sunshine," he murmured against my mouth.

His words pulled me from my lusty haze. We were in the kitchen of our shared apartment, and not thirty minutes ago, I'd been actively trying to avoid him. For exactly this reason. When I was with him, I forgot the rest of the world. Forgot how my actions could hurt other people, and how inevitably my relationships always ended with me alone.

I twisted my head to the side, breaking the kiss. For a long moment, I felt Adam's uneven breath against my cheek, then he took several steps back. I shivered at the sudden loss of warmth and had to curl my fingers into my palms to stop myself from reaching for him.

Adam held his hands loosely at his sides, but I could see the tension in his body. "So what's it to be? Do we go back or move forward?"

I froze, unable to make a decision. Could I go back? I didn't want to lose the connection I had with Adam, but I didn't see a way forward now that we'd crossed the line. Friends with benefits sounded nice on the surface, but what happened when the fall semester started and I became a distraction he no longer wanted? Or when Eva came home and discovered I'd picked up where she'd left off.

Icy cold fear slid through my veins. The thought of losing Adam already made my chest hurt, how much worse would it be if I let myself get fully involved? My reasons for refusing to sleep with him in the beginning were still valid. It was my resolve that needed help.

Adam was my weakness, and I couldn't resist him forever. He'd snuck under my defenses, making me want to take a chance. I wasn't ready. My heart pounded in my ears, and distantly, I knew I was reacting out of panic. It didn't matter.

Something had to change. I couldn't move forward with Adam without getting my emotions involved, they were already involved. Handling him one on one wasn't working because I didn't want to go back, so I grasped onto the one excuse I had to create some distance while moving forward. Our dating lessons. I needed to find someone else to distract me.

Still panting, I lifted my head to meet his eyes. "I think we should go out tonight so I can practice. On someone else."

He frowned, and an expression I couldn't categorize

flashed across his face. "You want to go out and try to pick up a guy tonight?"

I nodded, even though everything in me screamed it was a mistake. "Yes."

His expression lingered longer this time, and I was able to identify it—hurt. "If that's what you want."

I shoved my foot farther into my mouth trying to make it better, unable to stop myself. "I'm sure I could find a ride home if you don't want to wait around. I could use a ride there though."

His shoulders tensed slightly. "I'll bring you there *and* home, Blue."

My chest tightened with the absolute certainty I was screwing up even as I tried to fix it. "I'm sorry if I'm giving you mixed signals. I don't know what I'm doing. I understand if you regret getting involved, but I'm glad you're helping me, Adam."

He shook his head slightly as his lips pressed together into a tight smile. Nothing like the one he usually wore around me. "Sunshine, I don't regret one second of time I've spent with you. When you're ready to go, you know where to find me."

In a reversal of last night, Adam turned on his heel and left me in the kitchen without looking back. I slumped against the counter with my pulse still racing from his kiss. Suddenly, distance was the last thing I wanted.

18

Mac

I took a small sip of my beer and settled in at the bar for a long night. After the life-altering kiss in the kitchen this morning—followed by the quickest kick to my balls I'd ever experienced—I didn't see Blue again until she knocked on my door twenty minutes ago.

She'd put all our lessons to good use, pairing a funky, short summer dress with dark teal cowboy boots and adding a casual wave to her hair. The look said confident and fun, and best of all, it felt like authentic Blue. I'd wanted to yank her into my room and convince her she didn't need the lessons.

Then her eyes passed over my shoulder, and I remembered the speed with which she'd pivoted from me to literally any other guy. Friends, it was. I pasted on a patented Mac smile and ushered her to the car.

I didn't offer advice or encouragement on the way over —I didn't have it in me—but just before we went through the door, I slipped up and told her she looked beautiful. She'd given me a sad smile, and I'd made a beeline for the bar.

Johnny's wasn't as busy in the summer, and I was glad I didn't have to elbow anyone out of the way to keep Blue in my line of sight. She'd barely ordered a drink before a frat bro chatted her up. He nodded toward a table of bro clones, none of whom bothered to hide their shit-eating grins, and Blue shook her head. Good girl. She could do much better than that clown, though not-Archer might approve of his credentials.

Unfortunately, the idiot took her refusal as a challenge. He kept talking, and when she ignored him, he snatched up her beer from the counter. Raucous laughter came from the guys behind him as he backed toward his table, wiggling her drink like a cat toy. I prepped to intervene, but another guy at the bar beat me to the rescue.

He stepped between the asshole and Blue, then ordered her a new drink. I watched until the asshole shrugged and returned to his table with his stolen beer. When I focused on Blue again, she was smiling at the new guy. A real smile.

My fingers tightened on my glass, and I shoved down the bubbling jealousy. This was what she wanted. Practice. Alone. I took a swig and scanned the room blindly. My gaze ended up on a group of dancing girls who looked vaguely familiar, but they couldn't hold my attention.

Movement from Blue's direction had me swinging my head around. She'd tossed her head back with a laugh. A dark, possessive sensation exploded in my chest, and I suddenly had a better understanding of Noah's cranky ass.

He'd watched Chloe hook up with one person after another while he stood on the sidelines. I didn't want to watch Blue flirt with this guy, laugh with him like she did with me, give him the crooked smile I'd pulled out of her. I wanted to jump between them, stake a claim, beg for the chance to prove I could be the one for her.

But was I? Blue didn't seem to think so, or she wouldn't be smiling and laughing with someone else. The snub felt a little too familiar.

I forced myself to take a mental step back. We were here for Blue. My feelings didn't factor into this. Hers did. Even if it pained me, I wanted her to come out of this confident in her ability to make connections with people. As long as she came home with me.

They talked for a few minutes, and her smile looked genuine. I took stock of the interloper. He seemed decent enough at first glance. Jeans and a button down said he wasn't looking for a quickie, but I took away a couple of points for the tassels on his loafers.

The waitress led them to a booth closer to me, and Tassels gestured for Blue to sit on the inside. I smiled grimly into my beer. He'd hit the first test already. Blue always had to be on the outside in a booth. She said it was a safety issue, but I overheard her tell Eva once that having another person's body block her ability to leave made her feel trapped.

"I'd prefer to be on the outside."

Instead of switching places, he failed the test, laughing off her request. "Ladies first."

Blue's eyes flicked to me for a split second, then she slid into the booth, scooting all the way to the half wall. Something twisted in my chest at her clear distress. I wanted to rush over and toss Tassels out of the way to make Blue more comfortable.

Not my job. She wanted to handle this herself, so I needed to keep my distance. A reasonable distance. I couldn't see her face from my current position, and suddenly, my spot was unacceptable.

I made my way closer, using the increasing crowd as

cover, until I could practically reach her from the other side of the booth wall. If there was even a slim chance of her leaving with him, I was going to make an ass of myself by dragging her home. Fifty-fifty chance I'd tie her to my bed after for good measure.

Somehow, I made it through almost an hour of Tassels talking about himself while I fended off passes from random women on their way to the dance floor. Even if I hadn't been here for Blue, the promise of an emotionless hookup did nothing for me. Instead, I amused myself by counting the number of times Tassels mentioned his financial portfolio. How did this guy ever pick up girls beyond the first ten minutes?

From the corner of my eye, I watched him stretch his arm across the back of the booth to play with her hair. She liked it when I curled the colors around my fingers, and my jaw clenched at the sight of someone else trying it. For a second, I considered ripping his hand away. Before I could commit, Blue readjusted to face him, subtly pulling the strands out of his reach, and I let out a not so quiet snort.

Then I made the mistake of looking directly at them. Tassels met my eyes at the same time Blue flagged down the server for a third drink. I gave Blue a slow once over and sent him a sharp smile. He could make what he wanted from it, but judging by the lines bracketing his mouth, he'd picked up on my silent message.

I drained the last dregs of my warm beer and started coming up with exit strategies that didn't involve me throwing Blue over my shoulder or kissing her in front of the entire bar. As if she knew my dwindling patience was making both those options look good, she asked him to move so she could go to the bathroom.

He let her out and watched her ass as she walked away.

Not so decent after all. I saw my moment. The second she was hidden by the crowd, I slid into the booth opposite him.

In a move I should have expected, Tassels spoke before I could say anything. "I saw her first."

"You don't even see her now. Time to move along."

Annoyance lit his eyes, followed quickly by calculation. "And if I choose not to?"

I raised a brow and stood, drawing myself to my full height and crossing my arms over my chest. No lie, I may have thrown in a flex too. She wasn't leaving the bar with anyone but me.

Tassels held up his hands. "Fine. You win."

I shrugged at him. "Better luck next time."

He muttered something offensive under his breath, but his opinion meant nothing to me. I turned my back on him to search the room. No sign of Blue near the restrooms, but I spotted her at the end of the bar, half hidden behind the sign for the End of Summer Cosplay Karaoke party.

Instantly, I relaxed. Tassels couldn't see her from there. She'd already ditched the guy on her own.

Excitement and dread filled me in equal measure as I made my way over to her. Blue was probably looking for her next practice dummy, but two was my limit for the night. I was determined she'd practice on me or no one. With that in mind, I stopped holding myself back.

I braced my hands on either side of her, leaning down close enough to whisper in her ear. "Running away already."

Instantly, she rested her weight against me, tilting her head to speak over her shoulder. "If I am, I'm not very good at it since I only made it as far as the bar."

"I don't blame you for needing a stronger drink. That guy was only slightly better than the first one."

She sighed, and I felt it in my chest. "He was nice at first."

"We should have called it off as soon as you sat down."

"That wouldn't have given us much data to analyze for improvement," she muttered.

"It was clear from the beginning he wasn't right for you, which is all the data we need." Curiosity got the better of me, and I asked the question plaguing me for the last hour. "Why did you take the inner seat in the booth?"

Blue turned to face me, putting us inches apart. With me leaning on the bar, all she'd have to do was raise up a little to make contact. Would she taste as good as last time?

"You were watching."

I blinked and pulled my mind away from her lips. "What?"

"I sat on the inside because you were watching. If I'd wanted out, and he'd tried to stop me, you'd have made him move."

"Damn straight I'd have made him move. But for future reference—and my continued sanity—all dates from now on end as soon as you're uncomfortable."

"That's going to make it hard to date at all." Her mouth curled up into a tiny self-deprecating grin, and the last remaining bit of my willpower disappeared. "How were my flirting skills?"

"Two for two, so I'd say fantastic. Now we just need to work on your choice of targets."

Her face scrunched, and she stared down at the napkin in front of her. "Agreed. I'm averaging one hundred percent on the dick meter. What is it about me that attracts guys like that?"

I lifted her chin, pausing until she met my eyes. "It is *not* you. You're smart and funny and strong—and beautiful, which is all those guys saw. That's on them."

Her tongue darted out to wet her lower lip, barely missing my thumb. "How can you be sure?"

"Because I see all of you, and I'm nothing like those assholes. Right?"

She finally gave me a real smile. "You're certainly better with your mouth."

I dropped a chaste kiss on her, not letting myself linger despite her quick indrawn breath. "Fuck yes, I am. Don't you dare settle for less."

Blue nodded slowly. "I think I'm learning that lesson."

My next question came out rougher than I intended, but I was mentally preparing for a fight. "Do you want to practice some more?"

"I think I'm good for now," she said with a laugh. Her amusement didn't dim my satisfaction in the least.

The bartender set a glass of water next to my hand, nodded at Blue, then moved to the other end of the bar. Unlike the last time, I had the distinct impression he was watching me to make sure I didn't overstep. Come to think of it, I hadn't seen Scott since I'd told Lars about his questionable customer service.

Blue grabbed my water, but when she lifted it, the slick glass slid out of her hand. I caught it before it could hit the bar and douse us both. As a precaution, I leaned over to set it out of her reach, and the motion put us in contact from shoulder to hips.

Big Mac perked up at the close proximity, but I was done hiding my reaction to her. "You are such a lightweight. How many drinks did you have... two?"

She shook with laughter. "I'm not drunk, just clumsy. Now that you mention it though, I didn't eat dinner before we left. Too nervous. And between the beer thief and Nick, I couldn't order food."

Ah, so Tassels had a name. Belatedly, I realized Blue didn't stiffen or move away from me like she had with him. She didn't make excuses to run away. When it mattered, she'd trusted me to keep her safe.

"Do you want to eat? Only the finest pizza for my girl."

Blue tilted her head up at me with lazy comfort. "No. Take me home, Adam."

The words burrowed into me, a flash fantasy of hearing her say them in a different context—one where we didn't separate at the end of the night. Where she said them to me because *I* was the one she wanted to be with.

A dangerous train of thought, considering my history.

"Let's go, Sunshine."

The entire drive home Blue snuck glances at me I couldn't read without ending up in a ditch. The apartment was dark when we came in, and my steps got progressively slower as we crossed the living room. Tonight had been different, maybe because of the lines we'd crossed in the last twenty-four hours, but I didn't want it to end.

It wasn't about sex. Like I'd told her before, sex was easy. I craved everything else. The banter, the soft looks, the barely there touches, I wanted to curl around her, safe in my arms, and never let go.

We made it all the way to the hallway between our rooms before she stopped me with a hand on my arm.

"Thank you, Adam," she said softly. "For going, and for making me feel better after."

I couldn't do it. I couldn't let the night end here even though I knew I was risking a repeat of the Eva disaster. Blue was worth the risk. If she couldn't see me as more than a friend, I'd still take whatever she'd give me. Until I convinced her otherwise.

Before she could disappear into her room, I loosely circled her wrist. "Watch a movie with me."

She sent me a questioning look, then smiled. "Okay."

My room was too dangerous. Blue wanted me—that much was clear—but I intended to respect her decision this morning. Friends. Nothing more. The temptation to push when I knew she'd probably say yes would be more than I could resist. I tugged her back the way we'd come and pulled her down next to me. Without a second thought, she snuggled into my side under my arm. I flipped through the options, but when I stopped on my usual late-night comedy fare, she shook her head.

"Let's watch Wonder Woman."

I gasped dramatically, aiming for light and fun. "Are you trying to seduce me? Because this will definitely work."

She rolled her eyes. "If I were trying to seduce you, I'd be wearing considerably less clothing."

Big Mac twitched at the image, and I wasted no time cueing up my favorite movie of all time. Neither of us mentioned the heavy tension in the air caused by her blunt comment. By the halfway point, I'd stopped watching the screen entirely in favor of staring at the intriguing emotions passing across her face.

"I can see why you like her," she murmured, her eyes getting heavy.

Part of me was elated she understood my borderline obsession, but at the moment, even Wonder Woman paled in comparison. All I could see was Blue.

19

Blue

My pillow smelled like Adam. I tried unsuccessfully to roll over and realized my pillow *was* Adam. His long arms wrapped around me on the strip of couch we shared. One under my head, and one locked across my stomach. His thumb moved in a tiny circle against the side of my breast, and I woke up all the way.

When I'd fallen asleep, we'd been vertical with my head on his shoulder. How the heck had we ended up like this? How was there even room on the couch for both of us next to each other?

Despite the tiny thrill working its way through my blood, I remained still and took stock. The room was pitch black, and Adam breathed steadily behind me. Still asleep. Without his octopus grip, I might have face-planted off the couch.

Logic insisted I extricate myself and go to bed—alone— but I liked being tangled up with him. His chin rested on my head, and my foot was tucked between his calves. And I was warm. Inside and out.

Was this what it felt like to be more than friends with Adam? Like all I wanted to do was burrow closer, safe, surrounded by him.

After the horrendous experience at the bar, I thought maybe I'd made the wrong decision. I'd hurt him in a bid to protect myself, and he'd still been there every step of the way. Longing coiled in my belly.

I wanted Adam. I didn't want to miss another moment of what I could have with him, even if it was only friends with benefits. Even if he left me in the end.

The feeling fluttered in my chest, delicate and new. I held my breath waiting for it to fade, but it anchored into place near my heart, right under Adam's hand. Warning bells clanged in my head as I realized I may have already missed my chance.

Why would he still want to be with me when I'd basically thrown his offer back in his face?

The reminder of my stupid actions this morning convinced me to move. We should probably talk before I pushed things too far. My gut clenched in protest, but I tried to ease away from Adam's warmth without waking him up. I only managed an inch or two before his arms tightened.

"Don't go," he said softly into my hair.

I froze. "I'm not tired anymore."

"I'm not asking for sleep," he countered.

A shiver raced across my skin, leaving a trail of fire in its wake. Friends with benefits, a hook up, the inevitable conclusion to months of foreplay—whatever this was, he seemed to want it as much as I did. The evidence pressed against me in a hard line.

"Are you sure this is a good idea?" I whispered into the darkness, unable to stop myself from checking one last time.

"It's not a bad one. Sometimes the gray area is worth the

risk." His hand slid across my stomach, bunching my dress on the way, and the pressure of each fingertip branded my skin. "You going to take a chance with me, Sunshine?"

I wanted to. Desperately. And I was done denying myself.

My hips writhed of their own accord, urging him to slide his hand lower. My dress had already ridden up to the tops of my thighs, and judging from the heat flooding my pussy, it wouldn't take much to relieve the ache. With no second thoughts, I dove into the gray.

I covered his hand with mine and moved him myself, but he only gave my clit a single caress before linking our fingers, holding me in place between my thighs.

Adam brushed his lips against the back of my shoulder, the side of my neck, the spot under my ear. "What do you want? Say the words, Blue."

I spread my legs slightly as my inner muscles clenched. "Touch me."

He finally dipped below my panties, teasing me with our joined hands. "Show me what you like."

I guided his fingers to stroke myself, but with him the sensations were heightened. Stronger, more intense, and yet still not enough. I moaned at the light touch and tilted my hips, instinctively seeking contact, pressure, something. "Adam."

"Is this what you need?" He pushed a finger inside me, rubbing my clit with this thumb.

"*Yes*." I couldn't contain the whimpering noises coming out of my throat. My hips moved with his hand, driving me higher until I came with a flash behind my lids brighter than the lightning outside.

I was still riding the wave of tingling sensation when he rolled me under him and took my mouth.

"You're not done yet, Sunshine. Lift."

With a little help, he pulled my dress over my head and tossed it onto the floor next to us. My bra went next, then my soaked panties. Adam kissed his way down to my stomach, then leveraged himself up enough to yank his shirt off.

He lapped at my clit as he dropped the rest of his clothes, making me wild. When he pulled back to roll on a condom, I almost threw a couch pillow at him for stopping. My eyes must have adjusted to the dim streetlights from outside because I caught his grin before he made his way back up my body. I wanted a better look—naked Adam was my new favorite Adam—but I wasn't going to stop him when his weight settled between my legs.

I raised my hips to rub my clit along his hard length as he trailed kisses up my jaw. Every part of me was electrified, and I'd crawl through glass to feel him inside me. With a frustrated moan, I sank my nails into his butt, urging him forward. He chuckled, a rough, dark sound I wanted to hear again, and lifted my knee tight to his hip, notching himself at my entrance.

At the last second, he paused, his muscles twitching with the effort of holding himself back. "You sure?"

"Yes." And I was. One hundred percent. I'd probably burn in friendship hell for the decision, but I didn't care—I wanted this with Adam.

I was so wet, he slid home in one thrust.

His head dropped to my neck, and he shuddered. "Fuck, Blue. You feel so good."

Words were beyond me. He moved his hips in a sinuous rhythm, dragging his mouth down my chest until he captured a nipple in his mouth. I arched up off the couch when he sucked hard.

"God, yes."

I wasn't sure if I said the words out loud, but it didn't matter. Adam seemed to know exactly what I liked without trying, so I looped a hand behind his neck and held on. He gave the same treatment to the other side, and I thought I'd drown in pleasure. What had I been missing all these years?

He groaned against my skin. "I love the way you respond to me. And the way my touch makes you wild. The way your eyes darken when you're about to come. So pretty and perfect. Are you going to come for me again, pretty girl?"

His words sent me over the edge. I squeezed him tight, and he thrust to the hilt, his fingers digging into my hip hard enough to leave bruises. He buried his face in my hair, and I thought I might leave matching marks on the back of his neck.

I loved it. Every second of it. There was a good chance Adam had ruined me for any other relationships.

As I came down from the high, I realized we were naked on the couch in the middle of the living room. It was a little late for concerns about anyone catching us, but I'd have to scrub down the cushions tomorrow.

Adam nuzzled my neck. "Stop thinking about cleaning."

A laugh bubbled out of me. "Not my fault your thoughts are so dirty."

He leveraged himself up to meet my eyes, quirking a brow. "It is entirely your fault my thoughts are dirty."

I wasn't sorry. Adam might not be mine, but he wanted me. Now that he'd had me, a prickling sense of foreboding tried to push through the lovely endorphins. We'd rocketed past the friendship barrier, and I couldn't find it in myself to regret the decision. Not with his weight still pinning me to the cushions and the need I still saw in his eyes.

But I'd never had sex with my roommate on the living room couch before. Would we say goodnight and go to our separate bedrooms? Were we supposed to wake up tomorrow as friends and forget what happened in the dark?

I'd tried that scenario after the kitchen incident and utterly failed. Nothing about my feelings made sense, but for once, I didn't want to go my own way.

"What now?" I asked.

Adam's hand slid into my hair, and he kissed me softly. "Now I carry you to bed and show you what I can do with more than a foot and a half of space."

———

A WEEK LATER, I'd only returned to my own room to grab a change of clothes and my school bag. No one questioned the amount of time I spent in Adam's room, but Shaw and RJ were distracted running double training sessions for the team.

All but one of them Adam skipped. He'd had to meet Alex for a project yesterday, and this morning, he'd rolled over to shut off his alarm before pulling me against him again. By some miracle, no one had barged into Adam's room when he didn't show.

He claimed these were voluntary workouts, and he was making up the time on his own. I didn't want to interfere since I'd long ago lost sight of the boundaries in our relationship. Instead of pointing out where he *should* be, I stood in Adam's bathroom wearing nothing but one of his football shirts and examining the fading color in my hair.

Mom's engagement luncheon was in two days, and I knew Rob hated the bright streaks. I could leave it to fade or cover it with my natural color. It would certainly be the path of least resistance, but I hated the idea of muting myself. My hair was the one thing I splurged on in my life. The colors reflected the deepest part of my personality, including the stubborn urge to never give in to outside pressure.

Rob could suck it. He wouldn't factor into my decision.

I didn't see how I could do it myself though. Mom usually helped me redo the dye, and the process took several hours. Without her, my arms might fall off before I finished. She didn't have time to drive to Addison, and I wasn't in the mood to battle with Rob over the use of his bathroom.

Adam found me frowning at my reflection and wrapped his arms around me from behind. "What's wrong?"

"I'm thinking about letting my hair fade back to my natural color."

He scoffed. "Hell no. We're not doing that."

My brows went up. "We?"

"Yeah, we. I'm not letting my girl have sad hair."

"Lots of people have normal brown hair without being sad."

Adam brushed a kiss against my temple. "Not you. Your rainbow makes you happy. If this is about not-Archer, fuck him."

A smile peeked through at Adam's enthusiastic dislike for a guy he'd never met, all for my sake. "I'd already decided to ignore Rob's preferences."

"What's holding you back then?"

I sighed. "The amount of effort necessary. I could probably do it myself, but it's considerably easier with two people."

"Problem solved. I'll help you."

I turned to face him. "Don't you have practice later today?"

He shrugged, keeping his arms locked around me. "Official practices haven't started yet. I'm supposed to watch film from last season with Shaw and Noah, but I can do it on my own later. What do we need?"

As uncomfortable as I was with Adam skipping another football thing for me, I really wanted to feel like myself at the luncheon. "Okay. I'll show you what to do."

I tried to move away to grab the stuff I needed from my bathroom, but Adam didn't let go. He lifted my chin until I met his eyes.

"Talk to me," he ordered. "What else is going on in that beautiful head of yours?"

"I don't have a date." The worry erupted from me without warning. I hadn't even been consciously thinking about the problem.

We hadn't discussed the change in our relationship, but we hadn't gone back to practicing my dating skills either. I was stuck in the between space where I couldn't move forward despite my deadline creeping up on me.

"At this rate, I'll end up stuck with Shad, who seems inordinately excited for an engagement luncheon."

His brows drew together. "How do you know Shad's excitement level?"

I shook my head and pulled back. This time, Adam let me go. "He keeps texting me."

He followed on my heels to the bedroom. "He's *what*?"

"Texting me. Every couple of days, usually. Sometimes a week goes by and I think he's gotten bored, but then he starts up again."

"What kind of texts?"

I grabbed my phone, pulling up the chat to show him. "Here, look. They all seem innocent on the surface, but there's a pattern of innuendo."

Adam scrolled through, his mouth twisting down. "Did you ask him to stop?"

"Yes, but he ignored me."

"You should block him—or I could tell him to fuck off for you." Adam handed me my phone back, and I set it down on the dresser with a sigh.

"I'd rather just ignore him. When the messages come through, I don't read them. Yes, they're a constant reminder of his creepy fascination, but I feel like I should save them in case..." Now that I'd said the words out loud, anxiety twisted in my stomach. "What am I supposed to do? I have two days until the fancy lunch, and I'd rather not go than go with Shad."

"Take me."

My eyes shot to his face, expecting him to be grinning or laughing at his joke, but he was serious. "I thought you didn't want to get involved in another friends with benefits situation."

Now he did laugh. "Sunshine, we're spending all our free time naked in bed together. We've already covered the friends and the benefits."

"Yes, I noticed," I responded dryly. "But a lot of people end up naked in bed together without expecting anything beyond sex."

"Let me be absolutely clear here. This isn't just sex for me. For one, I'm worth more than that. For two, we were friends before Big Mac got involved."

I snickered at the nickname, but he only sent me a warning glance and kept going.

"For three, friends with benefits is literally sex with no expectations. The only difference between FWB and hooking up is you know the person you're fucking." He weighed the air in each hand, lifting one then the other. "Might get brunch together later, might spend an hour in bed. That kind of thing."

His explanation made a disturbing kind of sense, but I found myself caught on his first point. "This isn't just sex for you?"

He huffed and fell back onto the bed, tucking his hands behind his head. "No. I haven't been interested in just sex for a while."

"But you're always flirting."

"Only with you, Blue."

I threw my hands up. "I thought you were like that with everyone."

His face closed down a little. "No."

The quiet word stuck in my chest. I'd spent the better part of the summer with him, and not once had I seen him hit on another girl. Only me. He hadn't even gone out as much as usual because I was a homebody at heart. When I stayed in, so did he. In hindsight, the truth was obvious.

I knelt on the bed, and he rolled his head to stare up at me. "I'm sorry, Adam. It's not just sex for me either."

He unclenched his hands and reached for me, twining our fingers together on his chest. "I know. I'm trying not to push, but it's hard. The last time I felt like this..." Adam shook his head. "Honestly, I don't think there was a last time. I wouldn't risk my friendship with you if I didn't see the chance for a future with something better."

I'd never really considered my future beyond graduating and starting the yoga studio with Mom. But she'd started early and left me behind. A blessing in disguise, apparently, because I wouldn't have ended up here with Adam.

"The chance for something better sounds good, but you're not risking our friendship." I gave him a sly smile. "We're besties, right? Whether or not Big Mac is involved."

He kissed my fingers. "Even if I hadn't spent the night beating my personal record for orgasms given, I'd still want to go with you to your mom's lunch. I'll gladly be your arm candy, schmooze the rich guests, and stand between you and Shad. I'll even throw in a foot massage when we get home because whoever invented high heels clearly hated women, and I do not."

Warmth spread from my chest, rising up my cheeks and stinging my eyes. "Thank you."

"Anytime, Sunshine."

20

Blue

The next day, with my underlayers freshly dyed and Adam gone with the football crew for their rescheduled film time, I felt confident enough to tackle the one thing still bothering me.

Telling Eva.

I wasn't a good liar on the best of days, and I hated the idea of keeping important things from someone I cared about. Adam was going to pick me up before my class at the ABC, but I had plenty of time to find a way to explain I was sleeping with my best friend's ex.

Not just sleeping, either. I was all twisted up with emotions. Eva could probably untwist me, but asking her to help sort out my relationship with a guy who'd been hers not too long ago seemed unfair. Granted, Eva had ended things, but even I could see fleeing across the state wasn't the reaction of someone who didn't care.

Human relationships were hard.

After spending the morning procrastinating by cleaning every surface in the common areas of the apartment, I ducked into my room to grab a shower and a fresh change of clothes. My shirt was halfway over my head when I spotted a small, rainbow-covered box sitting in the middle of my neatly made bed.

I let the shirt fall back down and approached the box like it might bite me. My mom loved giving presents, but she always wanted to be around to see my face when I opened them. Secret gift-giving wasn't her style.

I picked it up, surprised by the light weight, and checked for a tag. Nothing had been added other than the big silver bow taking up the entire top of the box. I lifted the lid, then stared down at the contents.

Nestled inside sparkly white tissue paper sat a bracelet of shiny faceted beads the same colors as my hair. Interspersed between the beads were plain white letters spelling out *#1 bestie*. Adam got me a bestie bracelet. My heart flopped over so hard I had to press my palm against my chest to take a breath.

Under the bracelet, I found a folded piece of notebook paper. Fleetingly, I wondered if it had come from his Wonder Woman notebook. I hoped so.

SUNSHINE,

So you never forget I was your first.
Adam

I SHOULD HAVE REALIZED RIGHT AWAY it was from Adam. He'd been the one who suggested I call Eva from my room. Gingerly, I slid the elastic over my wrist and admired the colors.

No one had ever given me a present like this before. One steeped in meaning and emotion. Mom's were always trinkets that made her think of me. Sweet, but she got more out of them than I did.

Adam had picked out this bracelet for me to enjoy. Another first after he'd claimed so many.

The alarm on my phone went off, reminding me I'd run out of time to shower if I wanted to get in my visit with Eva before class. The bracelet glimmered at me, and I considered taking it off along with the shirt of Adam's I'd stolen to sleep in.

Eva preferred video calls because she liked reading a person's body language when she talked to them. It was almost as good as mind reading—her words—which meant she'd see my clothes and room. I ran my finger along the beads, then left it on my wrist while I changed. If she asked about it, I'd tell the truth.

I relied heavily on distraction and obscuring my face to hide my thoughts, but the whole point of the morning was to clear my conscience. I'd avoided her video calls up until now because I hadn't been ready to talk about Adam, and one look at my face would have assured the topic.

With a deep breath, I sent her a video request.

Eva appeared on the screen drinking coffee out of a glass bottle in a gorgeous coastal themed living room. Her blonde hair was piled on top of her head in a wild topknot, and her skin glowed with a deep tan. She looked relaxed and happy.

I knew her parents were wealthy—hello, beach house— but she made it a point not to bring up money. Suddenly, the discrepancy between her life and mine smacked me in the face.

An uninterrupted wall of glass behind her showcased the waves crashing under a bright blue sky. The scene behind me in my tiny video looked sad and dark in comparison. I glanced around my bedroom and realized I'd left the heavy curtains closed after essentially moving into Adam's room.

With a shake of my head, I leaned over to jerk the material aside, bathing myself in sunlight. Might as well give her a better shot at reading my mind.

Eva let out a contented sigh and smiled at me. "Hi, bestie. Miss me?"

Her question hit me with a visceral reminder of Adam asking me the same thing. The echo of his voice, warm with amusement, sent a shiver across my skin. This wouldn't take long if everything made me think of Adam.

"It's not the same around here without you, Eva." The wistful tone surprised me. I really did miss her. She always made me want to smile, even if I didn't show it on the outside.

"I'm sure you could find some trouble if you tried hard enough. Wrestle any mannequins lately?"

Case in point. The memory brought a flood of fondness for the day that changed my life. We'd met when she and Chloe had come into the shop looking for dresses. Chloe had wanted the one Mom put in the window, so I'd had to wrestle with Bertha, our best mannequin.

"No. The store is shut down for good. I hear the new cowboy bar is going to have a mechanical bull though."

"Challenge accepted." She took a closer look at me and set down her Frappuccino. "What's wrong? Do I need to come back there and castrate someone?"

I frowned at her immediate and forceful defense, guilt hitting me with a strong backhand. I shouldn't have waited so long to spill my secret. Would she react the same way if she knew I was actively trying not to think of Adam naked while I talked to her? Was I supposed to talk about it? The whole best friend situation was new ground for me.

"No, thank you. I can do my own castrating, disgusting as it is. Mom stumbled on a YouTube video once while making dinner, and I couldn't eat beef for months after." I paused, waffling about what to say.

Eva tilted her head and waited. She knew me well enough to sense when I needed a second to untangle my thoughts. I wanted to talk about my situation, and if I were involved with any other guy, I wouldn't hesitate to share with Eva. But Adam was different—in so many ways.

I'd already told her about Rob and Shad. She'd probably have a unique take on the wedding and my potentially insane solution. I'd never seen her shy away from a hard topic, and she was fiercely loyal to her friends.

Fiercely loyal to me. She deserved the same treatment.

My fingers twisted together below the scope of the camera. "I'm having... feelings."

"Emotional feelings or *feelings*?" She gestured toward her lap.

I snorted out a laugh. "Both."

"That's a good sign. Emotional involvement means he's probably not an asshole, though sometimes a girl just wants to be held down and fucked, with mutual consent of course —wait, I'm making some assumptions here, he or she?"

"He." My cheeks flamed at the image she conjured with her rambling. So much for not thinking of Adam naked. "And he's not an asshole, but he's surprisingly persistent when it comes to getting what he wants."

She bounced a little on the couch. "And he wants you?"

"Yes?" I grimaced. "We both agreed we should stick to friendship, but even with the best of intentions, we ended up in bed together." I shook my head. "He wants to come to mom's engagement lunch. As my date."

Her brows drew together. "Why is this a problem? We've

established he's not an asshole, and you'll definitely have more fun with someone who'll sneak you out for a quickie."

I frowned. "I don't think I could handle a quickie at a formal event."

She gave me a sly smile. "You're telling yourself no, but if he asked, you'd totally go for it. I'm proud of you, babe. It's about time someone revved your engine. What else?"

"I'm not sure he'll meet Rob's idiotic standards."

Eva's lips pressed together. "If your guy makes you happy, then Rob can shove his standards directly up his ass. You're there to support Hope, not prance around like a show pony. Look, you're not about subtleties. Show up as your bold, unapologetic self with a guy who treats your lady parts right. See where it goes with the date, and let your mom sort out her runner up fiancé."

"What if he's someone I'm not supposed to have feelings for?" I asked quietly.

Her expression softened into sad understanding. "It's Mac, isn't it?"

Panic made me freeze. I'd planned to tell her, but I should have realized she'd figure it out on her own before I'd work up the courage.

"It's okay, Blue. He was supposed to move on, and I'm glad it's you. I'm just sorry I didn't see it earlier."

"There was nothing to see earlier. This is a new development." I winced, completely out of my element. "Am I supposed to apologize? I don't know the societal cues for this situation, and I don't want you to be hurt or angry."

She laughed, but it wasn't mean, simply amused. "No, honey. Mac and I had an ill-advised fling, which may have firebombed our friendship, but I don't have a claim on him.

At least, not with you. If one of those manipulative ball bunnies tried to mess with him, I'd ruin her."

"I think your friendship can withstand the damage you've both done to it."

"Ouch," she said under her breath, then louder. "Well, if you're looking for my blessing, you have it. Out of curiosity and the need to patch up the holes in my spy network, how did you guys end up together?"

"THE NIGHT MOM, Rob, and Shad ambushed me with the wedding date ultimatum, I downed too much wine and walked out on dinner. Adam had the misfortune of giving me his phone number earlier in the day after we spent the afternoon together at a sorority party. I called him to pick me up in Dallas, and over late-night tacos, drunkenly convinced him to give me dating lessons."

Eva held up a finger as she shook with silent laughter. "I'm sorry. I'm not laughing at you. This whole situation is perfect. I couldn't have organized it better myself. Mac, being himself, agreed to help you, then he moved you in with him. You didn't stand a chance in hell of saying no."

"Thanks," I said dryly.

She wasn't wrong. Adam and I had been dancing around a relationship from the day in the sorority kitchen. I frowned. Come to think of it, most of my weak moments with Adam were in kitchens. He did have a habit of cooking without his shirt on.

Eva waggled her eyebrows, hopefully unaware I'd reverted back to thinking about Adam naked. "As much as I want to offer my own take on your *education*, it's probably best if I don't get involved. Mac can handle it."

I chewed on my lower lip, debating my next question,

but Eva waved her hand at me. "Go ahead and ask whatever it is."

"Why did you hook up with Adam in the first place?"

Her mirth faded. "I was lonely. My parents were being themselves again, dragging me into their drama. After a couple of shots of tequila, I just wanted to feel good. Mac was right there, going through girls left and right, and I thought it was my turn. We could have some casual fun without any of the mess."

I expected jealousy, but the anger on Adam's behalf surprised me. "Adam deserves more than casual fun."

"I agree. That's why I broke it off and left." She looked away, staring out over the waves for a long moment before facing me again. "You call him Adam."

"He's not Mac to me." I didn't have a better explanation than that, but Eva understood.

Her lips quirked up in a half-smile. "When things get tough, don't give up on him."

"What if he gives up on me?" I hadn't acknowledged the fear, but it took root in my mind anyway.

"He won't. Mac might fuck up sometimes, but he doesn't quit."

I could attest to the second part. With Eva's blessing, my guilt about overstepping disappeared. As far as I was concerned, I'd met my moral obligations as a best friend. Now all I had to do was get through the rest of the summer and Mom's wedding, then maybe I could focus on what a future with Adam might look like.

21

Mac

"Mac, stop yammering and get in here." Coach Gordon poked his head out of his office door and pointed as if I'd forgotten where I was supposed to be.

I still had to do a double take every time I saw his face. He'd shocked us all by returning from vacation without his bushy walrus mustache. The guys started a pool on why he'd shaved, and Taco Truck, one of our rookies, was trying to give me the rundown.

The large black man slunk away when Coach glared in our direction. I knew what was coming, but I'd hoped I could put it off until camp was over.

Training camp had officially started at the beginning of August, and despite knowing better, I'd been slipping—late to the facility, half a step behind in drills, distracted during film time. Coach was a laid-back guy for someone in charge of a championship D1 football program, but even he had limits.

I jogged over to him, hoping the effort would gain me some bonus points.

He eyed my sweaty shirt. "Did you finish your reps?"

"Yes, chef."

With a sigh, he ducked into his office. "I asked you to stop calling me that."

"And I asked you for a pony last Christmas, but neither of us got what we wanted."

Coach's chair creaked as he sank into it and nodded at the ones opposite him. "I'm not your damn Santa Claus, and that mouth is going to get you in trouble one day."

I'd heard the warning before. Up until a few months ago, I hadn't found any trouble I couldn't outrun. Turned out Eva had no problem turning my words against me. I wasn't worried about Coach, though, until Shaw slipped into the room and shut the door.

My roommate and best friend, the man who I'd personally helped land his girl, stood blocking the exit with his arms crossed as if he thought I'd make a break for it. Coach cleared his throat, and I already wanted to jump out the nearest window.

"Mac, if you don't get your head out of your ass, you'll be on the bench for the first game. Maybe more."

My jaw clenched as I stared at the bookshelves over his left shoulder. "I had an off week. It won't happen again." I'd make sure of it.

"It's not only this week. Shaw tells me you've been having a hard summer, and I'm sorry to hear that, but I need you to shake off whatever's got ahold of your balls."

I shot my former best friend a glare, but he gave me his fuck around and find out face. The betrayal stung.

"My schedule has been unpredictable, but I've been putting in the effort on my own time, Coach."

"It's not about effort, son. It's about building a single unit out of all you goofballs. You've been the heart of our team for the last few years, even before my time, but unless something changes, I have to follow protocol. You're sliding down the depth chart. I want you out there as a starter, so we need to address the situation now while it can still be salvaged."

I hated everything about this conversation. I'd chosen a long time ago to focus solely on football because I'd worried I wouldn't be able to handle more. The last few months may have proven me right.

Unfortunately, there wasn't much I was willing to change. Alex was depending on me to nail the competition audition, and I wouldn't let Blue down now that she'd finally admitted she needed me.

Shaw added insult to injury. "I know you're hurting because of Eva, but it's time to get over her."

Coach pinched the bridge of his nose. "Tell me we're not having girl issues. Again. You guys are adults."

I scrubbed a hand down my face, surprised Shaw thought I was still pining for Eva. How had he missed Blue coming out of my room practically every morning? I went over the last week in my head and realized he and RJ always slipped out early to get some alone time in the weight room. Our crew hadn't been as social since Eva left, but we always spent more time apart in the summers.

Apparently, Shaw wasn't the only one not paying attention.

I met Coach's gaze. "What do you need me to do?"

He nodded. "Hold on to that attitude for one. We still have a few weeks of camp. If you show up the way I know you can, you'll be fine. It would go a long way if you could work with Haskins."

Shaw pushed away from the wall and clapped a hand on my shoulder. "He's almost as fast as you, but he could use some situational awareness."

I grimaced, then added a half-assed salute. "Aye aye, Cap'n."

Haskins had transferred in for this year, and he had a bad habit of watching the defense instead of the ball. When he paid attention though, he was good. If the powers that be needed me to prove myself, I'd do my best.

"Anything else?" I stood before I'd finished my question because I couldn't actually handle anything else being piled on me at the moment. I just wanted to get home and convince Blue to join me in the shower.

Coach waved me away. "Go on. You're stinking up my office."

Shaw opened the door for me, and I surreptitiously sniffed my pits on the way past him. Damn, maybe I'd shower *then* convince Blue to get naked. After I talked to Haskins. And put the finishing touches on my final project for my summer class.

Once out in the hallway, Shaw knocked my shoulder with his. "Sorry for the ambush."

"No, I deserved it. I'm mostly over the Eva thing, by the way. I just have a lot going on right now."

He slowed down so we'd have a semblance of privacy before coming back into the main weight room. "Have you talked to her?"

A band around my chest tightened, belying my words a few seconds ago. "No. She's the one who left, so I'm not going to force anything. When she's ready to talk, I'll be here."

"Riley says she's coming back soon."

I nodded. "She had some workshops planned for her squad before she took off. I think they were supposed to start next week."

Shaw eyed me. "Real talk. What's going on in your head?"

I spread my arms, offering him a smile. "What you see is what you get, Shaw. You know that."

"Bullshit. Eva hurt you, and I'm sorry I didn't step up when she dropped you. I'm glad Blue has been here to make up for my shitty friendship."

"You're all good, man. Honestly, it hurt more that she left than that she didn't want a relationship. I know Eva. I should have realized she wasn't suddenly trying to settle down. She was right though. We would never have worked as a real couple."

"I'm not sure I agree, but I'm glad you're past it. If Eva isn't fucking with your mind, what is?"

My phone vibrated in my pocket, and I pulled it out to see a message from Alex asking me to stop by after training. I hadn't told anyone about the music competition, not even Blue. Shaw would understand to a certain degree, but I didn't want to chance him asking me to make a choice.

Other than RJ, football came first for him. Always.

I glanced down the hall toward our state-of-the-art weight room where Haskins was probably still finishing up. Even if I explained about the competition, and about Blue, it wouldn't be a good excuse. I was here to play football, and I needed to remember that.

"Nothing I can't handle." I rubbed my hands together. "Gotta go. I have a date with Haskins he's going to regret."

Shaw pinched the bridge of his nose, exactly like Coach had. "Don't traumatize him. Train him. TU is going to need a good receiver when you and Riley graduate."

"Noted. Minor trauma only. You can count on me."

His hand dropped, and he met my eyes. "I know."

The quiet words snagged in my mind as I turned away. Shaw had faith in me despite my piss poor performance and unwillingness to talk. I wasn't sure what I'd done to deserve this team, but I wasn't going to let them down.

————

AN HOUR LATER, I'd showered, set up a time to work with Haskins, and made my way to Alex's place. I texted Blue from the driveway letting her know I'd be late getting back, but she only sent me a frowny face. Her finals group wasn't pulling their weight, and she'd been cranky for days—not that it stopped me from trying to distract her at every opportunity. She was probably happy to hand me off to Alex for a while.

I'd met Alex my freshman year in our music theory class. At the time, he'd been a quiet guy with an unlucky dorm roommate and a horrible haircut. Since then, his hair had improved, and he'd managed to rent one of the houses close to campus usually reserved for professors.

Up until this summer, I'd only been in Alex's place twice. We usually met at Johnny's when we needed to work on music. The last few months, I'd been over here several times a week.

Johnny's was great when we were working on karaoke playlists or a school project, but Alex insisted we needed someplace with less distractions. I couldn't argue with him since I spent at least half our sessions eating pizza or talking to people who wandered over. His boyfriend, Luis, always insisted on making food, so I had no problem changing locations.

Luis answered the door and waved me toward the

kitchen. "Alex is in there. Pulled pork sandwiches on the counter. I'm going to Wildcat to study."

He hopped past me down the steps, looping his messenger bag over his head. I considered asking him to bring me a hazelnut latte, but I hopefully wouldn't be here when he got back.

"You here, X?" After one unfortunate incident where I didn't knock loud enough and Alex had pulled a kitchen knife on me, I'd learned to announce my presence well in advance.

"Back here."

I found him at the kitchen table hunched over his laptop with two notebooks, three pairs of headphones, and an uneaten bagel on a plate next to him. He didn't look up at me as I made a beeline for the crock pot of pulled pork.

When Alex was in the groove, it was best to leave him alone until he hit a breaking point. Unless Luis needed him. Luis could get him to do anything. Despite Alex texting me to come over, I knew where I stood on his priority list.

After I'd stuffed half a sandwich in my mouth, he leaned back in his chair and stretched his arms out behind him, grinning. "We got it."

I almost dropped my pulled pork. "What? The competition? I thought we were waiting to send in our entry until your perfectionist brain was happy."

"We did. I spent a couple of hours polishing it after our last session and submitted it. They emailed me today."

"The fuck, man? And you didn't think that would be relevant when you oh so casually asked me to stop by."

He chuckled and stood to grab another plate, covering it with meat without bothering with the bread. "I thought it would be more fun this way."

I checked my phone to make sure I hadn't missed a day somewhere and frowned. "I thought the deadline wasn't for another week."

Alex resumed his seat and shoved the bagel aside to make room. "It isn't, but they're not limiting the number of finalists, so if you're in, you're in. We're in. They loved our sample, and they can't wait to hear us perform live."

I sank down across from him, shock stealing some of my appetite. We'd been working on the sample all summer, but I'd never really considered what would happen if we made it to the next stage.

"I'm gonna be real here. I didn't think we had a shot in hell. I'm kind of freaking out right now."

He set his fork down. "Well stop. Sending in a demo is one thing, but playing it live in its entirety is another. We have a lot of work to do still."

"Right." I ran a hand through my hair and tried to wrangle my thoughts into some kind of order.

"Are you ready to tell people?" he asked.

I thought of Shaw's face when he'd asked what was fucking with my head and Blue's when she'd asked why I hadn't told anyone about my love for music. The risk was real if I told them. I could fuck up, fail, ruin everything for Alex... I didn't want another set of responsibilities piling on. Another place where I had to be Mac even though I was losing it inside.

No reason to add that pressure before we knew anything. If we won, I'd have something concrete to tell them. I'd have to because my life would change. Suddenly, I'd have an opportunity besides football to build my future, and I'd have to find a way to make space for it.

"No. I want to wait."

Alex shook his head. "If you insist, but you're the one swearing Luis to secrecy this time. I had to clean the bathrooms all summer. Maybe he'll go easier on you if you try it with your shirt off."

I laughed, despite feeling like I'd stepped off a cliff. "What can I say? He has good taste."

22

Blue

"Miss me?" The familiar refrain was accompanied by Adam sliding his arms around me from behind.

We'd made it through finals and half of training camp to arrive at Mom's first official wedding event. A lunch celebrating their engagement. I'd let her pick out my dress, and shown up with a dapper-looking date, as requested. Adam looked fantastic in his suit, but I preferred him at home in his ratty gym shorts.

I rested my hand on his and leaned back against his chest. "You were gone for five minutes."

"It felt like a lifetime with Dr. Blum talking to me about mutual funds."

I hid my smile with a sip of champagne and glanced around at the people mingling in the large ballroom. Mom had warned me her engagement luncheon would take place at a hotel, but I'd assumed in one of the restaurants.

Not fancy enough for Rob though.

His business connections mixed with faculty from TU

and instructors in the yoga community. I loved the diversity, but Rob's smile was strained at the edges. He had a death grip on Mom, carting her from one group in suits to another. Maybe I was petty, but those fine lines bracketing his mouth brought me an inordinate amount of joy.

Adam dropped a kiss on my temple, and I felt his smile catch on my hair. "Admit it. We were wasting our time trying to find you a date at the bar. I'm the best choice you could have made."

"You make excellent arm candy."

His fingers slipped lower and flexed, bringing my butt in full contact with the erection I suspected he was using me to hide. "How much longer before I can take you home and peel this dress off you?"

I pursed my lips, praying no one noticed the heat climbing my cheeks. "We could probably slip out now. I've met all my obligations, and I don't think Rob is going to let Mom go any time soon."

He let out a low, satisfied hum that made me wish we weren't an hour from Addison. "Good. I already had the valet bring the Jeep around."

I shook my head, amused despite myself. "Cocky."

"Fuck, yes." He nudged his hips forward once, a tease of what I hoped was to come, then released me to take my hand.

The gods must have been smiling down on me for once because no one paid us any attention as we left the hotel. As promised, the Jeep was waiting at the curb. Adam helped me inside and sent me a wicked grin as he jogged around the front.

Once we escaped the snarl of Dallas traffic, Adam turned down the music and reached for my hand. "One down, how many more to go?"

I scrunched my nose trying to remember. "Three, I think?"

He glanced my direction with a raised brow. "Before the semester starts?"

"No, the actual wedding isn't until the last Saturday of September." I was the maid of honor in name only, so I'd relegated the details to my email and forgotten them.

He winced, and I realized the problem. Football season would be well underway, so the Saturday wedding would be a game day for him.

"Crap," I muttered.

Adam squeezed my hand. "Don't worry about it. We'll work it out."

After the success of today, I didn't want to go back to trying to find a date. Adam was right. No one would live up to him.

I trusted him, but I didn't want him sacrificing for me. "You're not skipping a game."

"If it's an early home game or a bye, I should be able to make it. Unless they're psychopaths, and planning a morning wedding, in which case we should probably shun them."

"As much as I'd love to shun Rob, I don't think my mom would understand. Is your schedule already set?"

"Yeah, it's been set for months, but I don't have it memorized. Shaw would know."

I made a mental note to talk to my other roommate about their game schedule, but the reminder brought up another aspect I hadn't considered—the explanation of why I needed to know.

Eva was the only one I'd talked to about my relationship with Adam, and I had no idea if the others even knew. Usually, the football players did their athlete stuff together, and I studied. If Adam had free time, we tended to spend it alone. Naked.

No one had commented, which led me to believe no one had noticed. Now that I'd told Eva, I didn't care if they knew, but how did Adam feel about it? The last time he'd gotten involved with a friend, she'd left. Not just him, but the group too. Was he nervous about their reactions?

In my usual fashion, I blurted out the question without thinking. "Are you nervous about what the others will think of us being together?"

His eyes shot to me for a second before they returned to the road. "Do I *ever* give off the impression I'm nervous?"

"No, but that doesn't answer my question."

He stayed quiet for a long beat, and a quick slice of pain startled me. I frowned, trying to tug my hand away from him.

Instead of letting go, he lifted my fingers to his lips. "Stop that. I was thinking."

I let him lower my hand to his thigh. "Why would you need to think about a yes or no question?"

"Because I was trying to figure out what I'd done to make you think I was nervous. I'm not, to be clear."

The flare of hurt abated with his soft words, replaced by guilt. "You didn't do anything. I just wasn't sure if I was supposed to let Shaw and the others know we were together. We haven't talked about it."

"Let's talk about it now. I'll go first." He pointedly glanced my way to be sure I was listening, making me smile. "I didn't want to get involved with you in the beginning because I was afraid I'd drive you off the way I did Eva. That's why I agreed to friends without benefits."

"You didn't drive off Eva," I interrupted. "And you won't drive off me."

He nodded, rubbing his thumb across my wrist. "Good because the more I got to know you, the more I liked you. I wanted to spend all my time with you, and that hasn't changed. I want everything. Can you handle that?"

I nodded, staring down at my lap to try to find the right words. I didn't want my mouth to mess this up for once. "In my experience, people leave, or don't show up in the first place. It's fine when I don't have any emotional investment. You made it not fine. There's so much in here—" I stopped to wave my free hand over my torso. "It's scary and exhilarating and exhausting. What I do and say matters suddenly because if I'm not careful I might hurt you. I don't want to hurt you. I'd do a lot to *not* hurt you. I'd do a lot to keep you too."

"You don't have to do anything, Sunshine. I'm yours."

Warmth spread from my chest, and I scooted closer to lay my head on his shoulder. "I'm yours too."

Adam kissed the top of my head. "I know."

I giggled, relieved we'd made it through the conversation. "Cocky."

"As soon as we get home, baby."

———

For once, Shaw and RJ were in the living room when we came in the door. Adam pulled me to a stop, and RJ immediately zeroed in on our hands clasped together. She tilted her head at me in a silent question even I understood. Shaw straightened from his slouch, but Adam didn't give him a chance to say anything.

"Blue and I are together, and I'm pretty sure I'm in love with her. Deal with it."

"Shit," Shaw cursed as RJ laughed.

"Questions?" Adam continued. "No? Excellent."

I stared at him wide-eyed as he dragged me into his bedroom and locked the door behind us. "You're in love with me?"

He grinned as he yanked off his suit while I stood there with my mouth open. "Yep."

"I..." My brain declined to finish the sentence.

Adam dropped his pants, revealing Big Mac in all his glory, and chuckled. "You don't have to say anything—I just wanted you to know. And now I want you to know that I plan to eat that sweet pussy until you come at least twice."

I probably should have stuck with silence, but surprise made me ask, "Are you sure?"

"Come here, Blue." He didn't wait for me to act before peeling off my dress as promised. The stretchy material gave him easy access, and I helped by lifting my arms. My bra and underwear followed quickly after.

Adam crawled backward onto the bed pulling me with him until he sat against the headboard with me straddling his lap.

"Are you sure?" I asked again.

"I know what I want, Sunshine. Now grab the headboard and ride my face."

He wasn't asking. Adam slid lower and grabbed my hips, positioning me right where he wanted me. With one hand working my pussy and the other on his dick, Adam growled his satisfaction.

With my head thrown back and my legs wide, I gripped his headboard and did as he ordered. After two orgasms, my legs were mush, but I wanted more. I needed him inside me.

I lifted off him and muttered, "Condom."

He immediately reached for his nightstand. A few

seconds later, Adam scooted up until I was positioned above his sheathed cock. His eyes caught mine as he drew a nipple into his mouth, flicking the tip with his tongue. With my hands still gripping the headboard, I leisurely sank down until he was notched at my entrance.

He groaned, and his hands clenched my hips. "That's it, baby. Take what's yours."

I'd never get tired of that first moment of connection when he slid inside me. How he filled me perfectly, and everything felt right in the world. Like I'd been made to fit him. Adam cupped my neck and pulled me down for a slow, heart-melting kiss.

He let me set the pace, a leisurely exploration of pleasure that didn't stay unhurried for long. His hands roamed my body as the tempo increased. I rode him for all I was worth, muttering nonsense as I chased my release. With each rise and fall, he rubbed his thumb between my cheeks, adding a little more pressure every time I moved against him. A thrill zipped through me. I'd never tried anal play, but with Adam, I was up for anything.

"Yes," I moaned, and a second later, he pushed through the tight ring of muscle. I was hit with a new set of dual sensations that sent me rocketing skyward.

He swiped his tongue across my collarbone, my nipples, my throat, until I grabbed a handful of his hair and brought his mouth to mine.

I love you too. The words circled my mind, stubbornly refusing to be shared, but Adam didn't need them. He showered me with praise and brought me over a third time before finding his own release.

My heart pounded as I shuddered around him. The idea of love scared me—what was to stop someone from changing their mind?—but Adam made the risk worth it. He nuzzled my neck, holding me tight, and I couldn't imagine wanting to be anywhere else.

23

Blue

I was in déjà vu hell. The last time I'd come to a karaoke party at Johnny's, I'd been massively over-dressed thanks to a dress my mom insisted I wear. Adam had assured me I wouldn't have to worry about my clothes this time because it was a cosplay karaoke party. He'd wanted to go as mac and cheese, but I'd had a better idea.

Or at least, I'd thought it was better until it involved me arriving late in a skirt that barely covered my underwear. As if Mom knew I was returning to the scene of the crime, she called me just as I exited the Uber in front of Johnny's.

"Good news, honey. I found you a place to live."

"Hello to you too, Mom. I already have a place to live." I didn't tell her I only used my room as storage at this point, or that I wasn't sure what I was going to do when the semester started as Noah had only agreed to the summer.

"I'm glad Mac and Eva stepped up to help when you needed it, but we both know you need your space to thrive."

I wanted to argue, but historically, she was right. I'd

moved into my own apartment as soon as she'd let me. Granted, it was right next door, but Mom was a new age hippy who didn't have a tidy bone in her body.

Having my own space meant I could keep it exactly the way I wanted it without worrying about another person's needs. My brow furrowed as I realized I hadn't felt trapped in Adam's apartment the same way I had in Mom's, despite having more roommates.

A warm breeze blew past my legs, lifting the edges of the skirt, and I slapped them down again. Three guys in matching unicorn costumes came out of the darkness in the parking lot right as the other side flipped up. They slowed as they passed me, and one sent me a smile. I glared at him and turned my back. Dating practice was officially over. I didn't need to be nice or social anymore.

Mom kept talking when I didn't answer. "One of my colleagues has a little guest house behind her property. She usually reserves it for foreign students, but she was just telling me how by some miracle the college found housing for all of them. I'm reasonably certain she'd give you the same deal."

"Really?"

"Yeah, it's not huge—maybe four hundred square feet—but it would be all yours."

I blew out a breath, tucking an annoying curl behind my ear. "Can I think about it, or did you already call her?"

Mom's tinkling laugh rang out. "I already called her. She has a contract waiting for you. The house is empty, so you can move in tomorrow if you want."

I rubbed the space between my eyes. "Thanks, Mom."

There was no point in arguing with her. I could always explain to the colleague why I didn't need the house, and it would be nice to have a backup plan in case all my decisions over the last few months blew up in my face.

"You're welcome, honey. I sent you her information. Oops, I have to go. Rob wants my help picking out new curtains. Love you."

"Love you too."

She hung up, and I stared down at my phone. Did I want to move out? What would that mean for me and Adam? He'd said he loved me, but he hadn't mentioned living arrangements. The fall semester was almost here, and I'd need more than half a bed and a closet in another room. Honestly, the idea of getting all my stuff out of Rob's place had a lot of appeal.

People dated without living together all the time. Moving out didn't have to change anything. My gut twisted into a knot as I tucked the phone into my waistband. Communication was key, right? I'd just ask Adam what he thought.

The inside of Johnny's was loud, dark, and packed with sweating people. A woman in a cat costume stood on the stage talking into a mic. Despite the way he'd described it, I'd half expected Adam to be running the event like he had last time, but I didn't see him anywhere at the front.

A sinking sense of foreboding tightened in my chest as I scanned the room looking for a familiar face. My list of friends was fairly small, but I'd assumed the rest of the crew would show up too. Unfortunately, their usual booth was taken up by a group dressed as ninja turtles.

I tugged at the fake corset I wore and readjusted the gold lasso laying against my thigh as I started another circle of the packed room. The crowd at the bar was two deep, but I didn't think Adam would be there anyway. If he wasn't on the stage, he'd be near Alex in the DJ booth.

I battled my way through the dancers until I got close enough to see Alex was alone. Where the heck was Adam? I probably should have foregone the surprise and rode with him. Half of the people milling around wore masks, so I ended up squinting awkwardly at perfect strangers looking for a familiar face.

Alex spotted me as I emerged from the dance floor, and his gaze darted past me with a frown. The woman emceeing the event called up the next group, and he nodded at the space behind his chair. The song started as I skirted the half wall separating him from the rest of the bar.

Once I got close enough, he spun around and scanned the direction I'd come from. "Where's Mac?"

"I was going to ask you the same question. Have you seen him?"

"Not since we finished the live run-through last night."

I stopped searching the room and stepped closer. "Live run-through?"

Alex's gaze snapped back to me with wide eyes. "Shit. Forget I said that."

If he hadn't looked so guilty, I might have. "No. Run-through of what?"

"I can't tell you. You'll have to ask Mac. Honestly, I hope you ask him. He needs to talk about his shit. But don't mention my name, okay?"

I frowned at him. "He's going to know where I got the information."

"That's true, but I'm hoping you yelling at him will be enough to distract him."

My shoulders tensed. "I don't yell at people."

He shrugged. "Figure of speech. I expected him to be here before we opened, but he had a football thing earlier so maybe it ran late?"

I appreciated his willingness to give Adam an excuse, but I was starting to get the feeling I'd wasted my time. "Thank you. If you see him, will you tell him I went home?"

Alex hesitated for a long beat, then nodded. "You make a great Wonder Woman, by the way. I hope Mac gets to see your costume."

"Me too," I muttered, as he spun back to his laptop for the next song.

The easiest solution was to call Adam, but his phone rang until the voicemail picked up. Texting produced an equal lack of response. I sighed and waved at Alex as I made my way back across the room to the exit.

I didn't like the idea of Adam keeping secrets, especially after he'd made a big deal out of open communication, but I wasn't going to jump to conclusions. We lived together—slept together every night. It's not like I didn't know where to find him.

While I waited for an Uber to arrive, I took a quick selfie outside the bar. Just in case. Adam may have skipped cosplay karaoke, but I still wanted him to see the effort. The rideshare pulled up as my phone dinged with a new email.

My hopes rose and crashed in an instant when I saw it was from Mom instead of Adam. He didn't usually email me, but it hadn't stopped my lizard brain from grasping onto the possibility. I confirmed my address with the driver and opened the message.

Mom had sent a copy of the contract along with the number of her colleague. I could easily afford the rent with the money she'd set aside, and the pictures were adorable. It was basically a tiny house with crisp white paint and cute little black shutters. Best of all, it was within walking distance of campus.

To my surprise, I wanted to take the offer. I loved waking

up with Adam, sleeping with his arms around me, studying with my feet propped on his lap, but the apartment wasn't home for me. Noah's room was still unmistakably Noah's. Mom was right—I needed my own space, but I didn't want to give up Adam either.

As if in response to my thoughts, a notification popped up on my screen of a new post from one of Eva's friends on TU's social media. *#couplegoals Eva + Mac. Cheer queen and football star? Sorry, ball bunnies. Looks like this one's taken. [sad face emoji]*

The post included a picture of Adam holding Eva from behind and kissing her neck, the same way he'd done countless times with me. Eva's face was turned away from the camera, but their body language said it all.

The flare of hurt took my breath away. I wasn't stupid. I knew this picture was from the spring semester, but it was the first time I'd seen them together like that. They'd done a good job of keeping their relationship a secret.

It wasn't the speculation that bothered me...it was the similarity. The picture could have been of Adam and me—I'd seen the same look on his face.

The driver cleared his throat, and I glanced around, belatedly realizing we were in the parking lot of the apartment.

"Thanks." I paid him and gave him a good tip for letting me get lost in my thoughts without interrupting or murdering me.

A thought occurred to me as I hit the sidewalk and noticed Adam's Jeep in its usual spot—maybe Adam had simply traded in one Eva for another. And maybe having my own place was a good idea after all.

I wasn't sure what to expect when I opened the door, but

Adam asleep face down on the couch with a throw pillow decorating his butt hadn't been anywhere near the top. He was shirtless, as he usually was at home, but a hint of red peeked out from under the pillow, so he was wearing shorts at least.

Relief blasted through the apprehension. He hadn't ditched me on purpose. He'd fallen asleep after another day of practice on top of staying out late last night. Apparently working on a performance with Alex.

I shook my head, feeling stupid for not asking before. I'd gotten distracted with finding the last bits of my costume and hadn't thought twice when he'd texted he was still at Alex's. What else had I missed?

Adam muttered something about gravy, and I let out a quiet laugh. He was a heavy sleeper, so I grabbed the fuzzy blanket off the lone recliner and covered him. Tomorrow would be soon enough to hash out my issues.

I hated the idea I might be a consolation prize. Adam had never made me feel anything but special, and still, I couldn't shake the niggling doubt. I was secretly terrified the last few months had been too good to be true—that I'd lucked into the single best relationship of my life and my luck would change.

I was tired of waiting for the other shoe to drop...and I was tired of second-guessing myself. Adam hadn't meant to stand me up, but the drive home from karaoke had been brutal. A stark reminder of how precarious my emotions were. A tiny mix-up sent me searching for ways Adam was pulling away—even when I knew he wasn't.

He *was* hiding things though. Loving someone sucked when the vulnerability came back to bite me in the butt. My whole life was wrapped up in Adam at the moment, but it didn't have to be. I suddenly had other options for living arrangements which would make me feel a whole lot more stable and less dependent on someone keeping secrets from me.

I texted Mom's colleague and told her I'd take the tiny house.

24

Mac

The sunlight streaming through the living room window told me everything I needed to know about how much I'd fucked up last night. Practice had been a bitch with Haskins needing extra work after, and I'd been wiped after staying up half the night before with Alex.

Last night was supposed to be a fun date with Blue, but judging from the sore spot in my shoulder, I hadn't moved after I'd laid down to close my eyes for a second. I stretched with a groan and tossed the blanket covering me back onto the chair where Eva liked it.

It took a second for my groggy brain to remember Eva didn't come over anymore. I scrubbed a hand down my face, trying to wake up. Shaw and RJ spent the night in Dallas for a charity event, so Blue must have put the blanket over me. Before or after I'd stood her up at karaoke?

Probably after or she'd have woken me up. I stumbled into my room, already prepping my apology, but I pulled up short. The bed was empty and neatly made.

"Blue?"

I could see into the empty bathroom from my spot by the door, but I checked anyway. Everything looked normal except for the absence of my girlfriend. A low level panic started churning in my gut.

Belatedly, I realized I could hear low music coming from somewhere. The walls in our complex weren't particularly thick, but we'd never had a problem with noise crossing over before. I followed the sound across the hall and opened Noah's door.

A couple of boxes sat on the bed, half stuffed with Blue's things, and my girlfriend, who had spent the last countless nights in my room, in my bed, was carefully folding a pair of pants as she sang to the music. My heart tried to beat its way out of my throat.

I crossed my arms and leaned against the doorframe. "Going somewhere?"

Blue started and spun around with a hand on her chest as the pants fell to the floor. "Adam, you surprised me."

"I see that. Were you hoping to be gone before I woke up?" I hated the accusation in my tone, but dammit, she was packing.

"No." She bent to pick up the pants and set them aside. "I just wanted to get a head start. We need to talk."

Ah, the infamous phrase that usually marked the end of a relationship for me. Yes, I'd skipped out on our date the night before, but it was an accident and I'd thought she was happy. *I* was happy, up until ten seconds ago. Now I was having trouble pulling in a full breath. I'd thought I meant more to her than a missed date.

I hid the hurt with a smile. "Okay. You want to go first, or should I?"

She tilted her head to examine my face and her brows drew together. "Maybe you should go first."

My first instinct was to demand she unpack, preferably in my room where she belonged, but I reined in the caveman urge. An apology would work better than throwing her over my shoulder.

"Sure. I'm sorry about last night. I must have been more tired than I thought, and I hated waking up without you this morning."

I didn't realize how tightly I was holding myself, until Blue walked over and laid her hand on my forearm, making the muscle twitch. "I'm not upset about the karaoke thing, but thank you for the apology."

She tugged my arms apart so she could wrap them around her waist instead. The tight ball of anxiety in my chest loosened. I much preferred this position, especially when she locked her hands behind my neck, but I was definitely getting mixed signals. Was she leaving or not?

"What's going on, Blue?"

"I'll tell you, but first, I have a question. Were you ever going to tell me about your thing with Alex?"

The question felt like a test, and I knew I was going to fail. Dread spread through me like poison. "Yes. I just need a little more time. With football and Haskins and the shit with Eva, I didn't have a lot of bandwidth left over to dedicate to worrying about my project with him. It has nothing to do with us. You still get all of me."

"Have you considered how you'll be able to give your all to football and music and your friends and me once the season starts when your all is a finite resource? Something's going to give, and I'm afraid it will be me."

I opened my mouth to provide whatever reassurance she needed, but she pressed her fingers against my lips. "Think about it. Please. We're so far past friends with benefits, and I've never done this before. Everyone leaves. You stayed. It's terrifying—the hope for the future next to the fear it will all crumble."

Her hand slipped away, but I caught it and brought it back to kiss her palm. "I don't need to think about it. I have my priorities straight. Football and music are opportunities. I'll jump on them given the chance, but if I miss something, another chance will come along. There's only one you. My friends understand when to back off, even Eva, as evidenced by her current disappearance. Her and I need to talk at some point and see if our friendship withstood the power of my dick, but none of that comes before you. I love every colorful, blunt, sexy part of you. Don't leave me."

I'd never in my life begged a woman for her affections, but I'd do anything to keep Blue.

She sighed. "I'm not leaving you, but I'm moving out. Noah needs his room back, and honestly, I want something I did for myself for once."

There it was. I hadn't spared much thought for what would happen at the end of the summer, but I'd sort of assumed she'd simply transition across the hall to my room. I wanted her there with me all the time, and it had never occurred to me she might not feel the same way. A familiar shaft of pain split my chest.

"Am I holding on to you too tight?"

Blue shook her head with a smile. "No, I love the way you hold me. I love that you always reach for me and make me feel wanted."

"But you're still leaving."

"This was never supposed to be a permanent solution. My moving a few miles away shouldn't break us. You run that distance every morning for fun. Shaw and RJ are great, as I'm sure Noah is, but I hate feeling transient. I hate the constant change and uncertainty of where I'll be living next week. I'm moving out so I can give myself a level of stability, and so you can focus on other aspects of your life deserving of attention. I am in no way breaking up with you."

I cupped her face, and she kissed my thumb. Blue was so beautiful and earnest, trying so hard not to push me away while telling me what she needed. She wanted me. In her life as well as her bed. The vise around my chest loosened, but I needed to be sure.

"I don't want to let you go," I murmured.

"Then don't. Hold on tight. I'm not going anywhere you can't easily find me. Plus, I'm only a couple of blocks from Whataburger."

I laughed and stroked her hair, feeling lighter than I had since waking up. "That *is* a bonus, but I think I'm going to enjoy the privacy more. Another set of kitchen counters to test out."

Her blue-green eyes darkened with need. "I get the keys this afternoon."

"Let's get you packed then." I dropped a quick kiss on her lips, resisting the urge to linger there and prove my devotion until she couldn't remember anything except my name.

I let her go when she pulled away to grab the closest box, but the clothes reminded me why I'd laid down on the couch in the first place last night. She'd wanted to keep her outfit a secret, so I'd thought I had a little time before heading to Johnny's without her.

"Wait, I have one more question."

Blue raised a brow, waiting.

"What was your costume last night?"

A slow, wicked smile spread across her face. "I can show you at my new place."

God, I loved her.

————

I SPENT the next several days exhausted because my girl *really* liked her new house, and hell if I'd choose to sleep when I could have her naked and writhing underneath me. Shaw and RJ went with me on a special trip to Dallas to grab Blue's stuff between practices, Chloe helped Blue unpack, and Noah grumbled about having to clean two apartments now.

With surprising speed, we settled into yet another new normal, then the inevitable happened, and Eva came home.

She surprised me after practice when I'd been about to head over to Blue's. I wasn't proud of it, but my first reaction was to close the door in her face. My bedroom door, because being Eva, she'd walked right into my apartment like she lived there.

"I deserved that," she said as she barged through a second time, leaving the door wide open behind her.

I eyed the hallway. Probably a good choice. I'd been worried all summer she wouldn't come back, but with her in front of me looking like nothing had changed, the fear of losing her was replaced by anger.

Eva didn't seem to have the same reaction. She flopped on the bed, tucking her legs under her, while I went searching for a shirt.

"Blue's not here," I told her from the closet, pulling a random tee from the pile.

She snorted. "I know. I went by her place first. Cute. It reminds me of her."

I'd thought the same thing when I'd first seen it, but I didn't want to sit around talking about Blue when I could be with her in person. "What do you want?"

"To apologize."

That got my attention. I stopped stalling and faced her in the bedroom from a safe distance away. I wasn't taking any chances one of my asshole roommates, not counting RJ, would jump to the wrong conclusion.

In a weird repeat of the morning Blue had moved out, I leaned against the doorframe with my arms crossed. "I'm listening."

She clasped her hands in her lap, sitting up straight and losing her usual playful attitude. "I'm sorry for hurting you, but I'm not sorry for leaving."

"Your apologies suck," I muttered.

"I'm still going, jackass. We were better as friends. I'm not interested in giving another person control over any part of my life, and the pressure would have slowly destroyed us. I needed some time away to separate what we had from what we were dabbling in. Honestly, I could still use some time, but football season waits for no one."

My jaw clenched at the idea she still didn't want to be around me. I used to think she knew me better than anyone, but this summer had opened my eyes. She knew Mac. She hadn't seen Adam in years. I wasn't sure *I* had until Blue challenged me to be more than a rejected football fuckboy.

Still, it stung Eva had made all the decisions without consulting me. "Did you consider what I needed?"

"I did, and I knew it wasn't me. Had I known it was Blue, I would have gotten out of the way sooner. I'm glad you're happy." The smile she offered me felt tattered at the edges, but I knew she meant what she said.

I borrowed some of Blue's blunt honesty. "Why didn't you stay and talk to me?"

Eva's cheeks puffed as she let out a slow breath. "Because part of me wanted to give in and take the easy road. I already loved you—still love you—and I thought if I couldn't make it work with you, I didn't have much of a chance with anyone else. But that's a terrible reason to be involved with someone. Fear I'd never have the opportunity again? Pass. I couldn't do that to you."

To Eva, being in charge was as necessary as breathing. It would take a special brand of voodoo to convince her to hand over the reins in a relationship. In hindsight, I wasn't even close to that person. She'd seen the truth so clearly, and I'd totally missed the part where she was trying to protect me.

I hauled her off the bed into a hug. When she didn't hesitate to wrap her arms around my waist, one of the cracks in my heart healed. Blue made me happy, but so did Eva, just in different capacities.

"I'm sorry I wasn't strong enough to say no," I finally told her.

Eva let out a watery laugh and pulled away. "Please. Have you seen my ass? No one is that strong. Now tell me why Coach has you on his shit list."

"I might have skipped a couple of training sessions and fucked up a few times at camp. I had some other things on my mind this summer." I sent her a pointed look, to which she simply shrugged.

"Sounds like you weren't participating in team activities during the team building part of the pre-season."

"I was participating. Coach literally had to pull me away from the team to inform me I was on his list. If he hadn't interrupted, I would've had some money in the pool with the rest of them."

She raised a brow. "Which one?"

"Coach's mustache."

Eva grinned. "His wife found out she was allergic to

hummus when he got some stuck in his mustache then kissed her."

I swore. 'Wife made him do it' had been my first choice. "You couldn't have told me that last week?"

She shrugged. "You know my policy. I only use my powers for good or entertainment. Are we going to be okay?"

I hooked an arm around her shoulder and steered her out of my room. "Yeah, we're going to be okay. I missed you, Wildcat. Stay if you want, I'm heading out to see my girl."

She patted my bicep until I set her loose. "Nah, I have to go too. Henry's in the car."

I sent her an incredulous look. "The duck?"

"Don't start," she warned.

My shoulders shook with laughter as I remembered the way Henry had terrorized her and Chloe last semester. "Are you still putting him in those weird little diapers?"

She tossed her ponytail over her shoulder, one with a pink stripe I somehow hadn't noticed until just now. "Sometimes. He looks very dapper in his houndstooth. Speaking of dapper, tell Blue I need pics of you all dolled up for Hope's rehearsal party."

Oh shit. I stopped hauling her to the living room to cross check dates in my head.

With all the sex and football and rehearsals, the wedding stuff had become an afterthought. We'd done two of the events without a problem, but they were both low-key daytime parties where I only had to look good and say something witty once in a while. Not-Archer hadn't paid me any attention, which I assumed was due to him actively ignoring Blue as long as she wasn't making a scene.

The final event before the wedding was coming up this weekend, on the same night as the live performance with Alex, and I'd totally forgotten.

Eva read my face like I had subtitles attached and started laughing. "What did you fuck up?"

"Nothing I can't fix." I spun her around and shoved her out the door.

My mind raced with alternatives. We had a real chance of winning. Alex was a genius, and the judges had raved about our sample, but I couldn't be in two places at once. Or could I?

A hazy idea formed in the back of my mind. Alex would hate it, but I wasn't above forcing his hand. Blue was counting on me, and I wasn't letting Shad anywhere near her.

Eva stopped on the landing to get in one last shot. "Whatever you're planning, talk to Blue about it first. Remember what your mom always says."

I stopped with my hand on the door to meet her eyes, unable to resist the urge to tease her a little. "That I'm her favorite child?"

She pursed her lips. "Communication is key, my friend —and I'm definitely her favorite child."

Eva turned with a flare of pink hair and headed for the parking lot. I watched her get into her BMW, glad to have the old Eva back. Even if I was probably going to ignore her advice.

25

Mac

Fate didn't give me a choice. Instead of spending the next few hours naked with Blue, I drove over to Alex's, where I thought he might strangle me with one of his cords. After I explained my plan—and he yelled at me for a solid half hour—he agreed to do things my way. As long as I agreed to tell Blue about the competition.

Apparently, everyone was suddenly listening to my mother.

Five hours later, we finished our marathon session, and Luis kicked me out. At least he fed me first. Alex didn't even say goodbye.

Darkness had fallen while we were busy in the makeshift studio, and I winced when I checked my watch. Well past dinner time. Blue wouldn't be waiting for me, but I'd told her I'd come by after practice.

The drive over didn't take long, Addison wasn't that big, but for the first time ever, I was nervous to see my girl-friend. Blue didn't hide things. She didn't overreact either, but I still felt guilty for not sharing the big change happening in my life. Especially since she was the only one

I'd told about my passion for music—the only one who understood the twitchy feeling of Mac not being enough anymore.

Football was my life, and I had every intention of being drafted in April, but things inside me had shifted this summer. Blue had helped me realize I didn't have to be Mac all the time. I could let music be important too.

I could trust someone to want every part of me, not only the flashy outside.

A laugh escaped as I got out of my Jeep to walk around the big house. I wasn't interested in trusting a rando. I wanted Blue. More than anything else, I wanted Blue. Which meant Eva and Alex and my mom were right—I needed to tell her everything.

I was probably destroying my chance to level up with this crazy plan, but I wasn't going to leave her alone with Shad circling like a vulture. Her mom certainly hadn't stepped up to protect her, and not-Archer would just as likely offer her as a bonus to Shad if he hit his sales targets.

Music could wait—hell, football could wait—if it meant showing her she didn't need those assholes.

Blue opened the door to my knock, wearing one of my TU football shirts over cut-off shorts, and my brain short-circuited. There was something about seeing her in my clothes that triggered a possessive streak I'd kept buried deep. I tracked the tanned length of her legs, and when I got back to her face, heat darkened the blue green to the turquoise I loved.

Talking suddenly became less important. I closed the door behind me and reached for the hem of her shirt. Instead of lifting her arms, she back pedaled, almost toppling over the foot of her bed.

I shifted forward to catch her, but she held up her hands

to fend me off. What the hell? I stayed where I was by the door and tried to keep the hurt out of my voice.

"You okay, Sunshine?"

She let out a small humorless laugh. "Yes. I didn't mean to get dramatic, but when you touch me, my mind shuts off. Alex called me. He wanted to make sure you followed through with your end of the deal."

Yep, I was going to murder him for not trusting me. I shoved my balled-up hands in my pockets and rolled to my toes. "What did he say?"

"He told me about the competition." She tilted her head and studied me, like she'd done so many times before trying to work something out. "Why didn't *you* tell me?"

I wanted to hold her and erase the hint of sadness. Instead, I held myself still and hoped I didn't make things worse. "I don't know. Alex texted me about it the same night I had the idea for you to move in. I was going to tell him no like I always did, but something felt different this time. Like what I had before wasn't enough."

"You outgrew it," she said softly.

My lips twisted. "Yeah, that feels right. Then after I said yes, I was struggling to fit it all in. I didn't want to admit I couldn't handle it. I thought if I just pushed a little harder, nothing would drop."

She finally crossed the distance between us, tracing my jaw and running her fingers over my stubble. "I could have helped."

The urge to touch her became too much. I wrapped my hand around hers and kissed her fingertips. "What if you thought it was stupid? What if I lost my shot with you because I couldn't be Adam and Mac at the same time?"

Blue gave me a scolding look. "I deserve more faith than that."

"I know. Believe me, I know. Turns out, I *couldn't* handle everything. I don't know how much Alex told you, but we finaled in the contest. The last step is a live performance in front of the judges. I fucked up the days though. The live performance is the same night as your mom's party."

She frowned, but she didn't pull away as I'd feared. "Adam, that's fantastic. I'm so proud of you."

I used her hand to pull her closer, taking a chance by curling an arm around her waist. "I'm not going."

Her jaw firmed. "Yes, you are."

"No, I'm not. Alex will go with a video of me performing. We're last on the playlist, so he has plenty of time to try to schmooze the judges into letting us slide, or at least reschedule."

Frustration flashed over her features. "Adam, you have to see how this competition is more important than a party."

"It's not about the party. It's about showing up for you. It's about Shad making you feel hunted, and not-Archer making you feel inferior, and your mom making you feel abandoned." I patted my chest. "I want to make you feel loved. When everyone else is piling on, I want to be your safe place."

Blue dropped her forehead to my chest, shaking her head slightly. "You are impossible. Does anyone tell you no?"

I smiled at the feel of her against me. "Well, you still haven't agreed to marry me, so I don't *always* get what I want. Words are easy. Actions speak the truth. I'm not going."

She took a deep breath and nodded, lifting her head to meet my eyes. "I can't make you listen, but I can decide for myself. I'm going alone. You are officially uninvited. What you choose to do with your sudden free evening is up to you."

"Blue—"

"No," she interrupted me. "You're running yourself ragged trying to be everything for everyone. Stop. Take this one night for yourself. Actually, take every second between now and the performance. I don't want to see you until then."

My arm tightened around her, panic starting to churn in my stomach. "I *do not* agree to this deal."

"It's not a deal, and you won't get your way this time." She rose to her toes and brushed my mouth with hers, walking me back toward the door with a hand on my chest. "Once you've kicked butt at the competition, we can celebrate any way you want."

I cupped the back of her head, pulling her in for a real kiss. Blue sighed and tilted back, giving me the access I wanted. I breathed her in, the fresh green scent, and came back for more. The swirling, trembling emptiness sitting at the bottom of my ribcage insisted I take and take, like if I let her go, she'd disappear.

"I love you," I murmured, hoping it was enough.

She grasped my wrist, pulling my hand from her hair and kissing my palm. "Tell me again on Sunday."

Blue stepped back and closed the door between us, leaving me with no other option but to return to my Jeep. I tried to console Big Mac, but he pouted the whole way home.

———

SATURDAY DAWNED OVERCAST AND MUGGY. I didn't see the actual dawn because I'd stayed up worrying half the night and spent the other half having increasingly erotic dreams about Blue. We hadn't spent this long apart since the beginning of the summer, and I wasn't a fan.

I missed her. She was trying to give me space to get my shit together, and I was using it to mope around thinking about her. She wasn't even answering my texts, though I could see she'd read them. My saving grace was the temporary aspect of the situation. I could do anything in short bursts.

I'd spent two days waffling, pulling double workouts, and torturing Haskins. Alex didn't call me to come over for the first time all summer, and I thought I saw Luis cross the street to avoid talking to me during one of my runs.

Unfortunately, the time apart made me question my plan, which was probably what she'd intended. I'd made massively bad decisions before, namely getting involved with Eva, and I didn't want to lose Blue to my own arrogance.

I didn't want to lose Blue.

The last few days had made it abundantly clear my life was better with her in it. I wanted her cheering for me in the stands and arguing with me over breakfasts and lying next to me every night. I'd marry her in a second if she'd let me.

The time without her was making me grumpy. Shaw and RJ didn't notice, but Noah pulled me aside after morning conditioning. He tossed my water bottle at me, then waited until I was drinking to ask his question.

"What are you doing with Blue?"

I almost spit water right in his face. He would have deserved it. "Man, I know you don't need me to explain the birds and the bees to you. Then again after last semester's baby scare maybe you need a refresher."

He crossed his arms and raised a brow, serene in the face

of my teasing. "I meant why are you sleeping in your bed instead of hers. Are you okay?"

I wasn't. I very much wasn't. I was in over my head, and I needed help. Maybe it was time to admit the truth. "Fuck. No, I'm not. Blue is going to her mom's wedding party thing tonight, and I'm supposed to be her date."

He tilted his head. "Why is that a problem?"

I sighed, running my hand through my sweaty hair. "I'm also supposed to perform for a singing competition tonight. Her future stepbrother is a sleazy asshole who keeps trying to corner her, and the dad isn't much better. If I can protect her, I want to be there, but she told me I couldn't come with her. I'm worried if I show up anyway it'll drive her away because I didn't listen."

Noah clapped me on the back. "I know what I'd pick, but you know her better than any of us. If you need backup, I'm there. And next time you're in a competition, let us know. I want to make sure I set aside time to make glitter signs with your name on them."

"Thanks, man." I should have known better than to think these guys would do anything other than support me completely. We were family.

He nodded and headed off toward the showers. As much as I appreciated the reminder that I should trust my friends, I still didn't have a solid recommendation. Noah would go to the party. One hundred percent. If Chloe asked him to dress up in a chicken suit and dance the hula, he'd do it, despite his extreme dislike for being the center of attention.

The difference was Blue had asked me to stay away.

I made my way home and sighed as I realized I only had one option left for unbiased advice. Graciela Alvarez Mackenzie. Momma Mac.

After parking my Jeep, I dropped my head back on the rest and sent her a video request.

"What's wrong?" she asked, before her face had even appeared on the call. She'd cut her hair since the last time I'd seen her, so now the dark locks stopped bluntly at her chin.

"Why does something have to be wrong for me to call you?"

"Because when I ask for proof of life, I get a text of you flexing like a clown. Is this about the Blue girl?"

My mind screeched to a halt, unable to process how my mom could pick that information out of thin air. "Wha...How?"

She sniffed. "You think you're the only one who talks to me?"

Eva. I should have realized. "How much did she tell you?"

The camera jostled as she sat down at the kitchen table. "Enough for me to know it's serious. I'll forgo the guilt trip this time for not telling me about her, but I expect you to bring her home next time I see you. Now, how can I help?"

"I need advice. Blue needs me to come as her date to an event, but it's the same night as a music competition that could jumpstart my career."

She frowned. "You're finally pursuing your music?"

"Yes."

"Why does Blue need you at the event?"

"It's complicated, but the short version is I'm trying to protect her against a guy who's been harassing her. I have this plan for the competition that I'd put at a fifty-fifty chance of success, so I can be with Blue like I promised."

Mom propped her chin on her hand. "This girl means more to you than your music?"

I nodded.

"Your football?" she asked, her voice going up an octave.

"She means more to me than anything, but she told me to go to the competition."

Her eyes widened, and she made the sign of the cross over her chest.

I sighed. "Mom, you're not even catholic."

"So? You could use all the help you can get, *mijo*. You've been solely focused on football since you learned to catch a ball. If this girl gets you to follow your heart instead of your head, I'll pray to any god who'll listen." She leaned away from the camera to yell down the hall. "John, get the sage and a lighter."

I groaned. "Don't bring Dad into this. Besides, isn't burning sage for getting rid of negative energy or something?"

She faced me again with a sharp quirk of her eyebrow, implying that was exactly how she planned to use it.

"You're not funny," I muttered.

"Yes, I am. You didn't inherit your humor from your father."

From behind her somewhere, Dad yelled, "I heard that."

I suspected this was how my friends felt dealing with me all the time. "Mom, do you have advice or not?"

She scoffed. "You don't want my advice. You want permission to do the thing you're already going to do. Go forth, my son."

The alarm on my phone went off—the one I'd set way back when we'd been chosen as finalists. Time to leave for the Dallas auditorium.

"Shit, I have to go," I muttered.

"You kiss your girl with that mouth?"

I grinned at her. "Do you really want to know what I do to her with my mouth?"

Mom crossed herself again and hung up on me.

She was right. I'd already set the plan in motion, and Blue's direct order had been to take the night for myself. I intended to. Hopefully, my plan would work, but in the end, it came down to priorities. If I had to choose between the competition and Blue, she'd win every time.

———

WITH MY MOM'S BLESSING, I was heading to the hotel for Blue's party. It didn't take me long to get ready. I had to wear a suit to every game, so a fancy party was easy mode. Slacks, an open collared dress shirt, and a suit jacket. Done. Sexy without trying. Finding the hotel was a little harder.

I laughed as I pulled up at the valet and realized it was the same place she'd been the night she called me to pick her up. The party had a guest list, because of course it did, but Blue hadn't bothered taking me off of it.

I took the oversight as a sign I was doing the right thing. If she really intended for me to stay away, wouldn't she have made sure I couldn't get in? She knew how stubborn I was. Mom had taught me in no uncertain terms to listen when a woman tells you what she wants, but I was willing to ignore the lesson in this case.

Blue had made her decision, and I had made mine.

The modern glass and chrome of the posh hotel lobby looked cold and impersonal, but the ballroom was a little better, leaning heavily to generic black and gold flourishes with splashes of vibrant pinkish-purple flowers. I'd bet my starting position Hope had picked the flowers and not-Archer had chosen everything else.

People milled around in cocktail wear, and I waltzed right in like I belonged there. Technically, I did. By this time next year, I'd be prepping for my rookie season in the NFL with a first-round bonus under my belt. Half the people here would be begging me to let them invest my money.

I'd come a long way from the bottom of the private school social ladder. Funny, I didn't feel any different.

The crowd parted, and I caught sight of the woman of my dreams—literally—standing by the floor to ceiling windows overlooking the city. A simple black dress cinched at her waist and left her arms bare, but when she moved, bright colors peeked out from a split in the fabric. She'd curled her hair, letting the bulk of it fall freely past her shoulders, and the bracelet I'd given her glinted on her wrist.

Blue might be pissed, but when I spotted Shad eyeing her from a couple of groups away, I knew I'd made the right choice.

No regrets. Not a single one.

26

Blue

The ballroom was cold. Or maybe I was. Cold inside and out without Adam there. The maudlin sentiment pissed me off a little. I didn't think I'd been stupid to send him away, but damn, I missed him.

I rubbed the goosebumps on my arms and headed for the giant windows in the hope some of the heat from outside would seep in. Dallas spread out before me in a glittering cityscape. The view from the penthouse ballroom was impressive, but I wasn't interested in pretty sights.

We were both in town tonight. The thought circled in the back of my mind, teasing and taunting with the promise of ending my self-imposed solitude. All I had to do was sneak out and call an Uber. Alex had texted me the venue where they'd be.

The crazy urge to escape had only increased as the night wore on. I just had to get through a few more hours of blending into the wallpaper, and I could go back to the life I wanted. One without the constant threat of Shad appearing in the ABC.

He was lurking somewhere in the crowd, and I couldn't

shake the feeling he was watching me. I scanned the people around me, smiling at the strangers who nodded as if they knew me. No sign of him, but lack of visual confirmation didn't make me safe.

A waiter drifted by carrying a tray full of champagne flutes, blocking my view for a few seconds. I thought about grabbing one simply to have something in my hand, but I'd made a promise to myself to only have sparkling water for the duration. The liquid would still work to hide my face while I drank, but I wouldn't have to call Adam from the street corner at the end of the night.

Part of me was tempted to get trashed simply to have a reason to reach out to him. Probably not a healthy response, but I wasn't judging myself too harshly the last few days.

I'd tried to tell Mom I'd be on my own for this party, but she'd never returned my call. There was a time when we talked every day, sometimes on the phone, sometimes text, sometimes over coffee in the morning. I didn't go more than a few hours without seeing her, and my life was braided inextricably with hers.

Back then, she wouldn't have cared that I didn't have a date—or that I might say something embarrassing or wear the wrong thing. The changes had happened subtly over the last year, since she split with Archer. No, since she'd gotten involved with Rob.

Mom loved people, loved helping them find peace, and she shone as the center of attention. She'd called the asymmetrical layers of her simple off-white dress classy boho, and I dug it. Her tanned skin glowed from a summer of teaching outdoor yoga, and she'd done a fancy updo with her hair.

My mom was beautiful, and I missed her.

I didn't know how to traverse this new normal to reach

her, so I stayed in place by the window with my heart breaking. Maybe it was time for me to let go of the way things
used to be. Change wasn't always a bad thing. If Mom was
happy, I could find a way to be happy for her.

Maybe I needed a drink after all.

I turned and ran into a rock-solid chest. Strong hands
gripped my arms to steady me, and I looked up into a pair of
dark eyes. Like I'd conjured him from my wishful thinking.

"Miss me?" Adam grazed his thumbs over my skin, and a
shiver coursed through my body.

His grin had the dual effect of making me want to kiss
him while also kicking him in the shin for not listening.

"Dammit, Adam. You're not supposed to be here."

"Maybe not, but you're here, Sunshine, so that's where
I'm going to be."

I shook my head, throwing myself into his arms without
warning. He caught me, and I pressed my face into his
shoulder. Adam always showed up exactly when I
needed him.

"Thank you," I whispered.

I didn't get anything else out before I finally caught sight
of Shad and stiffened.

He'd been there every Tuesday and Thursday in the
ABC over the summer, but after the first time, Adam hadn't
let me walk into the building alone. Shad had kept his
distance, only following me with his eyes. Tonight felt different, like in this territory, Adam posed less of a threat.

He strode up to us like we should be bowing in his
presence.

Shad spared Adam a glance then gave me a once over
that made me want to take a shower. "Your mom asked me
to dance with you. Maybe introduce you around to the
prospective investors to give them a unified family image."

I couldn't tell if he was lying, but I had a lot of trouble believing my mom would give a crap about a unified family image. Shad didn't wait for an answer. He held out his short tumbler to Adam.

"Hold this, would you?"

Adam raised a brow at me, waiting for a sign of how he should handle this. I grimaced. On the off chance my mom actually cared, I could spare Shad one dance. How much harm could he do in three and a half minutes? Besides, Adam would be watching.

I smoothed his lapel, right over his heart, and hoped he could read my discomfort. "It's fine. I'll be right back."

Adam's smile turned sharp, and he accepted Shad's glass. "Sure."

Shad gestured for me to go ahead of him onto the dance floor, then gathered me close for the slow song with a hand at the small of my back. I thanked karma for not going with the dress Mom had chosen—a backless piece which would have given me zero protection against Shad's touch.

"Not drinking tonight?" he asked,

Unease skittered up my spine. "How do you know that?"

"I've been watching." Shad spun me in a sharp circle, casting a mocking grin over my shoulder.

With a slight twist, I noticed Adam cross his arms, his eyes locked on us. No drink in sight. Shad must have noticed too.

He pulled me closer so he could lean forward and speak into my ear. "Does he make you hold a football when he fucks you?"

I tried to move away, but Shad's grip held me in place. Unless I planned to start a wrestling match on the dance floor, I was stuck until the song ended. My silent response apparently wasn't enough for him because he spun us closer to the edge of the crowd away from Adam and came in for another round.

"What are you going to do now that his little cheerleader girlfriend is back in town? Are you the sloppy seconds or is she?"

I looked for Adam through the breaks between the dancing couples, but I couldn't spot him. He was tall and broad, but most of the people there were bigger than me. They formed a human wall trapping me in my own personal hell. Panic fluttered in my chest.

"You *do* realize we're going to be siblings in a few weeks, right?" I shot back.

His leer didn't abate as he scoffed. "This isn't the first time Dad's produced a ring to get some pussy. This time, I get to enjoy the perks too."

"You are beyond disgusting, and I hope you get a venereal disease." I shoved him away, trying to stay out of reach as I scooted around him.

I didn't like Rob, but I hadn't doubted the engagement until this moment. If he was playing games with my mom, I would use every weapon at Eva's disposal to ruin him. I made it four angry steps before I was hauled around by a hand on my elbow.

Shad's expression had lost some of the jovial sheen, replaced by cruelty hidden beneath a thin veneer of civility. "You're a stuck-up bitch, and one day, I'll give you what you deserve."

Screw the image, Mom would have to understand. I stomped on his foot with my stiletto and shoved him backwards when he released me. The last vestiges of Shad's mask dropped as he caught his balance. An ugly sneer crossed his face, and his eyes locked on me.

I was fully prepared to knee him in the testicles if he

touched me again, but he only made it a single step before Adam appeared between us. He turned his back on Shad to gently lift my arm and stroke his thumb across the angry red mark just above my elbow.

A little jolt of pain made me hiss. Shad must have grabbed me harder than I thought. Adam met my eyes, his own full of fury and fire. I shook my head.

Shad wasn't worth the trouble of making a scene. The dancers around us murmured and craned their necks to see what the commotion was, but I'd stopped caring about embarrassing anyone.

"I'm fine, Adam."

His jaw ticked. "This from him?"

"Yes." I didn't say anything else, but I didn't need to. Murder entered Adam's eyes.

"She's lying—" Shad made the mistake of taking a step forward, and in one motion, Adam turned and laid him out with a right cross.

Shad hit the ground holding his nose, and I had the disturbing realization that violence, at least against Shad, turned me on.

Adam shook out his hand with a grimace and wrapped his other arm around my waist. "You don't fucking touch a woman without her permission—and you sure as hell don't touch this one."

Goosebumps rose on my exposed skin, and I had the sudden urge to find a dark spot where I could get my boyfriend alone. He brushed a kiss across my temple, and my insides melted...for all of three seconds.

"Security, get the police," Shad called from where he was sprawled on the floor.

I stepped forward as far as Adam's arm would allow, pissed beyond measure. "Good. Then I can explain to them how I got this bruise, and how Adam prevented you from dragging me off against my will."

My version wasn't exactly the truth, but close enough.

Rob stepped between us, glaring first at his son, then at me and Adam. "There's no need for police involvement. I'm sure it was all a misunderstanding. Right, *Angela*?"

He put a special emphasis on the name I despised, and I felt my temper snap. "No, it wasn't a misunderstanding. Your son has been sexually harassing me for months, and tonight, he refused to listen when I told him no."

Rob's lips pressed together, and he gave a quick glance at the people still surrounding us watching the show. "Let's all calm down and enjoy the rest of the party. We can discuss this at home."

I snorted as Adam hauled me back against him with a distinctive growl. "I'm not going home with you, and especially not him," I jerked my chin at Shad, who'd regained his feet. "Never again."

"Your mother is going to be sad to hear that," Rob replied firmly.

Mom appeared on my other side. "Oh no, she won't. I'm perfectly happy with Blue's decision to create healthy boundaries and push back against gaslighting."

"Hope, we should discuss this somewhere—"

"No," she interrupted him. "Rob, we're done. I can't believe I didn't see what was going on before, but I see it now. You might want to take your son to get help."

Rob nodded once and hooked Shad's elbow, but Shad pulled his arm free.

He spit at Adam's feet, using his sleeve to mop up the blood on his face. "This is assault, and I'm taking it to the university. You won't play another day in your life."

I sucked in a breath as Rob towed Shad out of the room. "Can he do that?"

Adam shrugged. "He can try, but Coach doesn't like whiney assholes choosing his players."

Mom frowned at the door they'd left through as she patted Adam's bicep. "I knew I liked you. Take care of my girl while I deal with the mess."

"Always," Adam murmured, but I didn't think the words were meant for her.

27

Blue

Adam trailed his fingers down my arm, lifting my wrist to press a kiss next to my bracelet. "I know I said it before, but it bears repeating. From now on, we leave if a situation makes you uncomfortable."

An uncontrollable giggle rose up my throat. "And miss out on the chance to ruin a wedding?"

He chuckled. "All in a day's work."

I picked up his right hand and examined the red knuckles. "Punching him was dangerous. You need to take better care of yourself if you want to keep catching footballs for money. How did you not break your hand on his face?"

Adam flexed his fingers a couple of times, staring down at his hand. "I used to get in a lot of fights before I learned humor is a better defense than my fists. It's not really a skill you forget. Besides, I pulled my punch."

My brows rose. "I think you broke his nose."

"I definitely broke his nose. That was the goal. I'm sorry I didn't get there sooner." The guilt in his tone broke my heart.

"Adam..." I sighed, cupping his face. "You weren't even

supposed to be here. None of this is your fault, though you're paying for it. I don't want you to get in trouble with your team or hurt yourself so you can't play or miss an opportunity to pursue something that should be important to you."

"Not as important as you."

"Yes, as important as me. *You* are as important as me. This is not a pedestal situation—we're on equal ground. Go to your performance, you still have time."

His face shifted into the stubborn expression I knew so well. "I'm not leaving you here alone."

I smiled and nodded toward my mom who was talking animatedly to the catering staff. "I'm not alone. Despite recent events, I *can* take care of myself. Go."

Adam opened his mouth to argue again, but I stopped him with a soft kiss. He quickly deepened it, reminding me I hadn't had his mouth on me in several days. My pulse sped, and I let out a quiet whimper.

His grip on me tightened, and I knew if I didn't slow things down, I'd lose myself completely. With more than a little regret, I pulled back.

"Please, do this for me," I whispered.

He dropped his forehead to mine for a beat, then nodded once. "I'll be back to take you home, and I'm not leaving again. Stay with your mom, just in case."

Mom returned the second Adam walked away, confirming my suspicion she'd only left to give us some privacy. I kept my eyes on Adam until he turned into the hallway where I couldn't see him anymore.

"Whew," Mom fanned herself. "I don't remember him being quite so intense."

I didn't have any urge to discuss my sex life with my mom, so I stayed silent. She seemed to understand because she curled an arm around my shoulder, pulling me in for a hug.

"He reminds me of Archer a little. Must be an athlete thing."

I swung around to stare at her. "Why the hell did you break up with him then?"

She shrugged, like she always did when I asked. "Guess it's time to officially break up with Rob too."

About half of the guests had left, but those who stayed were all standing around on the dance floor where the action had taken place. Probably waiting for more drama. Mom didn't disappoint them. She kept her arm locked around my shoulders and raised her voice to be heard over the polite murmuring.

"I'm sorry to inform everyone I will not be getting married to Rob this September—or ever. Thank you for your support. Please stay and enjoy the rest of the food and drinks."

And that was it. A quick and easy announcement to mark yet another detour in her life. I watched her face carefully for signs of distress, but while her smile was sad, she didn't seem heartbroken.

"Are you okay?" I asked her softly.

She squeezed me against her and walked us back to my spot by the window where it was slightly quieter. "Yes. I'm angry at myself for letting this go on so long and not seeing the effect it was having on you. More than anything else, I'm furious at Shad. If that little fucker comes anywhere near you again, I'm going to have Mac break his kneecaps instead of just his nose."

I let out a laugh, then clapped my hand over my mouth. "Sorry. I probably shouldn't take joy in Shad's pain."

She waved my words away. "Yes, you should. He brought

these consequences on himself. I'm sorry I was too busy with my own life to see what he was doing to yours. We used to be a lot better at this mother/daughter thing. Maybe we can work on it."

I leaned my head against her shoulder, feeling lighter than I had in months. "I'd like that. I'm sorry I didn't talk to you when I was unhappy. Not for ruining the wedding though, that had to happen. Rob is the worst."

She sighed, her breath moving my hair. "He is, isn't he? All the times I let myself be quiet so he could take center stage keep circling my mind in a loop. Now that I'm looking, I can see the way I changed myself to please him, and it pisses me off. When did I let myself become a trophy wife? I should have known better, but the shiny new yoga studio was quite the distraction. Maybe I should take a break from dating for a while to focus on myself."

"Eva says she'll only accept a marriage between you and Archer, so keep that in mind the next time you agree to a date."

"On the positive side, all these events worked. I've secured the backing of several wealthy businesswomen who want to invest in my yoga studio. Laura quit yesterday and signed on with me full time." She laughed dryly. "I supposed I should have seen that as a sign."

With all the honesty flowing between us finally, I took a deep breath and told her the truth I'd been holding onto. "I'm glad the studio is still going forward, Mom, but I don't know if I'll be joining you after graduation."

She grabbed a champagne flute from a confused looking server still wandering around. "I had a feeling you might say that, and while I'd hoped you wanted the studio as much as me, I'm glad."

My head jerked back. "What?"

Mom gave me a sad smile. "We make a good team, and I think you'll like Laura now that Rob won't be around, but baby, running a yoga studio isn't your dream. Finish school. Try new things. If you end up working with me, I'll be ecstatic, but I want you to find something you feel passionate about."

Warmth flooded my cheeks as Adam popped up in my head unbidden.

She sipped her champagne and sent me a sly look. "I might know a certain football player who could use someone with your business savvy to help him balance life as a professional athlete and a musician."

I narrowed my eyes at her. "What do you know about it?"

"I know he showed up here when he could have been pursuing his own interests. I know he risked jail time and his spot on the team to defend my daughter. I know he has his heart in his eyes every time he looks at you."

"I love him." The words were infinitely easier to utter to my mom than they were to Adam.

She nodded. "Then go be there for him. I think your ride just arrived. Love you, honey." Mom grinned and kissed my cheek before striding toward one of her long-time students.

I frowned and scanned the room until I saw what had made her smile. In a little black dress I recognized because I'd sold it to her from my mom's shop, Eva waltzed past the security guards. No wonder Mom hadn't called me back—she already had all the information she needed from my sneaky best friend.

Eva ignored the waiter who offered her his tray, grabbed a water bottle from the bar as she passed, and held it up as she approached me.

"How many of these do you need?"

Shock rooted me to the spot. "What are you doing here?"

"I came to pick you up. Are we dealing with tipsy Blue yet or did Mac arrive in time to stop the nervous drinking?"

"I wasn't drinking tonight."

Eva smiled and hooked my elbow. "Perfect. Come on, the valets are holding my car."

I shook my head, trying to slow her pull on my arm. "How did you know to be here?"

"When Alex explained Mac's plan, I thought he might need a little help. Noah, Shaw, and RJ are waiting downstairs just in case."

"Alex told you?"

"Technically, Noah told me, but I got the details out of Alex. I assume you sent Mac to the competition venue?"

I nodded, speechless at the show of support.

"That's my girl. Don't let him have his way just because you love him."

First Mom, now Eva. It might be in my best interest to let Adam know I loved him since everyone else seemed to be aware. Eva raised a brow and sighed aggressively at my slow pace. I suspected if I dragged my feet much longer, she'd call on her army of football players to physically carry me downstairs to her car. She started tugging again, and I went willingly.

"How did you get Alex to talk?"

Eva sniffed. "Alex is a pushover—he didn't last more than a minute. I had a harder time getting past Luis. Now, are we going to go cheer on your boyfriend or not?"

"Yes. Absolutely." I didn't question how she could get us into the closed performance or why she'd waited until the last minute to spring all this on me.

The elevator didn't stop the whole way down. I was starting to think Eva might be part fairy godmother. We exited the hotel into the warm night, and I spotted her silver

BMW waiting at the curb with Noah, Shaw, and RJ stuffed into the backseat.

Eva thanked the valets, and they tripped over themselves trying to open her door for her. I slid into the passenger seat and twisted around.

"Thank you for coming," I told them.

Shaw snorted. "Like we were going to miss Mac's big singing deal after *years* of him dragging us to karaoke?"

Noah grinned and held up a white posterboard with *Go Mac!!* spelled out in bright pink glitter. RJ elbowed the sign out of the way to lean forward.

"If he wins, he'll never stop crowing about it, but we agreed to give him three weeks before we shove his head in a pillowcase."

Eva slammed her door, buckled herself in, and threw the car into gear. "Let's go show Mac what happens when he keeps things from us."

A wide smile spread across my face as I thought about surprising *him* for once. Yeah. I was ready to show him how much he meant to me.

28

Mac

My palms were sweating. Standing on stage in front of the five judges who could change our lives, I resisted the urge to wipe my hands on my pants. The auditorium wasn't very big, but with the stage lights on, I couldn't see anything in the room but them. I'd been singing in front of people for as long as I could remember—and I regularly played football in stadiums with tens of thousands of cheering fans—but this small audience made me nervous.

No. My inability to stay focused made me nervous.

I'd only arrived ten minutes before they called us back, and my mind wouldn't stop replaying the last hour over and over in stark detail. Blue flinging herself into my arms, the increasing panic in her eyes as she looked for me while they danced, the red mark on her arm. A big part of me wanted to say fuck it and go make sure she was okay.

If I tried to run out again though, Alex might hogtie me on the stage until our set was over. I could probably wait through the three songs we'd prepared to go running back to my girlfriend. And then, nothing was budging me from her side. I planned to have her naked in every spare second between now and classes starting. Maybe even after classes started. With the right angle, I could have a lot of fun while she tried to listen to an online lecture.

The thought made me smile, which was a huge improvement over the tight coil of anxiety trying to climb my throat. I took what Blue called yoga breaths—four beats in, four beats out—until my heart rate settled closer to normal.

I could do this.

In front of me, the judges sat at a long table talking among themselves. Right after I got a grip on my shit, the lady with short spiky hair sitting in the middle tapped her fingers on the stack of files, which caused the others to quiet down.

She called out to me. "Name?"

"Ma—" I stopped and cleared my throat. "Adam. Adam Mackenzie."

A smile slipped out as she flipped through the papers in front of her. "The football player?"

"Yeah." I raised my chin, prepared to defend my team if needed.

"Nice to meet you, Adam. I'm Lacey Duvall."

Surprise ricocheted through me, but I should have realized the big-name music producer would be one of the judges. She'd be working with the winning act, after all.

Lacey cocked her head, studying me. "I have to say...I'm impressed by the amount of work you put into this with your school and practice schedule."

"Thank you, but it was a shared effort with my partner, Alex."

She glanced behind me, nodding. "I understand there was a video component of your performance."

I could feel Alex's eyes burning a hole into the back of my head. "We decided we didn't need it."

The other people at the table, two ladies and two guys, shared relieved looks. Not a guarantee my plan would have failed, but not a good sign either. I definitely owed Blue an apology and an abundance of sexual favors.

"Excellent, if you're ready—"

A clatter from the darkness behind the judges interrupted Lacey, followed by a quiet curse I'd recognize anywhere.

"Eva?" I shaded my eyes from the bright spotlight and peered into the shadows.

The judges all turned around to look while Lacey motioned for the house lights to come up. Behind me, Alex snorted out a laugh as the disturbance became obvious. Taking over the center back row, my roommates, Eva, and my girlfriend started hooting and screaming.

I couldn't take my eyes off Blue, jumping up and down, smiling, helping Noah hold a ridiculous pink glitter sign with my name on it.

She blew me a kiss and mouthed *miss me?*

They came. My crew came. I grinned and tapped my chest over my heart. I'd been blessed with the best family in the world back home, one of the reasons I wanted so badly to take care of them, but the one I'd found here at TU was just as special.

Lacey turned to address the spectators. "I understand this is a special favor, but please be quiet while we're in session. Otherwise, I'll have to ask you to leave."

Everyone settled down except Eva, who let out one last shout. If Lacey could deal with this kind of chaos, we'd work well together. She shook her head and signaled for the lights to be lowered again, but she hadn't lost her smile.

After a few more formalities, including Alex finally introducing himself, Lacey gave us the go ahead. I stepped up to the mic and waited for the music to start. Three songs, now or never.

————

WHEN THE LAST BEAT FADED, the judges applauded, and so did our rowdy row in the back. I inclined my head in a little bow and shared a smile with Alex over my shoulder. We'd crushed it. I'd left my soul on the stage—I couldn't do better —and I was proud of what we'd made.

There was always the chance the other finalists were better. Strangely, I was okay with that. If this wasn't my time, I'd keep pushing and working until it was.

Lacey stood and approached the stage. "Well done. You should be proud of yourselves. We need to tabulate the scores and discuss—"

She stopped mid-sentence and sighed, which I saw but couldn't hear thanks to the noise my friends were making. When the ruckus didn't subside, Lacey turned, stuck two fingers in her mouth, and let out a piercing whistle.

She pointed at my cheering section. "You. Out. Wait for them in the lobby."

I caught Blue's eyes, and she pressed her lips together to contain her smile as they filed out. Even Eva, who'd no doubt organized the whole thing. Lacey waited until the door closed after them to continue.

"We need to tabulate the scores and discuss the options, but I think I can confidently say I'll be seeing more of you both. The competition organizer will announce the winners in the next twenty-four hours."

"Thank you, Ms. Duvall."

Alex echoed my statement, and she grinned.

"Call me Lacey."

I thought he might swoon. Just in case, I dropped an arm over his shoulders and walked him between the seats to the door. When my fingers closed over the handle, I hissed a little at the movement.

Now that the adrenaline had worn off, my hand ached. I needed to ice it, and maybe see the trainer just in case. Coach would probably give me the disappointed look I hated, but I'd take it this time. He'd find out why soon enough because I had no doubt Shad would try to follow through on his threat to get me suspended.

I laughed to myself. *Good luck, asshole.*

The second I pushed through the door, Blue launched herself at me. "I'm so proud of you. And turned on. You need to sing more at home."

Shaw snorted. "He sings all the time."

"Not like that, he doesn't," muttered RJ.

I hefted Blue a little higher with my good hand on her ass, fighting the urge to flatten her against the wall right there in the lobby. "I'll sing every day for you, Sunshine. You are the best girlfriend in the history of girlfriends."

"Hey—" RJ mumbled the rest of her sentence behind Shaw's hand.

I sent her an arched look. "You know our love could never be. My heart belongs to another."

RJ glared at Shaw until he shrugged and removed his hand. "Just trying to help."

Eva approached twirling her key fob around one finger. "My work here is done. I hope you get everything you want, Mac."

My arm tightened around Blue, who took the opportunity to plant her feet on the floor again. "I hope you find someone to make you happy, Eva."

She smiled. "Can't find what you're not looking for. I need to go relieve Chloe from duck-sitting."

"Yeah, me too," mumbled Noah.

I looked around at my ride or die crew—Shaw holding RJ, Eva holding herself, Noah holding his handmade sign—and felt something click into place inside me. "Let's get tacos."

"Shotgun," Noah said quietly, then took off out the door.

Eva pointed at Shaw as they followed. "No nookie in the backseat."

RJ laughed at Shaw's pouty face, but stopped when he sent her a sly look behind Eva's back. I shook my head. Even I didn't test Eva when it came to her car. The X7 was her baby. I decided on the spot to stay over at Blue's for the foreseeable future until Eva got her revenge on Shaw and RJ.

After the others left, Alex, Blue, and I made our way to the parking lot. We'd barely reached his car when Alex started making choking sounds. I spun around, and he was staring at his phone with his mouth open.

"You okay, man?"

He held the screen out to me, and I saw the word *Congratulations!!* in big letters. Everything in me stilled, and I met his eyes.

"We won?" I knew we'd kicked ass, but the possibility hadn't seemed real until just now. We'd only been gone fifteen minutes.

"We won." Alex started bouncing up and down. "We won. We won. We won."

I pulled Blue into a hug, and she squeezed me tight.

"I love you," she whispered, officially making it the best night of my life.

"I love you too, Sunshine." I cupped her head and kissed her for all I was worth.

The next few months would be hard with school, the internship, and football, but I couldn't wait to get started. With Blue, I had everything I wanted.

EPILOGUE

Blue

Three weeks later...

"You are utterly failing in your job to teach me to be a hottie." I pulled the mess of my hair away from my face and pretended to glare at my boyfriend.

"Who told you to say that?" Adam lay sprawled across my lap after waking me up with his tongue between my legs.

"Chloe. Though technically she said I was *already* a hottie and didn't need your help."

"She's not wrong." He nuzzled between my breasts, the action muffling his words. "How am I failing again?"

I threaded my hands through his hair, shorter now that the season had started, and tugged until I could see his face. "The TU social media harpies haven't picked up on our relationship yet. I don't care, but Chloe thinks if you took your hottie girlfriend out more often they'd stop speculating about you and every ball bunny within fifty feet."

Adam turned his head to kiss my wrist. "We're fixing that problem today, Sunshine. You're coming to the game."

Today was their first real game of the season after what he called a "cupcake" game in week one. I was slowly learning the terminology, but much of it didn't make sense to me. We only had about an hour before he had to head out to the stadium.

"You know what might help?" he asked.

I narrowed my eyes at him. "I'm not going to the game topless."

He laughed and pulled a jersey out from under his pillow. "How about in this then?"

I twisted my lips and spread it out to trace the letters of his last name. "You want me to go to a game with your name branded across my back?"

Adam sat up, propping himself on his fist. "Yes, but with less feudal undertones. You'll match Chloe."

"Chloe won't be wearing your name."

"No, but I want you to. I want everyone to know you're mine—and I want you to keep wearing my name when we graduate and you come with me wherever I get drafted."

My eyes cut to him. "What are you asking me?"

He picked up my left hand, playing with my fingers. "I thought I was pretty clear. You're my future. I know you need your space, and you want to build your own career, but I was hoping you could do that with me."

"You want me to move in with you," I clarified. "After graduation?"

"Unless you're finally ready to marry me," he quipped.

I leaned closer to brush my mouth over his. "Yes."

He stilled, pulling back to meet my eyes. "What?"

"Yes," I repeated. "I'll marry you, but we should probably wait until we find out what team you're going to in the draft."

For the first time, I'd struck Adam speechless. He framed

my face and kissed me, slow and sweet. I could spend all day, every day kissing him.

"Say the words, Blue," he whispered.

"I love you, Adam."

"And you're going to marry me." He punctuated the sentence with kisses along my jaw.

I laughed low. "And I'm going to marry you. One day, far in the future."

"And you'll wear my jersey to the game today."

"And I'll *think about* wearing your jersey to the game today."

"Good enough," he murmured, his weight settling between my legs.

————

I WORE THE JERSEY. After the guys and RJ left early, I caught a ride with Chloe and Eva, who gave me a disgusted look when I climbed into her car with Mackenzie across my back.

Adam had been right. I matched Chloe, happy and vibrant in Noah's jersey. Eva wore her cheer uniform and spent the entire drive complaining about her new living arrangements. She'd stayed with me for a few days, but a tiny house was no place for two women and a duck.

We met up with my mom and Archer—there for a friendly, non-date according to them—and split off. Eva hopped down to the field to join her squad warming up, and I had the weird sensation of being watched again.

For a split second, my lizard brain tried to insist Shad was there, a nasty side effect from the night of the party, but Shad was nowhere near the TU stadium. After he'd tried to get Adam benched, several TAs from the ABC came forward and accused him of sexual harassment.

I didn't have to say a thing. He was barred from campus. Eva wouldn't admit to orchestrating Shad's fall from grace, but she didn't deny it either.

As casually as possible, I scanned the area around us. It didn't take me long to find the culprit. A tall guy with broad shoulders, dark hair, and tattoos winding up his arms stood at the railing next to the field. We made eye contact, and his lips tipped up on one side in a humorless smile.

He looked vaguely familiar, but I couldn't place him. After the silent acknowledgement, he shifted his gaze to the cheerleaders. I kept my eyes on him. When one of the stunt team tossed Eva in the air and caught her with one hand, his jaw tightened.

I didn't get a dangerous vibe from him, but he was definitely watching Eva. I'd have to let her know later. Mystery guy left during the first quarter, and the rest of the game went by in a blur, ending with another victory for TU.

By the time Eva showed us where we could meet Adam and the others in the tunnel after the game, I'd decided her secret admirer was harmless. She had the same effect everywhere she went, and the guy hadn't done anything except watch the cheerleaders, who were *trying* to get the attention of the crowd.

My train of thought disappeared when Adam came out of the locker room doors, laughing with Shaw, RJ, Noah, and another guy he'd been talking to during the game. He spotted me and jogged over with a huge grin.

His arms looped around my waist, lifting me off the ground. "Miss me?"

"Always." I lifted my face for a kiss.

We'd decided to keep the marriage conversation between us for now, but it was all I could think about. This man with the wicked sense of humor and the heart of gold was coming home with me—would always come home with me. Adam was all mine.

From somewhere to our left, Eva groaned. "I hate you all."

Adam raised a brow in her direction without setting me down. "You owe me two bucks."

I smacked his shoulder. "Did you bet on me?"

"She tried to tell me I wouldn't convince you to wear the jersey. I had to prove her wrong, so she'd stop interfering." He tucked his hand under the silky material, then made a low happy noise at the bare skin underneath.

I laughed to cover my sudden shiver. "We should thank her. Without her interference, we might not be here."

Adam grinned and brushed his nose against mine. "Sunshine, you were made for me. We were always going to end up here."

———

Want more Mac? Get a glimpse of Mac and Blue's happy ever after with the exclusive bonus epilogue.

Click here for your free bonus epilogue!

**If you're having trouble clicking, go to http://www. nikkihallbooks.com/play-maker **

———

Want more of the Teagan University Wildcats?

Turn the page to see what happens when Eva meets the

coffee guy she loves to hate in Ice Cold Player, the first book in the Beyond the Ice hockey romance series.

ICE COLD PLAYER

Eva

Day one of my senior year in college, and I was homeless. Prospectless. Hopeless. Probably several other -lesses I didn't have the energy to conjure up. After a week of tireless effort—there's another one—not a single apartment, house, condo, or other would let me move in with my duck.

I didn't want to admit I was giving up, but damn, even my unparalleled manifestation abilities couldn't create an acceptable housing situation out of thin air.

Sweat dotted my forehead, and I tilted my face up to the blazing sun, hoping the heat would dry some of the tears. I hated crying, hated even more letting people see me cry, which was why I'd tucked myself away in a little-known courtyard behind the business building. The crumbling concrete fountain in the middle had seen better days, and most of the foliage was overgrown with weeds.

Except for the area bordering the edge of campus. Pine trees grew in thick clumps, but the azalea bushes had taken over the ground level in a riot of color. Teagan University had a beautiful campus, but this spot was my favorite.

The faint scent of coffee blew through on a light breeze, compliments of Wildcat Coffee right around the corner, and I could almost imagine this was any other day. If not for the constant calls from my friend group checking in on me.

I silenced my phone and set it next to me. They meant well, but they weren't helping. I returned to my sun worship pose, but my serenity didn't last long. Quiet footsteps marked the approach of an interloper.

A shadow blocked the warmth, and I sighed, accepting I wasn't going to find any more peace today. When I opened my eyes, my heart sank. Standing above me with his arms crossed was my coffee nemesis. Gavin King. Yes, I knew his name, but I refused to use it. 'Hey asshole' worked just as well.

He grunted and took up a position next to my spot on the wall of the fountain. We'd never had a real conversation, so I had no idea what he was doing here popping my solitude bubble.

When I peeked at him from under my lashes, he stared straight ahead at the azaleas, seemingly content to stand there and ruin my afternoon.

"What do you want?" I finally asked.

"You looked upset." He stated it as a fact, and my shoulders tensed up at the thought anyone had noticed.

Out of habit, I went on the offensive. "So you came out here to gloat?"

His lips tipped up on the end, but he didn't take the bait. "No. I came out here to make sure you weren't about to take a header into the fountain."

I glanced at the shallow green water and shuddered. "Gross. Why would you care?"

"Because I'd probably have to clean the fountain after.

This is technically part of Wildcat Coffee, and they hate their employees."

I hadn't known my favorite coffee shop owned my favorite piece of land. Like everything else around here, I'd assumed TU owned it.

"Maybe they only hate grumpy employees who've never heard of customer service."

He chuckled, low and slow, and I hated the way the sound shivered up my spine. "I think they're okay with me not handing out free espresso shots to all the girls who smile at me, Princess."

The nickname did it. I couldn't stand assholes who assumed since I was pretty and rich I must be entitled. The stupid sad feelings I hadn't been able to shake were banished with a flash of temper. "I smile at everyone, jackass."

"Not the way you smiled at me." His lazy, confident tone irked me to no end.

Yes, I'd thought he was hot the first time I'd seen him—I wasn't blind—but he'd been surly and rude. I didn't reward that kind of behavior with my good graces.

I clawed back the scathing retort he was no doubt expecting, choosing to gift him with my silence instead. Maybe if I ignored him, he'd go away.

His posture shifted as he cast a quick look down at me. "Might as well tell me what's wrong since I'm not going back inside until you do. No reason to prolong the torture."

I hated him and his confidence and his unflappable calm, but I my mouth went rogue and blurted out the story of my final appointment of the afternoon. Bob the office manager had laughed in my face when I inquired about a pet deposit for my duck and asked if I meant dick instead.

Then he'd offered me a discount if I was nice to him—his words.

Gavin's jaw tensed as I talked, and when I stopped for breath, it took a second for him to unclench enough to talk. "I hope you reported him."

"Oh yeah. I walked out and called the owner immediately. Despite apologizing profusely and promising to fire my good buddy Bob, he couldn't allow a duck as a pet in the complex." I sighed, feeling slightly better now that someone else had reinforced my reaction.

He shook his head slightly. "If your duck is the problem, why not leave it behind?"

My hands clenched in my lap. So much for feeling better. "I'm not abandoning Henry simply because things got hard. I'll find a place. Just probably not today."

He pulled a fuzzy, black, cat ear headband from his back pocket and sat down next to me on the stone lip of the fountain. "I heard you were engaged to that football player. Maybe you could move in with him."

I snorted. "No. Mac and I were involved for a very short time, and now it's over."

His head tilted just enough to meet my gaze. "He didn't meet the royal standards?"

My stomach did a curious flip at the direct eye contact. Gavin was objectively beautiful. Not in a shiny, perfect way, but in a gravelly, rough, fuck me against a brick wall kind of way. Too bad his personality ruined it.

"I don't know why you think I'm going to give you details about my personal life."

"You already did." He lifted one hand to tick off fingers. "I know you don't have a place to stay. I know you're irrationally attached to your duck. I know you have no problem metaphorically throat punching someone. And I know your last relationship ended because of you."

I winced, unable to hide my reaction fast enough. "None of this is your business."

He shrugged. "You're welcome to leave any time."

My hackles rose at the idea of him scaring me away. This was *my* place. He could leave. "And you're welcome to stop being an asshole. Looks like neither of us is going to get what we want."

He scrubbed a hand down his face, and I thought I caught the edge of a grin before he hid it with his fingers. "Whatever you say."

I shifted to face him, trying to decide if I'd rather strangle him or shove him into the fountain. "We didn't have the right chemistry."

"Still sounds like your fault. It's okay. It can be hard to work up a sweat for the peasants."

He was needling me. On purpose. I could see it in the subtle way he watched me as he let his barbs fly. I couldn't figure out if it was because he took joy in kicking someone while they were down or if he was trying to distract me from Bob and his ilk.

Honestly, his motivations didn't matter. Despite knowing what he was doing, I couldn't stop myself from responding.

I leaned in to poke his bicep. "I work up a sweat just fine. Don't judge my sex life based on your own lackluster efforts."

He turned to fully face me and grinned. "You couldn't handle me, Princess."

I wanted to wipe that smug smile off his face. I wanted to prove I wasn't a poor little rich girl incapable of passion. I wanted to kiss him. The thought shocked me, but I was too far gone to make a good decision.

Quickly, before I could change my mind, I fisted the T-shirt over his chest and closed the distance between us. Gavin didn't miss a beat. His mouth descended on mine as his hand speared through my hair, gripping tight.

Heat rushed through me, stealing my breath and making me tremble. I expected an angry, bruising kiss, but he softened. He explored and teased. I swallowed a whimper and released the clenched fabric to flatten my palm over his racing heart. So it wasn't just me.

Gavin changed the angle, coaxing my lips open. A flurry of what-ifs sped through my mind in rapid succession. What if I climbed into his lap? What if I dropped my hand a little lower? What if I'd been wrong this whole time?

No. Bad decisions happened when I let my lady parts lead the way. I shoved against his chest, and he backed away immediately. For a split second, I saw raw hunger on his face, then it disappeared behind his usual arrogant expression.

I stood and brushed imaginary dirt off my shorts as if I kissed my arch nemesis in a secluded courtyard every day.

"It wasn't me." I turned on my heel and followed the path out of the courtyard, willing my heart rate to return to normal.

A NOTE FROM NIKKI

Thank you so much for reading Play Maker! I'm always sad to see a series come to an end, but I'm glad we saved Mac for last. He didn't end up with Eva, but I think we can all agree he's better off. He needed someone to let him grow into the person he was destined to be.

And Eva. As Hope says, no one could forget Eva. She's up next, bringing her brash, sneaky, love bombing personality to a houseful of hockey players. Don't worry, she won't turn her back on her football besties, but sparring with Gavin is going to take up all her mental energy. This ending isn't even really an ending because I get to stay in Addison at TU with my next series.

If you have a second, please consider leaving a review. Even better, tag me with the review so we can be besties. You can find me on Facebook, Instagram, or TikTok. Finally, if you want updates on future books and other fun stuff, join my newsletter. I promise not to bite.

ACKNOWLEDGMENTS

I'd like to thank (in no particular order):

- Nicole Schneider, Liz Gallegos, and Megan Clements, for their editing prowess
- Velveeta Shells & Cheese, for those long nights when Mac wouldn't talk to me
- Angela Haddon, another beautiful cover, as always
- My various writing groups, you know who you are, for talking me down from the ledge with the deadline approaching
- The Hubs, look, I'm sorry about that time with the dishwasher—I forgot it was my turn and my brain was mush from three straight months of writing
- Southwest Airlines, your tray tables are the *perfect size* for my laptop
- San Diego, California, I needed that one quiet morning on the water
- All the coffee, everywhere, all the time, a caffeinated writer is a happy writer
- My readers, because you're the reason I get to do this—thank you for loving Mac as much as I do

ALSO BY NIKKI HALL

Wild Card series

Game Changer

Rule Breaker

Front Runner

Hard Hitter

Play Maker

Beyond the Ice series

Ice Cold Player

ABOUT THE AUTHOR

Nikki Hall is a smart-ass with a Ph.D. and a potty mouth. She writes stories that have spice and sass because she doesn't know any other way. Coffee makes her happy, messes make her stabby, and she'd sell one of her children for a second season of Firefly.

Want to find out when the newest Nikki Hall book hits the shelves? Sign up for her newsletter at www.nikkihall books.com/signup.

PLAY MAKER

Copyright © 2023 Nikki Hall

All rights reserved.

This is a work of fiction. Any similarity between the characters and situations within its pages and places or persons, living or dead, is unintentional and co-incidental.

Cover designed by Angela Haddon

Edited by Megan Clements, Waypoint Author Academy

Printed in Great Britain
by Amazon